Georgian Meads

Family life in the rural hamlet

Pease pudding hot
Pease pudding cold
Pease pudding in the pot, nine days old

Christopher Ward

Published by the author
direct from his keyboard and iPad 2023
Print run (c)

All photos and sketches are from the author's collection.
All characters in this publication are fictitious and any
resemblance to real persons, living or dead is purely
coincidental.

Paperback ISBN 978-1-3999-6945-1

Printed and bound in the United Kingdom by
www.printedwordpublishing.com
Hastings

Dedicated
to
Raffaele Amato

Contents

Chapter One

'Road to Meads'

Mud, mud and more mud will keep you company if you come the wrong way. Follow the white chalk and leave the stinking mud for others. Come along the old prehistoric track, high on the crest of the chalk downs with views to a silver blue sea and an open sky above you. Leave the low Weald mud for others who know no better. This high dry handsome track will lead you to the Road to Meads.

It is a road in the time of King George II. A time when when few silver crowns are taken from a purse to keep a road passable as there are few who want to pass. Those that do are on foot, on horseback or sit in an ox wagon and have little use for speed. For good or evil nature surfaces this road each season; soaking it into shallow puddles in winter and drying it into dusty earth in summer. The underlying chalk serves it well and saves it from the deep soaking mud of the Weald where boots sink almost to the knee. The road leads to a small hamlet where a measuring chain has been carefully pulled across the land by a stranger who is interested in the new scientific method. He has taken measurements where a plough boy has been busy with his yoked oxen; areas of opened ground where turnips and oats grow well on the south slopes. With compass and chainman for assistance he has noted all in a pocket book, returned to his Westminster address and prepared a detailed map of a manor. The manor is for sale. It is the Manor of Collstock showing the rural hamlet of Meads and is dated 1739 of the old Julian calendar.

On his return to the hamlet the stranger has been unlucky with his choice of inns. He has not had a good meal or good bed since leaving Westminster three days ago. He is tired and weary. Shouted words from an innkeeper have irritated his soul. With half closed eyes he gazes at candle light flickering in the polish of a walnut table. The candles burn in a silver candelabra, their golden light falling on a curling map that is carefully held open by a candle snuffer on one side and a pair of dividers on the other. His eyes occasionally rise and wander round a large high-ceilinged room. Oil portraits sit within moulded frames and classic fluted columns grace wide doorways. Fashionable mahogany chairs sit elegantly about on a smooth oak boarded floor. The candlelight brings colour to the smooth sculpted white face of a Greek Goddess that looks out serenely from below the mantel of a large decorative fireplace. The feeble light does not reach the extremities of this room; they remain dark and unknown.

He sits around the table with two wigged men; one showing rouge on his cheeks. He is skilled in the presentation of a manor in the form of an accurate financial document and the detailed map they are studying on the table showing the Road to Meads, strip farms, tithes and properties is the product of his labour. It is late into the night and all that can be heard is the quiet breathing of the men and the slow tick of a clock somewhere in the darkness. He is not far from sleep and dreams of a good bed, a maid for company and roast beef. They have been sitting in silence for some time; the air is fragrant with the scent of herbs and body odour.

'Surveyor,' a confident voice breaks the silence.

'Yes my, Lord.'

Pulled from his tired drifting mind, his foot slips off his footstool and he is awake. He watches as a chubby bent index finger with manicured nail descends and taps three times on the map.

'It says here ''Road to Meads,'' but where does it come from?' the rouged man asks.

'It's a chalk track my, Lord, I remember it well, it's just for the farms, ox wagons and cattle. The cottagers call it the Warren track it just goes up to what they call Meads Hollow to the grass waste and furlongs.'

'But it could go somewhere? I would be more interested if it did and had a coach or two.'

'There is nothing of substance up there my, Lord, just a few hovels and small farms. It goes along the coast to some havens that have fish. There are no turnpikes and thus no roads in this forgotten isolated waste.'

'Fish and spies no doubt. I suppose there is no coal down here. Better if there was. Just chalk, white chalk I presume.'

He turns his rouged face towards the surveyor for an answer. The surveyor looks up from the map and replies dismally,

'I regret to say it my, Lord, but coal is not under this soil. There is chalk, just chalk with a topping of grass and there is little timber here.'

'Chalk!' exclaims the rouged man, 'Is there any goodness or value within the chalk?'

'Some is burnt to plaster the lathes of grand houses, but little else,' replies the surveyor.

The third man who has been silent, looks up from his quiet meditation and interrupts.

'I can tell you that the decorations you see in this room come from the skilled use of the chalk.'

'Yes, that is so my, Lord. Italian marble dust and burnt chalk have been dressed into the shapes you see,' he says pointing to the decorative mantel where the face of the Greek Goddess looks out. 'Work carried out when this house changed its name from Bourne Place.'

The rouged man looks around the room, at the fluted columns and the face of the Goddess then at the surveyor. He smiles, yawns, then taps the map again.

'Is that something of worth. Who has it?' he asks.

'It is the Mansion House my, Lord. It is a farmer who has it. Known as a gentleman farmer who answers to the name Spendwell. Works as all farmers do.'

'Gentlemen farmers. Where have they come from? No quality,' musses the rouged man. 'What of the house. Is it of worth?' he continues.

'It is of old stock. Old Manor House that has seen its time. It has been inspected and requires a heavy purse.'

The clock ticks through a silence.

'These other things. What are these?'

4

'Just thatched hovels,' explains the surveyor. 'With stables and wagon sheds for trade. A small inn on The Street.'

'Nothing of worth here in this dismal waste,' decides the rouged man as he lifts himself off his chair. 'It's time gentlemen. I must retire now. I've talked, seen enough and will leave this manor for others and return to London on the morrow.'

With that comment the meeting ends. The surveyor picks up his dividers and drops the rolled-up map into a leather cylinder. He leaves the building to find a good bed. The others cordially 'Good night,' and go to their beds. A footman extinguishes all the candles except one, picks up the candelabra, leaves the room and closes the door.

ooo000ooo

We leave the map in its leather cylinder and look at the real, dusty, chalky 'Road to Meads,' with its creaking wagons, cattle and sheep that is just a few furlongs away. It sits in the moonlight of this summer night winding its dusty way down to the hamlet of Meads where the people dream unconcerned in their beds. Generations of people have lived, farmed and died alongside generations of forest on this spot of land. Trusted rural wisdoms direct the lives of the farmers, shepherds, innkeepers and others that inhabit this small isolated hamlet where they live and work on a green landscape of chalk downland. Living deep in this natural world has made them part of the nature that surrounds them. The slow rural clock is followed; its marks being sunrise, noon and sunset for their daily tasks while the seasons dictate and direct them through the years. Nothing is faster than a racing horse and the speed of a wagon is the speed of the slowest ox in the team. Added to their rural wisdom is the wisdom of the pulpit, delivered by eager clergy looking down on their flock, while the church warden assists in the absorption of the message by using a long stick to knock the heads of any of the congregation who give way to closed eyes and sleep in the pews. The pre-industrial enlightenment has dawned but in rural villages few can read, few can write; fingers, thumbs and tally sticks are their counting tools. Apart from growing turnips and clover in rotation, the great innovations, developments and achievements of their century are still distant ideas discussed in the coffee houses of London. Appreciation of childhood, empathy and compassion have instigated the writing of a royal charter for the construction of a Foundling Hospital in London, while its sentiment confronts the cheering crowds at public hangings.

The golden light of beeswax candles that the surveyor gazed at is gone. It has changed to the cold grey light of the moon that drifts over the hamlet revealing the rolling down land, with its neatly laid out small strip farms, hanger woods, orchards, hay barns, thatched cottages and quiet motionless sheep and cattle. It reveals the main thoroughfare of the hamlet, 'The Street,' where inn, Mansion House, dairy and meat yard find their place.

The road descends into the hamlet and passes a cottage where an oak sliding shutter has been pulled open to allow the cooler night air into a parlour. The light of the moon slips through this opening illuminating a night working spider spinning its web between the oak bars. In the cold grey light the valuable objects that sustain the lives of the Applegate family appear flat and colourless. A spinning wheel just inside the window casts an unrecognisable shadow on the hardened earth floor. In the middle of the room on a boarded table are a large clay bowl, wooden tankards, wooden dishes, a bone handled metal blade, some pewter spoons, a pack of alphabet cards, a small willow basket and a rounded chalk pebble. A small bench and stools are around the table. Along one wall is a wide blackened brick hearth with fireback and space for cooking and fuel. A three-legged iron cauldron stands over cinders, a potage pot on the hook of a chimney crane, andirons, and a few sticks of kindling can be seen. Leather bellows, birch twig hand brush, toasting fork, fire tongs and long handled skillet all hang from thick blacksmith nails driven into the wall. Long stemmed white clay pipes are displayed neatly in a wooden rack on the wall next to the swinging pendulum of a one-handed clock. A well-thumbed heavy book and small corked bottle with goose feather quill and sheets of rough paper sit in a recess of the wall. There are many objects on the narrow mantel over the hearth. In the dim light it is just possible to see two pewter candle sticks, a broken piece of hand mirror, a wooden tinder box and clay pipe with a broken stem.

An oak settle has been moved away from the hearth and sits against a wall. A twisted walking stick and besom broom stand in a corner. All these are the worthy necessary objects for the life of this family of eight. Although there is a window in the opposite wall it is in shadow and the other objects in the room disappear in the dim light. Boarded doors hang each side of the hearth; one is ajar to a lobby that leads to a kitchen and food store. The wheezing breath of a sleeper can be heard in the darkness coming from this kitchen. Lizzie, the eldest member of the cottage, lives in this kitchen where she sleeps and prepares food at the stone sink. She is the inherited family maid and is past counting summers; she stopped counting long ago. She had been told by her mother that she was born the day the big soldier in London was buried, but she has forgotten his name. She has recipes and rural wisdoms for every occasion.

The other door is open and in the dim light of the parlour it is just possible to see the lower steps of a clean wooden staircase, scrubbed with besom brush and sand. It turns as it rises to a narrow boarded landing that leads straight into the bigger bedroom that sits over the parlour. Here Martha Applegate sleeps alone in a wide bed on a deep mattress that has been stuffed with soft grasses, lavender and wormwood. Her shepherd husband drifts in and out of sleep next to his flock a mile distant on the downs. She dreams of a quill pen moving smoothly over paper leaving a scratch free alphabet of rounded letters. Self-tutored, she reads and writes and is one of the most sought-after women in the cottage community. Discovering this ability within herself has given her a sense of authority in a world where she has no representation. She lies on her back in a short sleeved linen shift, long black hair coils to her shoulders then hides itself under her body. Her weather tanned face gives more than the simple beauty of a perfect symmetry. She is a tall unhurried woman with noble features, a friend who seeks friendship. Her eyebrows are furry and dark on her brow while dark long eyelashes flicker with the movement of her dreams. One arm loosely stretches above her head to find coolness on this warm night, her armpit a wood of short fluffy black hair. Her other arm stretches out over the wide empty space beside her. Her hands are rough and her nails dirty but her cottage is as clean as she can make it. She knows every inch of it from the inaccessible holes where spiders, beetles, ants and others emerge, to the thinnest piece of thatch

8

where birds draw straws that leave holes for the rain. Her father had been violently taken for the navy when she was a small girl and she had grown up with her mother and three sisters. The singleness of her new life with an absent shepherd husband was accepted without apprehension. After a year of walking out with Barnabas, sleeping and loving in the warm long grass of summer they were seen by all as emotionally bonded. When she moved into the cottage on the death of his father they were seen as man and wife by the cottage community. But Martha's spirit had urged her for more and their names had been noted in the Latin Clergy Acts Book as married by licence and her fascination with seeing their names on the licence had led her to seek the knowledge to read and write. Child birth was life threatening for mother and child. She had trembled and fretted at her first birth as she looked at the pieces of tansy herb placed on her swollen belly to assist the birth. The following effortless and uncomplicated births had brought her tranquillity of mind as her family grew. In woven straw cots on the floor by her bed are her tiny daughters, Becky one summers and Ruby half a summer. Easy births and healthy children are what she had prayed for and that's what had arrived. Her older children had grown resourceful and fit; all had been sickness free through the winters and summers. She had seen and enjoyed thirty four summers.

In the same room, beyond a low wooden beam where the thatch slopes down, sleep Beth and Livy each with fifteen summers; the Applegate maids. These young women assist their mother with needle work, spinning and all maids work and loudly cry out against any suggestion of going into service. They regularly night talk nose to nose sharing their thoughts, comforting and consoling each other, whispering gently to each other to be out of earshot of Martha. Their rural wisdoms, myths and pulpit guidance are now augmented by the knowledge of some alphabet and although they sleep quietly with calm smooth faces, their minds work endlessly with emotionally selected panoramas, drifting through clothes, babies and spinning wheels to young ladies and young men in love. Their panoramas adjusting to suit their deeper fancies of how they wish to see their future. New glimpses of what might be that could take them anywhere.

Martha's husband Barnabas, away on the downs, lies outside his earth cover on this hot night gazing at the moon and stars as they roll across the heavens. He listens for noises in the night and thinks of his flock. Of the long hot dry spell of weather and the quality and dryness of their pasture. His dogs are asleep beside him. His large flock is free to graze over an unfenced downland waste that stretches to the horizon. He had spent a busy day with his dogs collecting loose sheep that had strayed and enraged a farmer by feasting on the green tops of his valuable turnips.

In the second smaller bedroom of the cottage that is accessed from a door on the landing are two male occupants. In one bed is Seth Applegate, a young man with many skills of shepherding, post setting, weeding and harvesting as the weather and season dictate. He is lying on his back, his legs and arms hang over the bed, his muddy toes twitch. He is strongly built and his heaving chest pulls in the warm summer air and pushes it out with a quiet whistle. Long fair hair curls around his smooth face and drifts down through a ribbon knot into a ponytail. His childish fun has almost slipped away and is now buried under practical reason gained from sixteen summers. He is deep asleep, his mind unconsciously searches for solutions, predictions and fulfilments. His dream shows him as a grown shepherd with a magnificent crook, looking at a vast infinite flock of sheep that stretches to the horizon. But he turns in his bed as his dream changes to the navy, sermons and young women.

The small corked bottle in the wall recess in the parlour is Martha's homemade brown ink made from crushed oak galls soaked in a rusty iron pot and filtered. Her pen she has carefully fashioned from a handsome goose feather. A growing local cottage industry has provided her with the rough paper. She is teaching Seth to read and write and he occasionally uses her pen, but he handles the delicate instrument like a pitchfork and squeezes the quill until the ink runs in rivulets over the valuable paper.

The other bed in this room is where little Jamie Applegate sleeps with just six summers of life and is now just four foot tall, vigorously learning the skills of life and proud of the letters he knows. He is not asleep; he is hot and fidgets. He lies on his back and can just see the beam above his head in the darkness. He wonders what shipwreck it came from and how many mariners had drowned. His body has started to tell him he is a little man, a change that is reinforced by his recent change from a skirt to his first breeches. Dry and dusty, square toed, any foot leather boots, woollen hose with leather soles, woollen breeches, shepherd's smock and a crumpled straw hat lie in an untidy pile.

The remaining member of the household is stretched out asleep downstairs on the cool door stone. He is a hairy sheepdog who cost a half penny a few hours after birth and now answers to that name. Communal cats creep into the cottage, creep out, and sleep where they will in their hunt for mice, rats and birds to torture. The night's silence is solid except for the quiet distant noise of grunting badgers, barking foxes, screeching night hawks and others out on their nocturnal journeys. Noises that do not trouble the sleepers who are too deep in their dreams to be disturbed.

The four Applegate rooms are part of a large ramshackle cottage that is divided in two for another family. Three or four similar cottages with an unidentified number of families are close by, all sharing one deep well. The cottages with their rustic extensions and additions form an intricate sculpture of the earth. Oak, chalk, stone and reed have been fashioned into a shelter that is now counting centuries. A sun faded soft earth colour has settled on the dwellings blending them into their surroundings. Moonlight slowly drifts away as daylight imperceptibly gathers in the east and the colour of morning slowly lights the distant sky. The swallows have already left their nests in the eaves, Halfpenny has left his hard bed and inspected his territory, the cock has crowed, a pig has grunted. A new day has begun.

Chapter Two

A red ribbon

Seth's eyelids flicker and slowly open as the first feeble light of day seeps into his room. The clock hand points to four as he slips carefully off his bed without disturbing little Jamie, pulls on his breeches and descends the stairs quietly in his bare feet. He slides the wooden bolt, opens the door and steps out into a fresh morning. Although the cottagers rarely drink well water it is readily lapped up by the cottager's pig, chickens and dogs in the heat of summer. He walks along a narrow herb lined garden path that wanders between adjacent cottages and leads to the well. The water is low at this time of year and as he winds up the bucket he is being watched by a small face, whose small body is just tall enough to look out through a cottage window.

'See you. See you. See youuuu.' the small face shouts into the morning then bobs down out of sight.

Seth knows the voice and smiles as he tips water from one bucket to another.

'I can hear a voice but can't see anyone,' he says out loud to himself.

'See you. See you. See youuuu.' the small face shouts again then disappears.

Seth turns and looks at the window where the voice came from, but there is no one to be seen.

'There's no one there,' he says again loudly to himself. 'It must be a ghost.'

'No! No! I'm no ghost,' the voice screeches and little Duffy's face appears between the oak bars of the window.

Duffy is a girl of five or six summers, rosy cheeked with a small piece of ribbon hanging in her tousled hair waiting to be tied into a bow. She lives within a neighbouring cottage and often watches for Seth in the first light of day.

'Feeding the Grunter?' she calls from the window.

'He must eat. We want a good fat pig.'

'The Grunter is awake. I heard him,' shouts Duffy.

'Awake for his victuals. Each day I look at him to see his fatness. The fatter the better, isn't that so, Duffy. If he's fat he can't fly away.'

'Nonsense! Nonsense!' shouts Duffy. 'Pigs have no wings. Pigs never fly.'

This pig named Grunter is a Tamworth with a long sandy coloured body. Random thick oak posts and boarding form Grunter's hog pen, but it needs regular attention as he is vigorous, fat and strong. He is under the close eye of the cottagers who regularly inspect their pig and pay much attention to his happiness and wellbeing. He is their assurance that there will be fresh meat and grease through the dark winter. Seth tips the water into the pig's bowl then wanders around the cottages collecting the contents from pig buckets at the cottage doors. He then drops the swill into the pen. Grunter is the first pig Seth has cared for and is always surprised at the knowledgeable way Grunter looks up from his food and looks at him squarely in the eye, as if he has something to say to him. Nell, the innkeeper of the Ship Inn, is the only other person in the hamlet who has pigs. She has three with piglets to see her inn through the winter. Seth returns to talk to little Duffy who is still watching him from her window.

'That'll keep him happy. I've been doing this for a long time and it will soon be time for someone else to take over?' he says looking into Duffy's small face.

'I can't do it! I'm too small!' she screeches out; glad of her size. 'I saw Fisher yesterday. He was over there,' Duffy points between the cottages to the other side of the Warren track. 'He was by the wall. He was looking at me.'

People's behaviour can often be simply explained because it is self-evident but sometimes it cannot. Fisher's cannot be explained. He is a mystery and has watched the children since they began to play outside. Dressed in his black fishing smock, hat and boots, he rarely speaks to anyone except the young people. He leans on a fence and watches or sometimes he would be high on the downs looking down on them. The eye of this figure in black disturbs the peace of the cottagers but to the children he is almost a friend. He is from the Fisher community who live on the harvest of the sea below the white chalk cliff.

'If he's a fisherman, why isn't he catching fish?' asks Duffy,

'Perhaps he has no boat,' replies Seth.

15

'He gave me a marble.'

Duffy's little fist pokes out between the bars and opens to show a brightly painted clay marble in the palm of her hand.

'It's good. I like it. Will he give me another?'

'I don't know, perhaps it's his last one', replies Seth as he looks over and sees Martha in the morning light standing by the cottage door with the bone handled knife in her hand.

She has pinned an apron over a short gown and slipped a white linen cap over her knotted and pinned up hair. She stands at the cottage door enjoying the cold of the door stone under her bare feet. The summer garden is in front of her with the opening flowers of the herb garden. Small white bells of sealwort are anchor points for a freshly spun web. Lavender, betony, rosemary and sage line the path with tansy, hyssop, wormwood and figwort close to the well. Broad beans, leeks, parsnips and salad leaves are nearby in a woven hazel enclosure. Beyond these is a small apple orchard, planted and shared by the cottagers that stretches beyond the cottages onto the waste open down land. Martha has seen this pleasant view of the garden many times. She holds the knife out to Seth as he approaches.

'To the stone with this, son. It's soft as a feather.'

Seth gets more water from the well, dips the blade into the water, pushes it across a sharpening stone then deposits the bucket of water into a bowl in the kitchen. A tap, tap, tapping noise is coming from the hearth where Lizzie is busy sending a shower of sparks onto a piece of tinder to light a small fire. It smokes, glows and crackles as she adds parts of a dried cowpat. Seth is labouring for the mansion this morning. He butters a heavy rye loaf then slips the sharp knife through it for a thick slice then cuts a piece of salted mackerel and drops

16

them into a straw basket with leather strap for his shoulder. On his way to the door he drinks some last night's ale from a tankard on the table. These will maintain him till noon when he will return to the cottage to eat and meet Abe, a wagoner, to take victuals to his father shepherding on the downs.

'I'm with Gaunt, setting boundary posts for manor,' he calls to Lizzie as he disappears through the cottage door into the morning.

A few furlongs east beyond Goodwin's barn is a tumbled cottage where Gaunt was born. It has stood for many generations of his ancestors and is now in the gradual process of returning itself to the natural world. The many insects feasting themselves on its wooden beams daily drop a brown dust onto the cottage floor where it sits unnoticed. A number of these partly consumed beams have collapsed allowing thatch to tumble onto the cottage floor where it lies holding countless nests, mice runs and green layers of soft moss. Fortunately for Gaunt the leaning brick chimney and hearth still stand. In this small remaining space of the cottage there is just enough room for his bed, table and a chest for his meagre clothing. The path to this half dwelling is just visible in the grass but it is of no importance as no one comes and no one goes except the solitary occupant. The women say he is a sad lonely man and that he needs a wife to escort his mind to more delicate ways. The men are less concerned and say he is just a man and do not trouble their minds with more thought. No one knows the answer to these presumptions except the man himself.

The ceremony of healing from the Kings touch had ceased and both his parents had succumbed to lingering scrofula which later took his sister away. He spent the time alone in his cottage with only the dim light of the moon to cheer him through the dark nights as he sobbed over his lost family. After many nights he decided to look at his world again and reappeared at the inn.

One afternoon when with close friends he told them of his lonely life and the dreams of spirits that visited him on moonlit nights. Fair maids with baskets of apples smiling and beckoning him as they stood by his bed but vanished to nothing when he woke. After this intimate meeting all his male friends agreed that he should take a wife to ease his lonely burden. His pipe and diet were eagerly investigated and many unsuccessful attempts were made to recreate his dreams as they were the envy of many men-folk. A smooth, innocent, honest oval face free from blemishes, spots and imperfections looks out at the world through large calm brown eyes. His hands hang away from his body to allow for the muscular thickness of his upper arms. Within this temple of strength, with some concern for its solitary life is a contented peaceable being. A man that presents himself to the world with the honest oval face, a ragged shirt, breeches and stockings all of with generous amounts of patches and stitching.

Lizzie, with a hot red face, is sitting on a stool watching fat melt in an iron pot for reed candle making. Thin pieces of meat are sizzling on a skillet. A white fresh apron is tied round her waist over a grey food-stained shift. When she walks she is in pain, her misshapen joints have set her legs apart and they descend from opposite sides of her shift.

'Let the Lord give me life and strength,' she whispers to herself as she lifts her apron to hold the hot handle of the skillet.

The sizzling continues, the meat is cooked. She lifts it out onto a wooden platter and tips the valuable fat into the iron pot. The Applegate maids tumble down the stairs laughing as they put on their spotless white linen caps, starched and pressed under the smoothing stone the night before. Martha and Jamie are already seated at the table. Lizzie places the cooked meat on the table.

'As we've fire for the candles some beast's been cooked,' she says knowing their preferences.

'You are a Godly saint amongst us,' says Livy as she smells the cooking.

'Don't blaspheme in this cottage,' Lizzie replies as she returns to the kitchen.

There is silence as heads are bowed and Martha whispers a few words.

The food of the British at this time is unsubtle as few French cooks have crossed the channel. Living on roast beef and plum pudding is the fare for some while others have rye bread and salt fish. These cottagers are at the salt fish end of the scale. From labouring, shepherding and cottage industry they have accumulated some surplus wealth; often counted in pennies after their tythes have been paid. Set out before them on the wooden table is a large wild yeast rye loaf, a bowl of butter, a plate of barley meal biscuits, a piece of salt fish, a pitcher of small beer, and a jug of milk. Some surplus wealth has provided the hot fried pork.

The sharp knife is busy around the table.

'Barnabas' victuals today,' says Martha as she slices the rye loaf. 'Get his victuals and barrel ready for Seth to take to his cover and don't forget his 'baccy and new pipe. Abe'll be here at noon.'

Livy looks at Martha and touches her hand to get her attention.

'Can I go with Seth this time, Martha,' she asks. 'I would like to see father and talk about the sheep. I haven't seen him for a long time,' she pleads.

'Yes and can I go too. Please, Ma,' asks Beth.

'Not today, Beth. It's your alphabet day. Today you can try the quill.'

'We can go together next time, Beth,' says Livy to comfort her. 'I'll tell you what the wagoner tells us and all about father.'

'When will we make tea Martha, you said you would get the leaves?' asks Beth.

'Water is to be boiled in a kettle,' explains Livy.

'We can boil water in those,' says Jamie pointing over to the black iron vessels around the hearth.

'No. No. No, Jamie. We are going to have a proper kettle and proper teapot with spouts and handles like ladies. I've been told to make tea properly a kettle and teapot are needed,' Livy says loudly, looking at Martha for confirmation of the proposal.

'Yes, a kettle and a teapot. That's what we'll get. Handcart has kettles,' says Martha as she nods her head watching Jamie push a piece of buttered bread into his small mouth.

'Hay! Hay! Hayricks! We'll have kettles and pots with spouts and handles, just like ladies,' shouts Livy. At this pronouncement they all loudly shout,

'Hay! Hay! Hayricks! - Hay! Hay! Hayricks!' and crash their wooden plates, tankards and spoons against the table in a loud chortling happy celebration. Halfpenny looks up at the ceiling and howls in agreement.

'What's all that for?' shouts Lizzie, just as loud from the kitchen.

'We'll be happy drinking tea. Martha is going to get leaves and kettle.'

'I've been told there's a town drink "Ladies Delight" that makes you happy. Like the other drinks in London. What does Vicar Lod say?' comes the voice from the kitchen.

After this comment there is silence around the table as judgement from a higher authority may need to be considered.

The sitters have satisfied their hunger. The victuals are taken from the table and stored in the kitchen in boxes of salt and various ground herbs to maintain freshness. Martha goes into the kitchen to get food for the little ones, Becky and Ruby, who have started crying in their hot straw cots upstairs. The girls sit by the window carding wool and waiting for Martha to start spinning. In the garden, as instructed by Martha, little Jamie has taken a hoe out of a tool store and is busy tapping at weeds between rows of beans with a hoe twice his size.

Out on the downs Seth and Gaunt have wielded their mattocks, dug post holes, fitted oak posts and packed them firm. Their meagre meal has been consumed and they lie in the grass under a hot sun. Seth's mind looks at younger days when he would play with Livy and Beth but now the girls play with girls and he plays with little Jamie. Livy's quiet smooth, honey voice now makes his ears and body tingle. When he hears her voice his eyes lose focus, he feels enjoyably perplexed and wonders why this is. These random thoughts flit through his mind as he looks at the blue sky and sweats under his ragged straw hat. His pony tail of fair hair descends midway down his back where it is easily trimmed straight across with sharp sheep shears. His square chin holds the start of a young fluffy beard that Livy watches with curiosity. His physical labouring has given him a strong body that moves with an easy sturdy directness while his voice follows the same design, solid and unhurried. Gaunt looks at the hammered earth around the post.

'That's good enough for a post,' he says in a slow deep voice, 'that's a post for many a year I'll swear,' he says after placing his large hand on its top and attempting to shake it. 'Strange fog and mist time o'year. Tells a bad winter to come,' he prophesies.

'Aye, I've heard that. Another one like last with furlongs under snow will get some wasted away. Get hay in early I'd say,' says Seth as he nods his sweaty forehead in the direction of the hamlet and they begin their walk back to their cottages talking of oak posts, turnips and snow. Hoeing between the beans little Jamie sees and shouts to Seth as he returns,

'He's back again, look. What's so special about us?'

He points across the track to the dark figure of Fisher who is watching him handle the hoe. Seth comes up to Jamie and holds the end of the hoe with one hand to provide additional force for Jamie who holds the middle. They attempt to tackle a weed together, but they cannot co-ordinate and the hoe misses the weed and swings high up into the air. Jamie's face creases with laughter.

'Ha ha!' he squeals and looks at Seth whose face is equally creased with a smile.

'Ha ha!' they squeal and laugh together.

'That was a good try,' judges Seth, looking annoyingly at the weed still upright.

'He's still there,' says Jamie pointing across the track again to Fisher, whose watching eyes annoy him.

'Has he ever given you a present?' asks Seth.

'Never,' says Jamie.

'Hey there. Are there no fish in the sea today?' Seth shouts to the man. But there is no reply, the man looks at the ground.

'Do the fish have a tale to tell us?' asks Seth shouting louder.

The girls carding by the window have heard the shouting. Livy puts her carding combs down and comes out to see what the shouting is about and as she comes into the garden Fisher strides across the track to her. He fumbles in a pocket of his thick black fishing trousers and takes out a roll of shiny red ribbon. It unwinds and hangs down in bright red shiny curls.

'This is for....ha....have this,' he stammers as he holds the ribbon higher.

She is amazed at the sight of the ribbon. Wide eyed she asks.

'Why is this for me?' but there is no answer.

Seth and Jamie have finished their fun with the hoe and approach the man, but he flicks his head to one side to turn them away.

'It's beautiful,' says Livy as she holds the dangling ribbon. Seth and Jamie have not gone away. They walk towards the man. He scowls, turns and walks away. Livy is left holding the end of the ribbon that she wraps around her neck and runs smiling back into the cottage.

Chapter Three

Warm wet grass

The track up to Meads Hollow is dusty. For many days an open blue sky has stretched to the horizon revealing a hot merciless sun that sweats the labourers, farmers, and shepherds out on the open downland. Livy and Seth sit on the grass in the shade of an orchard tree beside the Warren track to the Hollow waiting for Abe the wagoner. Livy has a straw basket loaded with victuals, a pouch of tobacco and Barnabas' delicate new pipe in a tightly woven straw bundle. Seth is delivering a cask containing the shepherd's ale which is on the grass beside him. This is a regular journey for the wagoner who delivers grain from Pashley Mill to Nell at the Ship Inn for her brewing. He then returns to the mill with the innkeeper's ale.

'Here he comes,' says Livy as she sees Abe with his lumbering oxen and creaking wagon turn up the track.

'Whoa my boys! A maid with you today, Seth,' he calls as his wagon shudders to a stop with its dry joints creaking.

He is missing a front lower tooth which has given him a useful opening into his mouth for the short stem of a pipe that jiggles up and down as he speaks. Long grey hair curls around his ears and stands in a large shaggy mass around his face. Under a ragged straw hat his wide friendly face with quick eyes looks out. The speed of his ox-team has seeped into his body, he has never been seen to hurry and believes haste is as bad as blasphemy; a moderating belief of many. His weather browned hands hold thick leather reins that lead to the neck of each of his beasts, while within easy reach is his long ox goad held vertical by being dropped through a hole in the driving board.

'And a fine maid she is,' answers Seth.

'Hot it's been. But some high cloud up there,' says Abe as he nods heavenward with his pipe rattling.

The two yoked oxen whip flies with their flailing tails as Seth hoists the cask onto the wagon and the passengers sit each side of Abe.

'You know my boys; Samson and Bob,' Abe calls as he points to his team. 'Step up!' he shouts.

The oxen push forward and the large wagon wheels slowly crunch against chalk and earth.

'Wagon's busy summer,' Abe begins. 'Bricks and load sawn lumber just gone to old Bourne Place, still working on parts. Summer time wagon's busy. Trunks, bags, furniture. Just taken two maids to Crewbragh and onto the Wells. Told me they were in service together at Kent Sheet. Both sad as night crying. No rest for some,' he goads his slow beasts and continues. 'Fine maids, sisters, best of friends, loved each other since small babes. But one saw the other dallying with the master in orchard, a hand in his breeches and told Mistress. She said she didn't care. She said her man Hickle was always a rogue and she had dallied sometimes. Miller Stone says grain looks like bad winter. Wife's lost child. Their seventh, bad news, what with others gone he needs some to work at mill.'

Samson has stopped moving, Bob immediately agrees and both beasts stand still until Abe goads the beasts again.

Seth turns his head and looks at the load the wagon is carrying.

'A good load for you this day, Abe.' he says.

'Aye. A good load. Small cask there's dark ale for miller. Innkeeper's got some in her cellar. Not to be talked of. Wheels turning now,' he says with a sense of great achievement on his hairy face as he glances down at the wheels slowly turning.

'So, what happened next with the maids?' Livy asks in earnest.

'Step up boys,' Abe shouts to the slow team. 'Mistress didn't heed the dallying. Master and Mistress content. But the two maids lost their fondness for each other. Shouting, screaming, throwing at each other. Started as friends but now green eyed jealous, broke things. Master said they had to go. They shouted and cried to Crewbragh but when we got to the Wells next day they were laughing together as good sisters.'

Livy ponders being in service with a frown.

'We overnight at Crewbragh the maids stay at the Cross. I sleep in wagon. It's a steady climb to Crewbragh and then another climb to the Wells. Way to Wells mud no chalk, bad as winter. Ruts deep baked hard, wheels get in the ruts and there's no getting out. Worst roads I know. No road in winter.'

'Heard any passing bells?' asks Livy.

26

'None have met my ears,' says Abe through his rattling pipe. 'Had journey to Horsham, delivering load of hides for saddles. Saw hangings by market. Big crowd. Six villains, ropes around necks, wriggling. Cloth cut off to remember them.'

'Oh, Abe. Do you stop and watch?' asks Livy.

'Can't wait. Wagon has to move say Dragoons.'

'My soul tells me it's the devils work to hang us,' says Livy.

'We'll be on our way,' says Seth as they reach the spot nearest to the shepherd's cover.

The wagon is now high on the brow of the hollow where the hanger wood stretches down around the hollow's steep sides.

'We're high like birds now,' says Seth.

'I love it here, look at that,' shouts Livy as she turns her head and looks down to the village below.

The wagon is high on the downs and stretching out below is the hamlet of Meads with cottages, strip farms, inn and dusty roads set in the living green of the downs. The view extends to the sparkling sea and then the flat bay of Pemsey coastal levels and beyond to distant wooded ridges below a blue sky. They look down at the small figures of labourers in the fields, some bending and planting, some hoeing, some digging. On a dusty track a loaded wagon creates a dusty haze that lingers behind it as it slowly moves on its way. Small figures walk the tracks while others gather round a handcart selling pots, pans, ribbons and smoothing irons, A pack horse is led by a small boy. Smoke drifts up from the chimneys of the Ship Inn where hot water is needed for the innkeeper's brewing. Abe has travelled many miles over this scene and points away to the horizon.

'And further on the orchards of Kent, the cathedral and the harbour,' he says excitedly as he points over to the horizon with the listener's imagination extending the view. After contemplating the magnificence of the scene the three draw themselves away.

'Good to ride with you, Abe,' Seth calls as he turns to head towards his father's cover in the earth.

'Step up,' calls Abe.

'Keep Samson and Bob merry,' shouts Livy as she watches the wagon wobble and rumble away.

A small knot of black hair twisted and pinned emerges through the back of Livy's white linen cap. Curls that had escaped the cap hang in delicate array around her temples and forehead. Her brown eyes look back longingly to the view then look at Seth. The straw bag she carries is bulky and unwieldy, but he has the cask over a shoulder.

'I can manage. It's alright it's not far,' she says hoping.

Seth listens to her voice and feels the hairs on the back of his neck lifting and tingling.

'I can take a handle of the bag,' he says enthusiastically.

They walk over the hot dry grass linked together by a basket. Livy laughs and runs down a grassy slope. Seth runs behind her struggling with the cask. The curves and dips of the downs are smooth and soft interrupted by scattered clusters of blackthorn.

'There it is.' he shouts nodding towards a grass covered mound.

The old earth cover that is Barnabas' home has already been here for generations of shepherds and ancient peoples.

Dug partly into an ancient barrow at Crapham Down, roofed with branches and odd beams. Then covered with thatched hurdles then with old sails and finally a layer of grassy sods. Its outside appearance has grown over the generations as any leak of water to the interior has resulted in fresh grassy sods being tossed over the whole structure. It is now an integral part of the downland with its grass roof a mass of flowering plants and buzzing insects. Close to the entrance a clay lined dew pond carries a meagre amount of water and over it flitting to and fro are pairs of mating dragonflies, their translucent silver wings vibrating above glossy emerald bodies.

'Something for you, Barnabas,' shouts Seth as they approach the door of the cover. We've got your new pipe and 'baccy.'

'Time for a smoke father,' adds Livy.

The door to this earth home is a random selection of tired sun-bleached boards hanging for support from a top hinge that a blacksmith heated and hammered in the distant past. There is no reply to the visitor's calls. Seth places the cask in the grass, holds and lifts the thick handle and manages to push the heavy door a few inches to give them access. It is a dim small elongated space, lit only by light that manages to pass the door. The straw floor is higher at the furthest end where it is covered with fleeces and rough hemp blankets to form a sleeping area. Tally sticks, wooden plate, decorated wooden tankard, pipe and metal tinder box are on a three-leg table. A wooden trunk, stool, cask and various tools make up the remaining items. Livy transfers the content of the basket into the trunk while Seth exchanges the casks.

'It's so hot in here,' she says in an exhausted voice. 'The dewpond,' she whispers looking at Seth.

They are soon outside. Seth scrambles onto the roof of the cover and searches the landscape for his father's flock. Livy gazes at the shimmering wings of the dragonflies then kicks off her thin leather shoes, lifts her smock to her thighs and wades into the dew pond. The mating dragon flies make way for her.

'Oh! The cool water,' she says with a thrill. 'It's alright, Seth. I've seen father put his feet in this water.'

She reaches for a dragonfly that disappears as her hand approaches.

'He's over that way,' shouts Seth pointing away.

They move towards tinkling bells, find the flock and two dogs but no shepherd. Eventually the tinkling bells have an added sound of a long deep snoring inhalation followed by a quiet relaxed exhalation.

'I can hear him. There he is,' shouts Livy pointing.

They find him stretched out on his back in the shade of a solitary tree with his crook beside him. A tranquil bearded face looking skywards, its eyes closed.

'We're here,' shouts Seth. Have brought the 'baccy,' but the shepherd snores on. Seth repeats his message a little louder but with the same result.

'He's deep away. I'll wake him,' says Livy looking around at the grass.

She picks a long stalk of grass with a small cluster of seeds at its end. She holds it out over the sleeping shepherd's face and lets the seeds gently bounce on the end of his nose as she controls the bounce holding the end of the stalk. The snoring stops, a hand jerks up, hits his nose and he jerks upright. There is an enormous cough, sneeze and bellow and the shepherd opens his eyes. The dogs stare and bark, distant rabbits scurry away.

'He can chase ferrets now,' says Livy laughing.

'You're....he.....here,' he stammers out loudly. 'He blessed me with my family. Two de....dear kin come to keep old shepherd eating and drinking,' he says in a dry sleepy voice.

'Pipe smoking too. Your 'baccy is fresh, and a new pipe to smoke it in,' says Livy, her face smiling with love for this unwashed hairy being. Although still full of sleep he struggles to his feet, opens his arms, hugs Livy then puts a hand on Seth's shoulder and gives him a fatherly shaking. His swollen joints pain him, he fears the locking of his knees and swelling of his hands will prevent him wandering the downs with his flock. His gait has become a jerky hobble supported by his crook and occasionally a second stick. He loves his son deeply and knows the day for the change is only a few summers away.

'Seth, my boy. Have you been ser....sermoned at church on Sabbath for me. I haven't been near pulpit and heard a sermon for some?' the shepherd asks.

'I've been there. In the pews on Sabbath. Vicar Lod says, "How is old Barnabas?" you're one of his flock that's got lost but not gone astray,' says Seth placing his hand on his father's shoulder. He is now taller than his stooping father.

'You'll be slee....sleeping out here when my body has done enough. When I'm fit for making....can....candles.'

The bare hot sun sits in a sea of blue sky. Bells ring faintly, skylarks sing, the air is hot, little moves, it is calm and still. Seth knows the peace of the chalk downs. Pride will sit on his shoulder if he has his own flock and dogs in this rolling landscape.

'When you wish father. When you are ready and when you feel it is what you want,' Seth calmly consoles his father.

Livy is happy. She smiles into the shepherd's eyes and runs her small fingers through his long beard and hair.

'Never been woken like that afore. All night with the dogs. There was something scaring them. I nev....never got si....sight of it that's why I was so deep asleep. Fresh cask and my 'bac....baccy, good girl Livy.'

'How have you been in this hot weather, father?' she asks.

'Hot and dr....dry like them,' he nods towards his flock. 'Going to new grass to nor....northern slopes on morrow if no rain. Dew ponds little. Grass dry. They're good for some wet,' his eyes move from his flock to the distance sky where a grey mass of cloud is slowly approaching, 'and dear Martha?'

'Martha say ''Tell him all is well,'' she says she has seen the cobbler for stitching your boots. And she is getting pots. Pots for tea. Pots to make tea.' says Livy excitedly. 'She is as good as always and gives you her love.'

The shepherd gives a double note whistle and the dogs rush over to a group of wandering ewes.

'Pots....pots for tea? questions Barnabas.

'Yes, Martha's getting the leaves and kettle to make tea. Just like ladies.'

When away in his cover he only splashes water onto his face when the dew ponds is full, his beard and hair get less attention. His beard with copious growth merges with his long thick hair as his weathered face peeps out through the encircling mass.

'Moon's waxing,' says Livy. 'What kind of bush is this?' she asks as she runs her fingers through his beard finding knots and picking out particles of a recent meal. 'Do you want a blade on this?'

The shepherd frowns slightly but smiles and nods approval. Livy runs back to the cover and returns with a sharpening stone and sheep shears. At the sound of the rasp of metal on stone the dogs prick up their ears, look skyward and whine an accompanying note. Barnabas leans forward towards her, her small hand holds curls, the blades slide together, curls drop to the ground and more face slowly emerges from the hairy overgrowth.

'More post and walling for some. Around Beacon Furlong now. Much to do,' says Seth.

On hearing this remark, the shepherd turns his head towards Seth. Livy follows his head still clipping with the shears.

'You been told by fa....farm, but it be the com....common land.'

'Told by farm I was. Mansion's getting flint and lime for walls.'

'Waste's being taken by farmer. Stops flock wand.... wandering but you and I stopped from going on wa....waste. Fencing for manor is stealing away common,' complains the shepherd.

After these remarks he let out a quick despondent sigh then his attention returns to the blades scraping together closer and closer to his skin.

'That be enough lass,' he says after some time has passed. 'I'm one...one of vicar's shorn flock now. Is it ci....cider or ale?'

'Pin of ale,' replies Seth.

'Worthy liquid I say. Te....tea heard 'tis maids' drink.'

'Not a maids' drink. It's a ladies' drink,' Livy corrects the shepherd.

After the beard trimming they sit on the grass carpet talking, thinking and listening to the sound of the downs.

'That lost man, Fisher, tha....that watches. Is he still hanging about like a bad spirit? No wor....work. Lost in his idleness ma....makes for evilness and wickedness.' The shepherd then repeats part of a proverb he had heard when a boy.

'He was there at sunrise,' replies Seth.

'Look at this,' says Livy drawing from her pocket the red ribbon. 'He gave it me this very morning.'

All eyes stare at the bright flash of colour. Seth frowns, Livy smiles, Barnabas looks solemn and mystified. They sit in silence.

'All is in cover, father. We will leave you now,' says Seth as he stands brushing dry grass from his breeches. 'Let's hope water is on the way.'

The two young people return to the earth cover, collect the empty cask and basket and make their way across the hot dry landscape across to Middle Brow back towards the Hollow.

'Is the cask really empty?' Livy asks as she feels perspiration trickling beneath her clothes.

'That does looks like some water.' says Seth as he notices the approaching dark clouds.

He pulls the bung, lifts the cask and holds it over Livy's face as she catches a few drops of liquid in her dry mouth. They reach the top of the Hollow and decide to take the short cut down the steep slope through the hanger wood. As they enter the wood they hear quiet clicks from the leaves overhead but pay no attention to it. They make their way down through the steep wood. Click, click, click. More dull sounds from the dry canopy of leaves above them. They look at each other with excitement and continue through the wood listening to the sound above them. The clicks have stopped and now a pattering sound can be heard overhead as the raindrops fall more quickly. Over this long dry spell, the trees have set up their defences. Stomata have sensed the dry moisture-less air and are closed. Sap has slowed and stopped as no moisture can be found in the parched earth. But now they quickly abandon their defences, open every pore to the rain and an enchanting scent drifts through the wood as the trees quench their thirst.

They arrive at the edge of the wood. The noise of the rain has risen to a powerful roar and as they step out of the wood they are in a drenching waterfall of cooling raindrops. They walk down the grassy slope, look skyward, open their mouths and drink the cooling rain into their hot bodies. It soaks into Livy's clothes and she feels the cool rain touch her hot skin. She drops the basket she is carrying, pulls off her bonnet and pulls the pin from her long hair and lets it fall to her waist. Her clothes are now sticking to her and she feels trapped. She struggles and pulls them off until she can feel cool raindrops over her whole body. Seth watches her white body as she turns towards him and shouts through the torrent.

'It's magic, Seth. Magic. Come on!'

Seth throws the cask off his shoulder and struggles out of his wet clinging clothes. They run down the slope in gay abandon as the empty cask tumbles and bounces its way down the slope in front of them. Livy falls to the ground and lies flat and still.

'Rolling. Rolling in the rain, Seth, remember?' she shouts as she lets her body roll over and over down the slope in the warm wet grass. Seth remembers how they played when children and he slips and rolls down the slope beside her. After several rolls laughing and shrieking their bodies stop and they try to stand, but dizzy spinning heads make them lie still in the grass. After a few moments Livy lifts her head.

'My clothes!' she shrieks. 'Where are my clothes?'

The rain drops are now smaller, falling with almost no sound. Their recreational partner is drifting away high above them. They look back up the slope to their scattered clothes lying in the wet steaming grass. They look at each other with smiles of confusion and silently collect their clothes and dress themselves as best they can. For Seth it is impossible, for as he pulls on his breeches there is a loud ripping sound. The basket and barrel are collected and they walk on silently towards their cottage.

'What was that!' exclaims Seth excitedly after some silence.

'Some magic rain when it was needed. Just rain. Wet and cool,' she says in a matter-of-fact voice that makes Seth feel he has played alone.

They continue in silence until they reach Martha who knows of their plight and is waiting with some clothes she has found in a wooden chest.

'These were your grandma's,' she says as she hands Livy a rough smock with moth holes and a generous decoration of unknown indelible stains. She sits on the door stone. Seth is given a rough grey hemp blanket to wrap himself in and sits beside her as they watch Martha spreading their clothes over garden bushes to dry in the hot sun that has returned. Martha knows their childhood is passing, she knows Seth's deeper voice but she is more concerned with his torn shirt and breeches. The end of daylight is approaching and Martha is on a stool beside the table with Seth's dried clothes. Little Jamie is scribbling with a piece of chalk on the stone floor around the hearth.

'Come here and bring that chalk with you,' she calls to him. 'Get on the table. I want to see how big you are.'

He clambers on the table and stands up.

'Give me the chalk. Lay down and stretch your arms out.'

Martha takes the chalk and draws a chalk line around Jamie's small torso.

'That's you,' she says pointing to Jamie's outline. 'I'm going to give you a new shirt.'

Seth's torn shirt is turned inside out, the collar removed, distressed seams snipped off, fullness and gathering allowed and the cloth is trimmed to Jamie's outline. Beth is given the collar to unstitch and resize while Livy makes double thickness small cuffs, sets button holes and sews the bone buttons. They stitch away and as the daylight fades a rush candle is lit and then the shirt is finished.

'Hayricks!' shouts Jamie as the shirt is held up by Martha.

'Slip it on,' she says.

They study the shirt with the critical eyes of self-reliant cottagers. The capable and nimble skill of the shirt makers has overcome any crude method of creation and the shirt is neat and fitting.

'You're for a new shirt too,' Martha tells Seth who has been watching the seamstresses.

They move out of the cottage as dusk falls and sit on the cool door stone. They sit in silence. Bats have woken and flit through the dusk while night scented plants add fragrance to the air. Dim light from a glow worm is on a blade of grass. The large nightly orb has returned with its grey light settling once again on the cottages to relieve the darkness. The Applegate maids are on their bed.

'The rain was so beautiful we wanted it on our bodies. We rolled and rolled. I was so dizzy,' Livy whispers to her bed companion as she turns to face her.

'We were watching for you as the rain fell. You both looked so tousled I knew something had happened.'

'Dressing in wet clothes is awkward. I heard Seth's shirt rip and he laughed,' whispers Livy.

'I think you feel for Seth,' says Beth. 'You always go with him and laugh together.'

'I can like him if I wish. I think he would be a good man to live with.'

'Where is a man for me?' asks Beth

'If I could marry, I would be happy. A real marrying with a vicar and papers,' says Livy. 'I would be happy.'

Her sleepy eyes slowly close and she drifts into a dream with her happy thought.

The moon is dimmed behind thin cloud. The night is dark, the cottage waits in silence for the morning sun. All are sleeping soundly except Seth who twists and turns on his straw filled bed as dreams come and go. In his dream he is on the downs, where he had been that afternoon. The rain is heavy, he feels hot and anxious. The rain has made a translucent mist where shapes move and twist. He hears her honey voice, she is coming towards him dancing in the rain as she had that afternoon. He sees her soft white body, she is close to him, he stretches out his arms to hold her waist and lift her. But his hands clutch the air and she vanishes. He trembles, shudders and suddenly wakes. He is bolt upright in his bed, sweat is pouring off his body, his heart pounds in his chest, his head throbs and his bed is wet with the sweat. The noise has woken little Jamie who sleeps nearby and who whispers.

'Seth, are you alright? Are you poorly? You have been moaning.'

'Yes Jamie. I think I'm alright. A spirit is playing with my body.'

'Is it good or evil?' asks Jamie.

'It might be both,' is the reply.

Seth falls back down on his bed, his head drops on the pillow and he tries to think of nothing. In time his troubled mind slowly settles and he begins to drift into a comfortable deep sleep. But in a while a new dream slowly drifts into his sleep and he shudders and twists again in his bed. He is sitting on a stool in the aisle of a church. The congregation is a wall of contorted faces, scowling and grimacing at him. His peers are judging him. He can see a pulpit where a clergyman is pointing at him and he hears the words of a sermon.

'Lewdness of the flesh. Lewdness of the body! Yea, and the mind. The garden, remember the garden. Their nakedness brought the devil to tempt them with an apple. A simple apple. Repent! Repent!' comes roaring from the red-faced clergyman.
A large heavy bible floats in the air, its pages flicking over then it slams shut and tumbles out of sight. He sees the gesticulating clergyman and pulpit slowly being swallowed up in a thick fog. The faces remain to stare, turn more hideous, then they too are lost in the fog. Seth opens his eyes, he is hot and sweaty again, lifting his head he looks around and is relieved to see the

familiar thatch and beams over his head and a small spider swinging on a thread in the dim light of the moon.

Chapter Four.

Jollyboy

The long days of summer are the Applegate shepherd's delight; they are his heaven. The freezing hands and feet of winter are distant memories. It's time to enjoy the summer warmth and on this particular day he is especially pleased as the buntings have arrived in large numbers. It is time to be busy. Shepherds would set as many coops as possible for a demand that rarely reached satisfaction.

'Look at them, Seth! More th....than I've ever seen,' he says with amazement as they watch thick flocks of buntings circling and landing over the downs. 'We'll catch the lit....little white arses tomorrow. Bring all, and lit....little Jamie too. He can set traps now. I've set a few already. Will be a go....good harvest.'

Rain fell that night but the morning held clear blue sky. The young members of the family are carrying sacks and spades and meet up with the shepherd just after sunrise.

'Come with me. I want to sh....show Jamie a trap set some days ago,' says the shepherd.

They arrive at a small tunnel in the grass marked with a large field flint. They crouch down and a turf is lifted. Flap! Flap! A startled white breasted bird with black flashes on the edges of grey wings is captive in this small tunnel.

'That lo....looks plump. A good bird,' he says with some satisfaction. 'Look Jamie see the noo....noose.'

'Yes, Pa.'

Barnabas extracts the bird from its horse hair noose and quickly twists its head; there is a dull cracking sound.

'We can easily get hu....hundreds on these grassy slopes and six pen....penny a dozen at the inn. Best pri....price at the old Lamb,' he says as he drops the limp lifeless bird into a sack.

Beth, who is closely watching the proceedings squeezes and contorts her face.

'That sound is evil. I hate it. Errrrr,' she squeezes out through gritted teeth.

'Don't fret so, Beth. It's just a bird,' says Livy.

The Shepherd carries out this termination of life without any emotional concern. His swollen joints give him pain but the thought of a bird feeling pain is not in his mental universe.

'Set the no....noose like this,' he says looking at Jamie. 'Then the turf ba....back over.'

He then ties the sack and points to another nearby coop.

'How many will we get today?' asks Jamie as he ties a noose.

'I've watched the....them arrive. Good few. Could fill sa....sack.'

As they settle around the next coup and begin to open it a small dog jumps into their crouching circle, pushes its nose into the tunnel then energetically jumps up at their surprised faces. The sound of an approaching horse is heard.

'Jolly!' a voice calls. 'Jollyboy! Jollyboy! Has he caused any trouble, he's got energy to spare. He's sometimes a nuisance stealing birds from the coops,' shouts the rider who leaps off his horse and comes over to the group.

'I'm from the house. The old Mansion House but most times I'm in busy London.'

He is a young lad of about sixteen summers, dressed in a tailored coat, waistcoat, breeches and riding boots. Although all his clothes are slightly worn and frayed, they all speak of underlying serious quality. A linen cravat is loosely fluffed and tied around his neck. Above this cravat is an eager face with pony tail of fair hair under a floppy old-style hat. A wig can be seen stuffed into a pocket.

'If you're selling you can deliver some to the house. Cook asks about them every summer, they're good for the table,' he continues looking at the Applegates one by one.

'Well lad, sir. I've go....got orders,' says Barnabas.

Beth looks at Barnabas with a puzzling frown.

'But there's   al....always a few dozen to spare. I'll gla....gladly talk with cook and leave what she needs, sir.'

'That would be good,' the lad replies.

The turf is moved aside and both nooses have wheatears.

'A good haul,' says the lad as he looks over their shoulders at the flapping birds.

The shepherd puts his hand down to lift one of the birds but it suddenly violently flaps its wings, wriggles its body, slips out of its noose and flies up with a slapping noise and disappears into the air at great speed. They are all startled as much as the bird. Suddenly there is a loud scream from the lad.

'Jollyboy Jollyboy. He's gone over!'

The coop is about four yards from the cliff edge and the bird has sped out over the edge chased by the friendly dog that has made everyone doubly aware of his presence but is now nowhere to be seen. The lad drops to his knees, crawls to the edge of the cliff and peers over.

'He's there. I can see him. Jollyboy, Jollyboy,' he calls down to his dog but it doesn't move. 'Oh Jollyboy you dullard of a dog. What shall we do?' he asks looking anxiously round at the bird catchers who are still crouching around the coop.

The Applegates previously happy are now shocked at this sudden tragedy. They cautiously approach the edge, look over, and see the terrier lying on its back a dangerous distance below.

'We must get ropes and help. Someone could be lowered down,' says Seth as the lad looks around the cliff face trying to discover a way down.

'Over there. I can get down over there,' he says pointing to a nearby chalk ledge on the immense chalk face. He runs to it and begins to descend.

They watch partly in admiration and partly in fear as they know the chalk could not be trusted like other stone. But the lad reaches his dog safely and sits beside him gently stroking its belly. Looking up at the faces peering over the edge he shouts up with relief.

'He has breath in him. I'll sit here with him.'

After a short time, the dog's legs begin to twitch and then his body wriggles. He springs to his feet, jumps up to the lad and licks his face as if nothing had happened. There is laughter and shouting from above which slowly went quiet as they considered the lad's next move in this tricky canine rescue.

As the bird catchers look down the lad tucks his coat into his breeches then buttons up his coat with a few buttons open at the top thus forming a pocket. He puts the dog into this pocket and buttons up the remaining buttons. He then begins his ascent as the onlookers watch again with some dread as the lad tests footholds, then gives them his full weight and then searches for another. He reaches the top of the cliff but as he reaches for his last foothold, the dog that has been quiet up to now, begins fidgeting in the lad's coat and suddenly manages to poke his head out. He barks and licks his master's face. Jollyboy is no doubt getting short of air in the pocket and not being aware of what is going on has innocently taken remedial action. It is too much for the lad, he loses his grip, falls backwards into space and plunges down to land back on the ledge. The dog lands beside him and runs about yelping. The onlookers screech in horror.

'This ain't Chris....Christian,' the shepherd says in a quiet voice to himself. 'Poor lad,' he then suddenly has a momentary feeling of guilt. 'Can't be us. Not us put him there,' and the feeling disappears.

'The dog is lucky. But what about him,' says Seth peering down.

They look down and see the lad begin to move, he stands up, shouts out in pain, hops about then suddenly falls over.

'Are you hurt ba....bad, lad,' the shepherd shouts down.

'My leg. My leg. I can't stand on it. It pains so much.'

'We'll get you up, sir,' shouts Barnabas lying flat at the cliff edge as the lad looks up and sees a row of faces anxiously peering down at him. 'Some....something's to be done, Seth.

Take his ma….mare, get to the house and get someone with ro….ropes. I'll climb do....down,' says the shepherd.

'You're not right with that, father. That's not for you. What's your name, lad?' Seth calls down.

'Wood, Charles Wood,' is shouted back.

'I'll go down on the le….ledges and tend him,' continues the shepherd.

'You're not going down there, father. It's not for you. Beth, you ride to the house and tell them to come,' instructs Seth.

'I'm away.' shouts Beth and she scrambles onto the lad's mare.

Seth climbs down onto the chalk ledges while his father looks on with a face of anguish. He successfully reaches the lad who puts his arms around Seth's neck and Seth climbs back up the cliff face. As he negotiates the last ledge Beth is back with an earthy gardener and a tidy lady. Seth lays the injured lad carefully on the grass.

'Oh! Charles. Charles. What has happened?' the lady looks around for an answer as she dismounts.

'He we….went over for his dog, my….my lady and tried….'

'But are you hurt, Charles?' she interrupts.

'I can't stand. It's my leg,' he says in pain.

'We must get you a surgeon. Your humours need to be balanced,' the lady says kissing him on the cheek. 'Put him in the saddle, Johns. Gently now,' she says to the gardener, 'and send for the surgeon.'

He is carefully lifted onto his horse and slips one foot onto the tread of a stirrup while his other foot hangs loose. The gardener begins walking the horse back to the house.

'What about Jolly. He's still on the ledge down there?' the lad shouts as his horse is being led away.

'The surgeon at the Wells must be got with all haste. Will you be able to collect the dog as you have done for my boy?' the lady asks looking at the shepherd.

'Yes. We will de....deliver him to the house, my lady,' he replies with a slight bow.

'We will expect that. Be sure he is safe, my boy loves the dog. How did this happen?' she asks.

She is informed of the dog's unsuccessful attempt to catch a wheatear and the details of the successive events that followed. She thanks Seth profusely for his brave rescue, gets into the saddle and gallops off after the invalid.

The sun is high. A cool breeze drifts in from a silver blue sea. Above are climbing masses of white cloud that drift slowly across pure blue. They sit silently on the grass green cliff top and gaze out into the immense blueness. Livy and Beth sit side by side as their voices blend together.

We country lasses wait to wed
Some country lad who works the land
Who knows the oak and loves a wood
With nature's reeds tight overhead

So send him me this royal land
With lips to kiss a'merry to be
Make my band with straw of gold
And place it on this true loves hand

Here nature crowns us with delight
With garlands from the buds of May
Golden corn ears fill our sight
While flowers scent our winter hay

There are no poor men I am told
Who live within this.....

The sound of their singing delights them all as it drifts on the air in this green, white and blue paradise. After a period of silence they peer down to the ledge below where Jollyboy has spent his surplus energy barking and trying to run up the steep cliff and now sits licking a paw.

'We're coming now little dog,' calls out Beth. 'We'll have you safe back at the house. I want to go for him. I can climb easily, Seth.'

Without waiting for a reply Beth lifts and ties her smock around her waist, climbs over the edge and makes her descent. They watch her descend to the ledge, put the small nervous dog in the tied-up smock and ascend without incident to the cliff top.

'We can't set him down till we're away from the edge,' she says as she pants from her exertion.

'I'll carry him,' says Livy taking Jollyboy in her arms and stroking his nose.

'You can carry him but I'm taking him to the house,' Beth says staring at Livy.

'You can. I didn't like him,' Livy replies.

'Didn't like the lad. What's there not to like about him,' Beth says with some surprise.

48

Livy is too busy stroking and patting the dog's nose to continue.

'Half a sack Th….that's enough for now,' says Barnabas after more coops are opened. 'We'll leave the re….rest for morrow.'

The bird catchers walk back to their cottage and transfer the few wheatears they have into a wicker basket. Jollyboy is given to Beth and with her father they make their way to The Street and the Mansion House.

Like a giant oak in a wood of smaller trees the Mansion House stands proud. Perhaps these smaller trees are also oaks struggling for the light and waiting for their turn to be thousand-year-old oaks. The house of course is not a thousand years old. It is more than a century old and its origins lie possibly somewhere in the century before that or perhaps before that. Soft Weald mud has been thrown into wooden brick moulds, pressed, trimmed, stacked, kilned and carted to this sheltered green location where it has arisen as a rural outpost of aristocratic grandeur in quiet tranquillity. Romantic flourishes of a travelled architect have dictated its form. A wisp of magic comes to passers-by when eyes alighted on the mystical conically topped round tower with lancet windows growing out of the south wing. Old customs have changed in this old manor. Gentleman farmer Spendwell is the head of the house now. He loves his roast beef and plum pudding. He loves his wife, loves his dogs and loves his maids. His wife loves her perfume, dresses, hats and dearly loves her horses. Their right-hand man used to be called a Bailiff but is now called a Constable and there was a court room here but the old court room is now a library waiting for its first book. Tithe collection, administration and a court for local misdemeanours is now accommodated in the marble floored hall. Fines and time in the pillory keep the peace. Aggrieved persons release their aggression on felons by pelting them with rotten vegetables, rotten eggs or bad fish or anything that takes their fancy as he or she occupies the pillory in The Street for a day.

Today The Street is hot and dusty. The smell of fermentation drifts out from the Ship Inn along with shouts and laughter. An old bull is led by the ring in its nose to its fate in Butcher's cherry coloured yard. Jollyboy barks in Beth's arms as she holds him tight while Barnabas carries the basket of fresh wheatears. They pass Bridger's field and reach the house garden with its tree lined boundary. Barnabas's eyes fall on the pillory post with its empty hand and neck holds cut into oak boards and its wrought iron lock that carries out the Constable's sentence. Barnabas has seen the Constable lock old Moe in this pillory where a flagon of ale and biscuits were left for him when his time for release came. Not all those pilloried were the target for rotting vegetables or similar foul things. They pass an elderly fisherwoman sitting on the ground next to a fish laden basket. She watches them approach.

'Fresh herring. Fresh herring,' she calls with a strong voice that has called the same words since childhood.

''Tis not the day for su....such victuals,' shouts Barnabas.

'For the beast in your arms if not for you,' she replies. Beth shakes her head.

It is now late afternoon. The courtyard of the mansion and the easterly elevations are in shadow and before they reach the wrought railings of the courtyard, they head for a partly open door that looks directly onto The Street where Barnabas knows staff enter and leave. He puts his hand on the studded oak door, pushes it gently and it silently opens. He looks in. Jollyboy wriggles in Beth's arms.

'Be still Jolly,' she exclaims. 'You're almost home.'

'Hi-ho! Hi-ho!' calls Barnabas as he looks down a long passage. There is no answer so he repeats his call. They can hear the rattling of plates and cutlery and eventually a head appears around a door to a passage and a kitchen maid stands in the passage wiping her hand on her apron.

'Wait there. Someone will come for you.'

She disappears back into the kitchen and they hear her say, 'It'll be the dog.'

The noise in the kitchen subsides, there is the scraping sound of a wooden stool being slid back on a tiled floor and a footman walks slowly to the door.

'Yes. What is your business with the house?' he asks with small crumbs of pastry still on his lips. His collarless coat, waistcoat and breeches are a dull vermilion with grey brocade buttons. His white stockings fall into clean shiny black square toed shoes with shiny brass buckles. Beth eyes this man with a certain envious delight.

'This morning I rescued Jollyboy after his fall. He belongs to Charles and I have brought him back. Charles was hurt and asked....,' Beth fires out proudly but before she has finished her tale the footman interrupts.

'Two good people and a dog and it is young master Charles' dog. We all know the dog very well. We try very hard to keep him out of the kitchen,' he says carefully as he brushes the crumbs from around his mouth. 'I have been told all about it. And you. What have you got in there?' he asks Barnabas looking at the basket.

'Wheatears for the kitchen as pro....promised.'

51

'Good. Give those to me,' he says. 'You follow me,' he says to Beth and closes the large door with Barnabas left standing outside.

He leads the way down the passage, hands the basket in at the kitchen door where the maids are busy, past more doors, a left turn and then they are in a two storey panelled hall with massive doors to the courtyard.

'Wait here.' he says in a commanding voice and ascends a wide staircase that curls down to the hall from a corridor above.

Although Jollyboy struggles to get away from Beth she still holds him tight and the dog has to be content with licking her face. Her eyes wander over the wainscoted walls and decorated hangings. A painter with a narrow brush is painting the letter 'L' over one of the doors. After a short wait she hears a door open and shut and the lady they met in the morning looks down at her over the balustrade.

'Oh good,' she says quietly to herself, then calls down, 'Please come up.' Beth climbs the polished staircase.

'Charles will be so happy to see you and Jollyboy. He is resting in his rooms in the south wing. He's distressed because he can only walk with a crutch, poor boy, and cannot ride without pain. But what of Jollyboy, is he hurt from his fall?' she asks as they walk along a dim corridor.

'He is his usual self,' replies Beth.

She has not been in the big house before. She has heard talk of the house as a fine place and she is now discovering what the word 'fine,' really meant. She had seen a silver crown once but never a two-guinea gold piece. It was these pieces of metal that had resulted in this giant oak in the woods but the process was a mystery to her. They stop at a door, the lady opens it. Beth's tired arms are opened, the dog jumps down and runs barking into the room. The lady indicates with her hand for her to enter. The room is large with south facing windows that just catch the late sun and look out over South Dean and the green downs cut with strip farms and onto the sea beyond. All now with a golden glow as the sun moves lower. The morning's events for Charles, although a great misadventure are relieved by the presence of Beth and of course the return in good health of Jollyboy. He has been thinking of the two girls he met as he reclined alone in his room. It is a long narrow room, with high backed carved walnut chairs. A writing desk stands with chests and small tables along the back wall where a small fire grate with dying embers lets wisps of cherry wood smoke drift into the room. Tall windows give a bright light that bounces off mirrors to fill the whole room.

'That's enough boy,' says Charles trying to keep the dog from enthusiastically licking his face and knocking his injured leg with a busy tail.

'Come in. I must thank you for rescuing my dog. He's my constant companion while I'm away from home. I come here in summers, ride the downs and sometimes join the hunt.'

'Father has left wheatears for the kitchen,' says Beth.

'Good. They'll make a good table. Back to Richmond in a few days. Before I go you must visit and we can talk about the sheep, wheatears and all country things,' he says with a smile at Beth.

The lady has gone over to a corner of the room and is searching a figured walnut cabinet.

'I want to meet everyone working the land, find out what they do. A complete impossibility I know but I want to know farming,' he looks over to the lady in the far corner and whispers,

'I need to escape sometimes,' he says in a hushed voice. 'But you must sit down,' he continues pointing to a nearby chair. 'As you have been so helpful, I must invite you to tea. I can show you how it's made in London. Come to the house tomorrow.'

'You must visit our cottage as we too will be having tea. We have decided to buy a teapot,' Beth says in some eagerness. 'Would you come?' she asks.

They try to make conversation but it's not long before they are silent. Eventually the lady, who is still opening and closing the cabinet comes over to them.

'My name is Michelle,' she says. 'We come to the sea each year. Gentleman farmer Spendwell is a family relation. London is so stinking it's good to flee the place. Get away to some quiet green land. You should get rest now,' she says looking at Charles. 'You can go home now. I'll get someone to see you out,' she opens a window and calls down to a gardener to send someone up. A short while later the footman appears at the door and holds it open as Beth leaves the room. As the door closes Beth stops for a moment as she can hear Michelle talking.

'That's all. To tea then that's all. These people are good working poor, but you shouldn't be seen out with them. They are shabby, untutored....'

Beth turns and walks away saddened and disappointed by what she has heard and knows she will weep silently in the night. They descend the staircase into the hall. There are people in the hall talking in a strange language. They suddenly stop talking, a moment of silence, then a sound reverberates around the old hall. Stretched silver wound strings are vibrating, nimble fingers press to frets, fingers pluck, fingers wander over a keyboard and fingers seal over sound holes. A quartet of two lutes, box clavichord and flute send clear crisp notes into the air. The hall is filled with an enchanting delightful sound. Beth cannot believe her ears, she has never heard a sound like this before, she stands, listening and staring at the strange instruments.

'This way,' the footman calls pointing to the way out down the passage. The sound follows them down the passage until the clattering noise of plates and cutlery interrupts their enjoyment. As she steps into the daylight Beth turns to the footman and asks.

'But what was that sound in the hall?'

'Music. 'Tis the gentleman farmer's music. He heard it when in the Netherlands, and has the musicians here to play for mistress,' he says as he closes the heavy door.

'I would love to hear that music again,' says Beth to the footman as the door closes.

'Perhaps that will be,' he says through the closing door. 'We all like the sound. The scratchy fiddles that some use now are not his taste,' and the door closes.

She listens to the music in her head as she walks homeward back along The Street where the fisherwoman shouts at a disgruntled customer but she hears nothing but the sound of the music playing in her mind. The notes from the lutes are still with her as she thinks of the strange instruments and the fingers of the musicians that worked them. But as she nears her cottage the sound drifts away to nothing and her mind is back to her simple cottage existence.

The mysterious night time visitor has risen again to drop its grey light over the hamlet. Beth looks at the embers of the fire as the words of the lady haunt her mind. She is with Martha in the parlour where the embers are slowly turning to ash. Martha has visited the Mansion House as a juror and sat in the hall where Beth had heard the music. She has been told all the events of the day and has experienced similar unworthy distinctions.

'It's just tittle-tattle, Beth. Take no notice. She's from the city. Just like city folk to be afraid of us village people,' she says to Beth. 'Don't let it fret you. I am sure she did not mean unpleasantness. She may be a good woman below her sad talk. Tell the lad on the morrow what she said. He'll tell you if she really is a bad penny.'

'I won't like to. I think she's his mother,' replies Beth as she leaves the hearth and climbs the stairs.

She is not looking forward to the night. Her emotions well up inside her and as she reaches the top step her tears are falling.

'Oh, Beth. Don't weep so. The lad invited you because he likes you,' whispers Livy as she hears Beth's sobs.

'She will stop him seeing me. I know she will,' says Beth through her sobs as she sits on the bed.

'Come and lie down. You poor sad girl,' says Livy.

Beth lies silently crying as Livy looks into her eyes and strokes her forehead.

'I will go on the morrow. If I'm ragged, he doesn't mind. He said he would show me tea,' she says with a sob.

'Did he try to kiss you?' asks Livy keen to know Beth's experience.

'We were never alone. The lady was in the room all the time. She was worried about his leg and said he should rest so I had to leave. When I left I heard the music players. It was such a beautiful sound.'

The two girls are silent as they listen to Martha's footsteps on the stair.

'Go and see the lad on the morrow, Beth,' Martha whispers across the dark room as she drops onto her bed. 'Forget about the sad lady.'

The girls are silent until they hear Martha's sleeping breath.

'Did you want him to hold you?' asks Livy.

'I don't know. I didn't think of holding. We talked about how lucky Jollyboy had been after falling so far onto the ledge,' replies Beth.

'I know Seth wants to hold me. When my clothes were off in the rain he watched as if he wanted to hold me,' says Livy. There is silence until she whispers. 'Shall I comfort you?'

'I am sad. No. Not this night.'

'I want Seth to hold me,' whispers Livy.

'Babies! You will have his baby. He's your brother,' says Beth in a louder voice.

'Shush! Ma will wake,' whispers Livy.

'Some say it's sinning.'

'Some say it isn't.'

The grey visitor drifts across the night. A grey face seen by all over countless millennia. New born babies look at it, old folk look at it, the blind feel it, and the seas are rocked by it. It silently watches but says nothing and fades as the light of a brighter visitor rises in the east.

Beth wakes with weary eyes, her night has been long and dismal. She is pleased to see the light of day through the open shutter. She thinks of his words, 'come tomorrow.'

At noon she finds herself in The Street, looking at the people around her, 'Are they shabby?' she asks herself. A Fisherwoman is here with her catch.

'Fresh lobster for you today, love. Pull the flesh from this claw,' she shouts as she holds up a cracked lobster claw.

Beth shakes her head with eyes closed. She wants to see Charles's face again. She is at the side door of the house. It is open. She knocks with her knuckles but the solid oak door makes little sound.

'Visitor for Charles,' she calls down the passage. She can hear the sound of the kitchen again as voices echo around tiled walls.

'Visitor for Charles,' she calls again.

'Someone's here,' is shouted. Beth expects to see the footman she saw yesterday but a kitchen maid looks into the passage.

'It's a girl,' says the maid.

'Charles told me to come,' Beth says down the passage.

'Charles said you should come?' repeats the maid.

'Yes,' says Beth. The maid returns to the kitchen, Beth hears their voices.

'Charles said she was to be here.'

'She's for blacking the boots, cook.'

'No, she's already in the boot room. Go and see her, cook.'

'I'll see her,' says cook leaving a wooden spoon in a pudding mix.

Beth waits. A large woman comes into the passage and looks Beth up and down.

'What are you here for, love,' says the cook.

'I've come for tea with Charles,' The cook looks at the pudding mix on her fingers then looks with kindness at Beth.

'You've missed them, love. Not here now. Went early, all of them with Charles and the dog. You the girl who brought the dog?' she asks.

'Yes, I brought Jollyboy here,' replies Beth.

'Well, I'll tell you. He came into the kitchen last dinner and told me about you. He said to tell you he had to go with the others. They come regular love, so he'll be here again.'

Beth's emotions are adrift on a large sea. A storm looms on one horizon, jagged rocks on another. She searches for some still water to stop her tears.

'Gone?' she asks. 'Have they really gone?' she asks again sadly.

'Of course love. I'm always true,' says the cook. 'And he told me to say the shepherd's wheatears satisfied the table.'

Beth did not want to hear about wheatears. She walks slowly back along The Street without seeing anything. She can hear the voice of a flower girl singing.

Fine orchids, rosemary, betony, rue
In dappled gardens eternally true
Flowers to bring joy mirth to your door
To brighten the sky so'll never go poor
My flowers to buy!
My flowers to buy!

She does not go to her cottage but to a fallen tree.

An old tree where a few branches have been cleared to expose its thick trunk that has been worn smooth by many who have sat here. This is where she sits as warm tears trickle slowly down her cheeks.

Chapter Five

Murdering spirit

The days float by. The harvest is in and the seasonal clock slowly takes the days away. The sun is no longer the brilliant cheering illuminator but a feeble fleeting visitor that leaves the cottagers early and plunges them into dark nights where rush candles bring little comfort. Heavy night frosts turn the green downs to a crisp silver-grey carpet that crunches under boots. Days have softened Beth's sadness but the lad who stole her heart is still a loved memory as the girls assist Martha with preparations for the snow and ice of winter. Wet mud and twisted straw have been forced into crevices and gaps. Stacked logs fill the inglenook. The food store has been loaded with earthenware jars of butter, honey, pickled onions, boxes of oat cakes and a barrel of salted fish. Untapped barrels of ale sit in a corner of the parlour. Today is a special day for Barnabas. It is the day he will return to his cottage, sleep with his wife and the next day being the Sabbath he will hear Vicar Lod's sermon and nod to him as he leaves the church. He'll feel his place in heaven has been saved. The sky is a blue grey endless sheet that sheds an eerie light on the rolling downland. The wind has shifted to the east and at midday a stinging cold wind drifts across the downs silencing wildlife that retreats to the protection of its domain. It stings Barnabas' face as he works in sheepskin leggings, over-smock, hood and mittens.

He is setting up a sheepfold by Crapham Hill next to a hay-barn that has roof cover for sheep. It is close to his cover and he will provide them with winter feed from the barn if the need arises. The first flakes of snow drift down in the early afternoon as he and Ebb, a fellow shepherd, whistle their dogs herding in the stragglers. They work on as the snow falls and soon the downs are covered in a crisp freezing whiteness. They have worked before in these conditions and there is no concern. The snugged cottages are ready when this freezing whiteness descends. Their solid oak shutters, always closed in the long dark winter days and nights, turn the cottages into cold dark caves where life is difficult. Lizzie is busy tallowing with mutton tallow. She vigorously rubs it into everything of leather; boots, shoes, clothing and the important fireside bellows. The single hand of the clock is at seven when Lizzie has finished tallowing. She stirs a simmering thick vegetable pottage with a heavy ladle. She melts and pours hot fat from a heavy spoon onto a long, partly peeled rush on a wooden tray. The pith absorbs the fat that will give a wick that will give light for an hour. Little Jamie is chalking his letters on a stone slab in the floor by the hearth. Beth and Livy decorate their caps with red ribbon bows. Seth sharpens a scythe blade on a stone. Martha has put woollen blankets over the babes in their cots and has come into the parlour. The wind whistles round the cottage, the shutters rattle, the roof beams creak and the fire smokes.

Out in the freezing wind and thickening snow Barnabas is making his way to his cover where he will collect the cask and then make his way to his wife and family at his cottage. But the deepening falling snow is becoming an obstacle to movement. Half way to his cover Barnabas stops to look at a small mounds of snow that he can see in the failing light.

'Heaven sa....save me,' he mutters through tight cold teeth, and he pushes his wet heavy leather boots through the snow towards the buried sheep.

Seth in the cottage listens to the howling wind and puts down the sharpening stone.

'It's a bad night!' he exclaims.

He pulls a wooden plug from a small spy hole in one of the shutters, gusts of wind and snow blow into the room. He peeps through the hole. Although he has seen many winters this was something he had never seen before. Large flakes of snow are falling quicker than usual, They fall and are then snatched by the wind that turns them into a swirling dancing white mass that is pulled away into the black night as more flakes fall.

'It's murderous bad!' he exclaims again, as he plugs the spy hole.

After several rush candles have burnt away they hear hammering on the cottage door and a shout. Martha slides a shutter and peers out into the swirling snow.

'Is Barnabas with you?' a voice calls. 'It's worse up there,' shouts a horse rider pointing his crop up the track.

It's the Riding Officer who works along the coast.

'Saw Ebb at the hay-barn. Told me Barnabas had gone to his cover but he wasn't there. I always talk to the shepherds along here to see if they've seen anything in the night. Looked around couldn't see him anywhere. So thought he'd be here.'

'No. No. he's not with us,' Martha shouts back.

'Must get to the stables.'

The horseman turns his horse and slowly disappears into the night. Martha is anxious as she slides the shutter closed, she looks at the clock hand and sees it almost vertical.

'Where is he?' she asks with a worried face.

'He's worked in the snow many winters. He'll be here in due time. He'll not want to miss the vicar,' answers Seth in a calming voice.

The wind and snow continue their freezing dance. Only Seth and Martha are in the parlour with a single light. Martha's feeling of helplessness in the face of nature and the knowledge that her husband's life may be in danger has raised anxiety to fear. Her lips are narrowed and pinched.

'Where is he now?' she asks to comfort herself knowing that there is no answer. 'The Officer says he can't find him, he's not in cover. Where is he?'

The wind as if answering Martha's question roars and screams outside.

'There must be foul weather up there,' says Seth with some dread.

'Seth. You must go. See that he is out of this weather. He would do the same for you. Tell them at the inn.'

'I will. I will. Barnabas will be in his cover. Not out in this.'

Seth's voice is just heard against the howl of the wind. He takes another look through the spy hole then pulls on his sheepskin clothes, squeezes his hands into mittens and slowly opens the cottage door. The outside is in chaos. As the door opens piled snow falls onto the cottage floor and blows into the parlour. The grey face of the moon looks down then hides itself behind black cloud as the wind continues to howl like a beast.

'When I find him, we'll shelter in cover. When the wind's gone we'll come down,' he shouts as he makes his way into the snow and wind as Martha pushes the door closed behind him. He tries to walk but the snow is deep and still falling heavily around him.

He reaches the Ship Inn, tells his story to the few companions he finds watching the dying embers in the hearth and leaves with Full and Acorn, both middling in their count of summers but reliable and eager to assist. With these men older than himself he feels less anxious and more confident in finding his father. Full lights a lantern as they leave the inn but as soon as they are in the night its flame is whipped out by the wind.

'If he's not at the hay-barn he must be in his cover,' shouts Seth to his companions as they push their way through the snow up the Warren track towards the barn. They hammer on the barn door and after a few moments Ebb shouts through the door.

'He's gone. Only me here now with flock to watch. Gone back to his cover.'

'What's to do now, Seth?' asks Full in an exhausted voice.

'We must go to his cover,' shouts Acorn.

'Yes. Yes. We shall find him there,' agrees Seth.

'Must a'gone past the first hour now,' shouts Full.

'We'll get over to his place and meet him there. He won't be out in this weather,' shouts Seth as he leads the way.

They slowly stumble along in the dark feeble light of the grey moon that watches. Seth stops and points to a small mound of snow.

'That's a buried sheep. I'm sure of that,' he shouts. But there is no reply. 'I'll have to give it breath,' he says to himself. He looks to check his volunteers are still with him and can just make out their shapes in the darkness.

'The sheep should all be by the barn. Must breath!' he says as he pushes a hole into the mound with his arm to give the sheep air.

His volunteers catch up with him, more buried sheep are seen and the three struggle in the snow to giving the sheep air. The snow still falls in large soft flakes. The fierce wind blows the snow into swirling ghosts that sting the eyes and freeze cold lips. The murdering spirit of winter is watching them as they struggle unaware of exhaustion approaching.

'I'm done. I can do no more. I must go back. Hands are well froze and will not work,' Full shouts in desperation.

'To the cover!' shouts Seth pointing. 'It's near!'

They stumble, confused, freezing and wet towards the shelter. Through the falling snow Seth sees a short snow covered post. A solitary post that puzzles him. Who has fixed such a post in this spot. He pulls himself through the deep snow to the post, stares at it then brushes snow off the top. His face creases in horror and he falls backward into the snow and tries to shout but his voice will not come. He tries to shout again but cannot. Eventually he manages a yell and points to the post. The volunteers come over and look at the post as their faces fill with horror.

'I know it. It's his. The shirt. It's his cloth!' Seth manages to screech out.

They all look with dread at a frozen hand.

'It's his! It's him!' cries Seth.

They stand speechless as the cold closes around them. Seth frantically clears the snow from the upright frozen arm. The sudden horror has brought them to their senses and they madly clear the snow from around the body. The shepherd's sheepskin is rigid, the fur hood frozen to his hair. His beard is a mass of thin silver threads of ice and snow surrounding a ghostly frozen face of bluish purple with sunken hollow cheeks and thin purple lips. Seth is still in shock as he looks into the face of his father. Contraction of muscle and tissue has left the body twisted and distorted. One foot is twisted, trapped between snow covered hurdles. The horror has thrown the three rescuers into an enchanted state. The grey face of the moon peers down at the freezing mortals and the murdering spirit of winter looks for more victims.

'A murderer is about tonight,' Seth whispers to himself.

The group stand in silence looking with fear at the sight in front of them until they become aware of the numbing coldness sinking deeper into their bodies.

'We must get him down from here,' says Seth. 'We must get him to his cottage. There will be beasts out.'

They are too exhausted to carry the stiff frozen corpse and they drag it through the snow leaving a long furrow in the icy white. The freezing killer watches as they struggle through the freezing white downland with one of its victims. Seth tries to think of what to do next, but his mind is frozen. The snow has ceased falling but the coldness of the night is still with them, they are almost ready to collapse with fatigue into the white soft snow that tempts them. They manage to pull the body to the top of the Hollow and begin the descent through the wooded slope where the snow is not so deep but touching a branch brings down more snow. They reach open ground and drag the frozen corpse to the cottage door. The noise of the wind has stopped and it is deadly quiet. Martha opens the door and stares into the night. Seth hurries to her and wraps her in his arms as she looks over his shoulder at the rescuers strange load lying in the snow. Her eyes widen with incredulity and disbelief as she recognised the frozen clothes around Barnabas' body. The horror of the scene makes her sick and weak. She stumbles backwards into the cottage as the corpse is taken in and the cottage door closes on the roaming killer. The corpse is laid on the floor. The rescuers shed their freezing clothes and stand about motionless with horror. Lizzie is first to move, she hastily adds to the glowing remains of a fire with kindling and logs and there is silence as the sad group try to believe what has happened. The rescuers are still in agony with stiff fingers that throb with acute stinging pain. Lizzie fills a large wooden bowl with milk and sets it on the table.

'Don't put your hands near the fire. If you do they'll kill you,' she shouts. 'Put your fingers in this to save them.'

The girls and Jamie have come down the stairs to see what is happening. They stand and stare wide eyed at the frozen corpse of the man they knew so well. Martha's tears fall as the family looks on.

'It's Barnabas. He's frozen dead in the snow,' she explains in a shaking voice.

Seth slips his frozen hands into the cold milk and feels some relief from the pain.

'It's father,' says Jamie in a strange silent voice.

'What are you doing with the milk?' asks Livy when she sees Seth looking painfully at his wriggling fingers in the bowl of milk.

'Fingers are frozen painful,' he says.

Livy slips her fingers into the cold milk.

'I'll squeeze and warm them,' she says. 'This is a fancy way to warm fingers. Is that warming them?' she asks in a shaky voice as they squeeze their fingers together.

After a few moments as Livy stares at the frozen corpse her emotions overpower her. She screams, pulls her fingers from the bowl, bursts into tears and runs to Martha.

'It's Barnabas!' she screams hugging Martha. 'It's father. What shall we do?'

Martha hugs her and the cottagers stand in fearful silence. They hear a drip of water. The frozen sheepskin has thawed. A fold falls open and Barnabas' blue distorted face is visible. Loud screams of horror fill the parlour.

'We must see to him. We must get a good box. A door, Seth, lift the door off,' shouts Martha.

Seth lifts the stair door off its hinges, puts it between two stools and the warming corpse is placed on the door covered in a linen sheet. Martha takes her eyes off the corpse and returns to looking at the live licking flames. Her body shudders as thoughts of Barnabas bring spasms of tears and despair. Nothing was sufficiently important to break the quiet crackling noise of the fire as they sit in silence looking vacantly at the flames. Eventually Martha begins to resurrect Barnabas. She talks of when they first met, how they had courted and loved in the green folds of the downs. She had loved him dearly. When she thought of the death and his absence, she felt emptiness and loneliness. She looks across at the linen sheet, not believing it is now a shroud for her husband's body and tears fall from her eyes.

'He must be cared for proper. A box of fresh wood must be got.' she whispers wiping her tears.

'Two hours and the sun will be up,' says Seth.

They sit around the fire looking at the flames turning wood to ash. Nothing is important. The moment is fixed. Silence is peace. Many logs are burnt through before anyone speaks.

'My old feller was boxed up and tidy in elm wood,' says Acorn after the silence. 'Grave diggers told stories of graveyard, all magic and devils they talk of. I'd rather be put in hole somewhere else, in some field to sleep away the time.'

He rubs his stubbly chin and starts to fill his clay pipe. The name a vicar wrote for him thirty five summers ago was Albert Corn. He lacks a few teeth, he is the youngest of six brothers. He has a square spotty face and strong square chin.

'Some field,' he continues. 'No parsnip field. A wheat field would be right.'

'Vicar won't bury you in no field,' says Seth. As he says the word vicar he gets a flash image of his dream with a preacher shouting at him from a pulpit and he looks at Livy and thinks of their rolling in the rain. The intrusive thought disappears. 'He won't bury you in no field, parsnips or wheat. You'll be in cemetery by church,' says Seth .

'In church yard surgeons may come with a spade and torch for my bones,' says Acorn frowning into the fire.

Beth holds little Jamie who looks at the frozen corpse. Martha looks into the flames.

'Who'd want your bones,' remarks Full.

'You go up or down you won't be in cemetery. It's the soul that floats about and goes to a good place or bad place,' says Seth.

'Barnabas will be buried right and proper deep. Night diggers for the dead with torches and spades never been in St. Mary's,' says Seth with some optimism on his face.

'Don't know that. Been said they come as pilgrims, all secret. Stay at Pilgrims' House by church then dig quiet as mice. Sometimes just take heads and go on their way. Get good money for a head I've heard,' says Full. 'If they come some summers away, they find nothing. Box is rotted. Body rotted. Flesh gone to earth.'

Livy looks at Jamie who looks at Martha but nothing is said and they screw up their faces at the dismal tales and hope they are not true.

'Horrors. Horrors. We want to sleep, not stay awake with ghosts in our heads,' shouts Livy, and the maids and Jamie leave the fireside for their beds. Acorn's pipe is out. He takes a stick from the fire, relights his pipe and continues.

'Fights at hangings I've seen. A body is nobody they say. Whose is it? Brothers and sisters say it's theirs. Surgeons grab it and cut it open, say it's theirs. Some vicars say it belongs to church.'

'My Barnabas is not nobody,' protests Martha.

'Buried in a field of wheat I'd belong to nobody but myself. Quiet and peaceful,' says Acorn. 'Bodies be earth. Parsnips, turnips all grow from the earth, so earth may be mighty worthy muck of folk.'

'No, that's not right. Creatures and spirits of the soil, will get you and disturb your sleep.' says Full satisfied that he has an answer.

'Worms will get you in field or cemetery. We should be buried in lead coffins. Sealed up tight. We'd be there till end, when we all get up and walk about, as the vicar says,' adds Seth who finally feels his body warming.

Martha looks up from the fire.

'All walking about?' questions Acorn, 'I'd be the only one in my field.'

'No more!' shouts Martha, 'I don't want to hear you talk of the dead like this. Barnabas is here with us. We must get a new box. I don't want him in something made from old cottage furniture. We'll talk to vicar. Put candles round him and get proper burial in churchyard. I've heard enough of these evil stories.'

'Well my old feller was....,' starts Full.

'No more talk of death. It's not wanted,' says Seth quietly with his arm round his mother.

Lizzie has quietly gone up to Martha's bedroom, opened an old linen chest, returned to those sitting around the fire and placed an object on Martha's knee. It's a black widow's cap. Martha shudders and her mind is numb with disbelief as she looks at the cap. She is now a widow in a world charted by men.

'You will think of your husband everyday but when you stop the thinking put it back in the chest where it belongs,' advises Lizzie from experience.

Soon after sunrise Martha attends to her two babies in their straw cots while Seth heads towards a barn where a carpenter repairs cottage furniture and can prepare a four sided box coffin. It is the Sabbath but care for the deceased will not provoke the vicar. The snow lies silently like a thick white blanket. Thick on the cottage thatch, thick on Gunter's hog

72

pen, thick on the hen coop. Any sounds fall into the snow and vanish. The world is strangely hushed. The low sun in the east brings little heat. Livy, Beth and Jamie have insisted on going with Seth to select the final enclosure for their father and they make their way through the snow as their breaths leave small clouds in the freezing cold air.

The carpenter is a thin man with the name of Reuben. Each Sabbath he has listened to vicar Lod and wrestled with the meanings from the testaments which resolve themselves into good, evil, heaven and hell. These have added to them the unanswered questions outside the church; the myths of good and evil spirits that are everywhere. He is a man who cares for his soul and finds negotiating a suitable route for his life's journey through this brew of mysteries a difficult one. The brew has left him nervous and confused with eyes that roll about in his head as if trying to find the right path.

They arrive at a large door wedged open by snow and walk under the cover of a roof where they find stacks of seasoning wood and pieces of cottage furniture sheltering from the snow. Reuben's father had been a successful timber merchant and when he died his son took on the craft but he found difficulty securing any contracts and he now spends his time repairing cottage furniture and contemplating. Seth, Livy, Beth and Jamie inspect heavy wooden chests, chairs, stools and tables. Seth calls for Reuben.

'There has been a passing. A box is wanted.'

'Don't know anyone in village gone. Who's this for?' asks Reuben blowing his breath into cupped hands.

'Barnabas. It's for Barnabas my shepherding father,' says Seth with some distress. 'Last night we found him frozen dead up Crapham Down.'

'Aye. I knows Barnabas. Not seen him much but knows him. Worst snow ever. Look these,' the carpenter points to his sheepskin hat and his body buried under thick sheepskins and wrapped round his legs. A loose pelt is tied round his waist. 'Getting some old now, need all this sheep wool,' he says as Seth looks at his unusual bulk. 'Ground's ice hard at church yard. Some job for diggers. Got to be buried. Does vicar know?'

'He'll know when he gets messages from the souls that are moving on. I will be going to see vicar when Barnabas is in his box.'

'Can fix that to be a box for a man. Good old oak that,' say Reuben pointing to a deep wooden chest. 'Could make it not so deep but longer for his size. Oak lasts in the ground.'

'We don't want old wood. Needs to be fresh for his soul.'

'Have some fine pit sawn ash there.' says Reuben walking over to a wood pile and lugging out a thick board. 'See that. Good stuff. A box of this be five shilling for wood, pinned with coloured stuff, neat pattern to top all for five shilling. You pay me four I get one from parish. A four side box that is.'

'Martha will see you right,' says Seth.

'Must see vicar,' mutters Reuben. 'Need to know what wood is best for their souls. Ash will be good for Barnabas. But I have elm wood.'

'My father can spend his time in ash wood,' replies Seth as he sees a strange shaped piece of wood held in a wooden vice.

'Bat for crickets,' says the carpenter following Seth's eyes.

'For crickets!' say Seth surprised.

'That be right. I want to get in team, 'Men of Meads' summer. This bat will get me to play,' says Reuben hopefully as he looks at the bat.

A few days later he delivers the finished coffin box to the Applegate cottage and talks to Martha. The sheepskins are lifted off Barnabas' body, his limbs straightened as best they can, his hair is trimmed, his body placed in a sheet and carefully lowered into the simple coffin supported between two black coffin stools. Tall stands, each with a rush candle, are placed each side of the coffin. The coffin lid stands in a corner, the small piece of mirrored glass is covered. Over the next few days friends and neighbours call to see Barnabas in his coffin, drink ale, eat bread and biscuits and give condolences to the Applegate family. A fiddler has played, there has been some feasting and Lizzie has knelt beside the coffin leading groups of wailers to frighten away the spirits of death and its mysteries. His corpse has been washed and wrapped in a woollen shroud tied at each end. In the shroud one hand holds a piece of wool. His face is bloated, his eyes bulge, fluid ouses from his nose and mouth, his body is swollen and smells. The family in mourning clothes have kept vigil. The vicar has attended. Blessed water has been sprinkled. The deputy Constable has rung the passing bell in The Street.

Martha greets all visitors, says a few words and feels numb and empty. She wants the present moment to last a long time as the unknown future makes her turn on her pillow and weep. Dressed in a black widow's gown and cap, she feels as though her life is over and the world has finished with her. She fears she may be homeless, a burden on the parish in the workhouse with her daughters in service unhappy and distant. What would happen to the babies? Barnabas had died intestate, would Seth now take his father's place as shepherd? Would he inherit or was he too young? What would she do without her children? These thoughts drift through her mind as she whispers to mourners and as she tries to sleep.

'All the ups and downs, accept them to feel better, dear,' says Lizzie stoically as she hugs Martha. 'Even very, very bad times.' She says as she looks towards the coffin.

The snow lies deep and crisp. The air is still. A blue sky lets sunlight turn the snow silvery gold. The day is cold and Seth watches the small clouds of his breath in front of him as he pushes through the snow on his way to St. Mary's church as he knows the gravediggers will be busy today. He walks in the snow following a horse's tracks surprising starving rooks and jackdaws that fight to pick at the horse's droppings. Cawing and kacking they rise into the air and descend again when he has passed. The snow is piled in drifts at the churchyard wall and against tall gravestones. The footpath to the church porch has been cleared by the church warden but Seth's path to where he hears the sound of digging is still covered in snow. In a corner of the churchyard behind the church, where wooden crosses lean at angles he finds the diggers. One stands in a grave wielding a mattock, another leans on a spade. Bundled up in layers of cloth tied with leather straps, leather boots and elf like pointed sheepskin hats with ear flaps that jump about as they dig. Their hands have been bound in cloth to beat the cold, but it has become unravelled and fingers are exposed.

'Spadework, Eliza,' says the man with the mattock as he steps out of the grave which is only knee deep. The man with the spade now steps into the grave and frozen earth and chalk are tossed onto a pile close to the grave.

'Cold and frozen. Chalks like rock, sir. But vicar gives

extra penny for digging in snow,' mattock man mumbles to Seth as they both stand watching the spadework.

'I'm ready for some. It's my father's,' says Seth. 'It's for Barnabas; the shepherd. My father,' he says again quietly.

'God rest his soul, sir. Shepherds don't see much of church, a Sabbath or any day. Work on Sabbath they do.'

Mattock man cups his hands and blows into them. The wound rags over his fingers are cold and wet. He passes the mattock to Seth who takes it in his sheepskin mittens. It is not long before the spade man steps out of the grave and Seth steps into the trench and wields the heavy iron blade. The chalk yields to the blade while Seth's mind brings images of his life with his father and he soon is thinking of his future.

'That's enough lad!' shouts a voice. Seth is pulled out of his meditation and looks at a large mass of loose chalk at his feet that he cannot remember cutting and feels his freezing hands. The work continues, the night closes in. The grave is dug and snow begins to fall and the grave diggers prepare to depart. Seth looks at the snowflakes drifting down into the grave.

'He must lie in a place of goodwill. Take these,' he says.

Seth's mittens are gratefully accepted and the men are gone. The dark night descends and the snowflakes continue their fall.

The funeral procession of coffin bearers and mourners moves through the thick crisp snow to the churchyard. Martha in her black gown and cap on this funeral day is arm in arm with Seth. The maids and Jamie hold hands. For a short moment, sermons, sins and punishment flit through Seth's mind. Is this death his punishment? He has been given a small oak cross that has no name and spent an evening cutting letters that Martha has advised into the wood. He gives it to a grave digger he finds in the church yard to set it securely in the frozen earth.

'It'll be in the ground a hundred summers.' says the grave digger reassuringly. 'If not taken for fuel.'

The winter is one of the worst for many, many years. A winter that people remember and talk about. The freezing north east wind blows until May. Few had fuel enough for their fire or nourishment to see them through this period and many lives were lost. Livestock froze to death in cold barns and stables or on the open downland where the wind showed no mercy to birds freezing on their perches. In the cities meat was roasted on fires lit on frozen rivers where people gamed, danced and refused to yield to the murdering spirit of winter.

Chapter Six

The Ship Inn

The Ship Inn had been built on the remains of an old medieval hall; a two storey space with rooms at one end, an open fire in the centre of the floor and a hole in the roof for the smoke. Each new innkeeper fashioned this old hall to suit their trade. A brick chimney at one end with large inglenook now manages to clears most of the smoke. A floor had been inserted into the two story space giving a large parlour and an extension at the back held a large brewing area with cellar and barrel hatch. A wagon shed and stables are around a cobbled yard. The original medieval hall had been built with thick oak crucks that had survived the centuries and still leant across the space like the embracing arms of two great companions. Soot covered with notches and holes these companions impart a mood of timeless security to the short lives of the mortal drinkers who now frequent their shelter.

Just across The Street is Butcher's cherry red yard and below the white cliff is Fisher village with its harvest from the sea; both serving the inn with fresh victuals. This is what Nell Broad discovered when she became innkeeper.

The natural decoration of her parlour walls changes with the seasons. Green winter mould creeps up from the dampness forming mystifying shapes that revert back in summer to an equally mystifying grey whitewash. The rammed chalk floor is annually levelled with fresh sand and scattered pudding grass that gives way to aged worn brick and stone where it stretches into the inglenook. During the snows this inglenook was the refuge for many who crowded round Nell's blazing fire; saving many from frozen flesh that would wither to black. In the parlour on high beams beyond drinkers reach hang salted and smoked joints of meats, smoked herrings and bunches of onions. On ledges are hard cheeses, freshly baked pies and large loaves all sharing the space with flagons of various strength ales, all ready to satisfy Nell's customers. Wooden bowls are temporarily filled with herbs as they wait for the seasonal arrival of apples, pears and wild berries. In a central and privileged position above all these on a short pole is the smiling brown head of a smoked pig; all that remains of the biggest and fattest pig that has seen the inn through the freezing winter. Its central privileged position is the way the survivors of the winter demonstrate their gratitude.

The innkeeper is a generous unsparing spirit when dealing with the needs of those who visit her inn but she has a shrewd eye on her purse when trading for its necessities. Hunger and thirst have never visited her or her forbears and nature has rewarded this good fortune by giving the innkeeper a hale and hearty spirit with a body that is visibly taller than the usual sixteen and a half hands of other local mortals. She has full wide lively lips the corners of which point to heaven if she is pleased but to the other place if something is amiss. Usually they point to the right place as she laughs and jostles her way between the many that gather round her tables. An embrace from her strong arms leaves you in no doubt about your new companion. She is an experienced woman who is skilled in the management of people. She has shouted at sword fighting drunkards with words that have removed them peaceably from her parlour to continue their fight in The Street and save her parlour furniture from damage. She brews and cooks, knows all her drinkers' names and has analysed their eating habits to always have what they want which includes her London recipes. She has married, given birth and become a widow. She is familiar with coins and knows that sometimes goodwill is more important than cold metal.

All these essential attributes exhibit themselves in this large comely woman that all approve. Her daughters Blossom and Barley rise early each morning and tie bunches of fresh green herbs to the lower beams, grease bellows, clear uneaten food from the tables and polish a lucky bell with salt and vinegar. The bell was found by the Fisher people attached to a mast that had been tossed onto their beach after a night of storms. Nell bartered her ale for this bell and it now hangs in the inglenook of her parlour. On this particular spring morning a narrow beam of morning sunlight slips through a crack in a shutter and falling on the polished bell throws a soft radiant glow to complete Nell's aspiration of a comfortable inn.

Many summers ago when Nell was working in her brewing cellar she discovered a small orphan boy asleep on sacks behind the barrels. He was a very scrawny thin and pale individual and when she heard him wake she tried to talk to him but he would say nothing. To try and resolve things she placed a warm churdle pie next to him on the floor. This he quickly attacked with his small hands, and he was soon licking the dish.

'Do you want more?' asked Nell smiling at the lost child.

He nodded his head and smiled back. After the boy had consumed a number of biscuits she asked him.

'Are you full now?' He nodded back to her and she left him.

The next day he was there again between the barrels. He ate another pie and Nell asked the same question.

'Are you full?'

This motherly attention continued and Nell was pleased to see the small boy put more flesh on his bones. He is now a grown man of considerable size who lives and sleeps between the barrels of fermenting grains and various liquids that are now the mediums of his art. Around his waist hanging from a wide belt are his pewter measures together with small leather purses of secret ingredients. He may now know more than Nell in the art of brewing. He is now a large plump hearty man whose generous girth determines the spacing of the parlour tables which he delicately negotiates distributing tankards of ale. He had never told anyone his name and Nell was pleased to give him the name of Full to complete her wish.

Chapter Seven

Fishers

The nightly visitor peers down. Its pale grey light falling on the white cliff that drops steeply away to the Fisher people's village. A perilous village that spreads along the base of the cliff trapped between the enormous chalk cliff and the relentless moving sea. A different harvest is gathered here; a harvest with perils, a harvest that uses strange tools, a harvest of creatures from the deep. Huddled along the base of the cliff are their fragile shacks, built from parts of broken boats, driftwood and sail all tarred black as the night. They know the nightly visitor as their timekeeper but they also know that it can pull a roaring sea up their beach to destroy their simple shacks. But this is where their mothers raised them. This is their world where they live their hard lives at the mercy of the natural world.

On this night the moon is large. It slowly drifts across the heavens heralding a threatening high tide but a good harvest for hungry fishermen with mouths to feed. It watches in its dim light as the fishermen prepare their boats and slip them into the water to drift slowly away to deeper water. Nets are lowered and the fishermen wait as myths, dreams and tales of strange creatures trouble their minds. Strange creatures that pull men down deep into their unknown dark world. A tale of three brothers lost in a thick mist. Then tossed one by one into a raging angry sea where they thrashed about in the water until pulled to below. The last brother gasped and choked as the foul water slipped into his exhausted body. But providence looked on him with some sympathy and he managed to stay afloat grasping the upturned boat. He was found the next day delirious. The creatures had taken his mind.

A staircase rises up the steep cliff giving the Fishers access to The Street above where they parade heaped baskets of their harvest. A dark night finds others on this staircase. Others who arrive in the dark on small boats carrying casks; threatening men who disappear like shadows when daylight arrives. But the Fisher people know it is better to look at nothing and say nothing as the dark stuff comes ashore.

A clear pure water spring issuing from the white chalk of the cliff brought this village into existence in prehistoric times. Constantly eroded by the sea it moves to a new spot with every generation. It has brought with it folklore and myth. It is a constant good spirit that does not disappear in dry summers as it gushes into rivulets that run down the cliff face and gathers in a wide pool shaped by the villagers. Constantly refreshed, the villagers drink it with great relief from their salt laden atmosphere. It has been given the name 'Hollywell.'

Chapter Eight

Men of Meads

Reclining on a settle and herb filled cushions in the large inglenook of the Ship Inn is old Moe. His eyes flicker and open and he looks at smiling cherubs holding garlands dancing on a wide black fireback that has kept him warm through the night. He rubs his eyes, blinks several times, picks up his stick and uses it to knock the ship's bell that hangs below the mantel. Barley in the passage hears the ring.

'That coat you got there would look better on me,' she says surveying Moe in his handed down clothes.

'From mansion it came. Bright colours and piping strange to me. But it does,' replies Moe as he smells baking. 'The smell of that is the smell of heaven. I'm sure of that,' he says as he sniffs the air.

'Some of us are nearer to that place than others,' says Barley.

'Near or far bring some cheese and ale to keep me on earth, good maid.'

Moe gets his victuals and the sun creeps higher into the sky. Full brings his large body into the parlour and slides a shutters fully open to let sunlight in as night insects scurry away to dark corners.

'What dreams have visited you in the night?' he asks Moe after clearing a spider's web from the opening.

'No dreams. Thoughts are on a good hit. Much to do and tell for first knock,' he replies.

'First knock of the summer needs to be good and worthy to set team up,' says Full as he moves tables and stools to their normal places. 'Some barrels will be emptied today.'

'Good number want to get in team, poor souls,' says Moe. 'Seven agreed with Bourne so seven it's to be,' he finishes his ale and cheese and plays with last year's tally sticks. 'Team to be chosen. They'll be here afore long smiling and winking at me.'

The sun creeps higher and as it reaches the top of its arc the parlour of the inn is full of eager aspiring players. Many small creatures that live in the inn share the relief that winter is now past and have decided to find new quarters. Small furtive brown eyes look out from a small hole in the wall of the parlour. They look across the sanded earth floor and register surprise at what they see in front of them. A sea of worn leather shoes and boots, most with square toes, a few with round toes, some with buckles, some bursting from missing stitching, some with pattens, all agitated with excitement. Some tapping, some jerking, some rising and falling, some scraping grooves in the sandy floor. The parlour floor is this mouse's extensive table and as it views the scene with alarm it changes its plans and quickly disappears back into the protection of its winter hole in the wall.

The wives and maids of the village have perceived subtle changes in the behaviour of their men-folk who are on an emotional journey and today is the first day of that journey. It manifests itself as quiet suppressed energy, more pipes while discussing sober considered opinions. Idle chatter gets no response. The husbands sit about like pensive gravestones while the wives wait for the journey to end. They know that it will end with the men-folk secretly weeping or turn them into raucous shouting merry makers. Unshaven proud earthy mortals with their pipes, ale and body odour filling the air of the inn with its homely familiar richness. It is time for the selection of the Men of Meads.

'You know our men, Moe. Will it be ours this first knock?' asks Spendwell who has called at the inn to advise Moe that he wishes to be included in the team.

'We need some good knocking. All things in their time. Like the seasons. Some good, some bad,' answers Moe with no answer.

'Be a good man and select winning men. Get Gaunt. None got him out and he knocked on till dusk. He can knock but get others to do the running,' pleads the gentleman farmer. 'I'll knock with them. Watchers from the Wells, paid for, will be here and Fordingbrook will be down for the knock from Westminster. He said he'd bring a chair.'

'I'll get them up to Welcome Field and we might this time have another good knock,' replies Moe, thinking it's a long way to bring a chair.

Old Moe is at the front of the village mortals' queue. He can truthfully be described as 'old.' as no living soul in the village was at his birth. All people in a queue watch and mentally note who is before them but Moe has no need for such things as there is no-one before him and he is not concerned with late comers. His longevity has given him wisdom which he generously distributes to his followers. It ascends from the knowledge of tending parsnips, turnips and how to pull the teats of goats to the vital knowledge of herbs and their medicinal properties. Which on some occasions have saved lives. He is privy to the curious thoughts and activities of all. He does not judge the morals of a confidence he has been given nor apportion blame or uprightness. His eyes are bright wells of alert contentment, longevity has not dimmed his spirit or his senses. His wellbeing is a concern for all in the hamlet who clothe him and always want him at their table. Some call him just Moe others call him old Moe depending on their closeness.

His authority on this important day gives him a rush of quiet energy. He stands with his back to the aspiring throng in the parlour of the inn looking at the cherubs on the fireback again to assist his thoughts. He ponders last year's games, performs mental calculations with the help of his fingers, thumbs and the notches on tally sticks and after a short contemplation period he turns and faces the throng. There is silence and all eyes look towards Moe.

'Ball will be out, Saint Marks,' he says loudly. 'Cuckoo Day. Knocking against Bourne's seven men,' he looks around identifying faces in front of him. 'So we want seven stronger, to send them back like turnips and fools to their wives.'

Glad of some relief a rowdy cheer bursts out. Tankards are raised and banged in agreement. When all have satisfied their passion Moe proceeds.

'We need the day to be ours. 'Tis a battle for our worth,' he pauses and holds up a tally stick. 'This one put us right,

Gaunt,' he shouts. 'Gaunt knocked them, you know the game, hitting he was till the dark came on.'

Some sitting round the rough wooden tables bang their tankards again and shout his name.

'Where is he? Is he here?' Moe asks hopefully looking around.

A loud throaty voice can be heard from somewhere in the throng of drinkers.

'Aye. I'm here a'right.'

As if by magic the packed bodies move aside until there is a clear line of vision between Moe and Gaunt who has his large body balanced on a three legged stool. Blossom, following Nell's instruction, has placed a hot churdle pie on the table in front of him; the lonely bachelor's first meal for a number of days. His face looks down, savouring the pie, but his eyes flicker up and focus on Moe and he looks like a bull ready to charge.

'You want some hitting done again this summer?' he asks down the line of bodies to Moe.

'That's what it is. That's what's to be my friend. You can knock till nightfall if needs be,' replies Moe relieved the big man is present.

'That I can do for you, Moe. But I need a good stick. Last one broke with my hitting and pieces flew about. Get me out at the time as I sleep like an oak in winter,' he says as his eyes return to the churdle pie.

'We will get you afore sunrise with wagon if there is need. Saint Marks it be.'

Moe begins to search for other familiar faces in the crowd. The previous evening Hickle Stone, a slightly impetuous man, had looked into his wife's brown eyes and spoken as sweetly as he could manage to her but to no avail. His springtime thrill of life has got him into trouble. A sleepless night has made him irritable and he is sore with blue bruises on his forehead and around a swollen eye delivered by Mavis Stone who does not yet share his springtime thrill of life. He draws on his pipe, fills his lungs with smoke, stands and roars out to the gathering in the parlour.

'My passion for crickets is strong as most. It is time my passion found me in team!'

He made this honest but unsubtle request each year. All listen with a grain of compassion and great understanding as many shared his predicament.

'My wife says, ''You not in team again, Hickle. Go tell them you're as good,'' and here I be. I'm to be in team. We got to get a win!' he bellows out in a cloud of his own smoke. 'If not tell me now. Don't keep me from my plough!'

He takes a deep swallow from his tankard and feels less irritable. He is unaware of the quiet meetings, conversations, small gifts and pleasantries that have been showered on Moe by the other aspiring players.

Reuben the coffin making carpenter has been fashioning his willow bat for some months. He has not played crickets and also has a passion to be in the team. The willow bat is between his legs. He is carefully carving a decorative pattern on the face of the bat with a small sharp knife. He has watched crickets on Welcome Field and hopes the bat will demonstrate his passion for a place in the team. He stops to listen to Hickle. He is anxious for the selection to proceed and he decides to demonstrate the strength of his bat. He raises it above his head and slams it down with a deafening crash onto his table. All ears are in pain, all eyes turn to him, he points the bat at Hickle.

'We're here for old Moe to talk, Good Hickle. Be a good man, sit down. Let old Moe say what's to say,' he says loudly in a shaky voice. Hickle looks across to him, draws more smoke and roars again,

'We got to get a win!'

'Sit down you turnip head.' is shouted from someone in the crowd.

'Good Hickle, I never mock you. Take no notice of those who do,' replies Reuben. 'This bat's fresh seasoned off the willow, best wood for a win. So good Hickle sit down and let old Moe tell us the team.'

Hickle snarls a grunt and sits. He has been pacified and is slightly esteemed by Reuben's polite request. Moe continues.

'Up on Welcome Field. Good grass for eight bowls apiece.'

A stranger has worked his way through the gathering and stands close to Moe. A tidy man. Clean breeches, coloured tailored coat and buckle shoes. He rolls a ball across a table. He is a discerning cobbler and in his small workshop he has beaten out triangular pieces of leather, these he has stitched together with greased jute twine to form a sphere. Within this sphere he has packed course wool and musket balls for added weight.

'The new ball,' he proclaims to the eager onlookers.

'Is stitching better than last and finished for game?' asks Moe.

'It is that.' the man replies. 'It has weight to be hit. Hit it hard, Gentlemen,' he passes the ball to Moe who inspects the stitching and weighs it in his hand.

'Should take a good knock and go further,' he says holding it over a table and dropping it with a loud thud.

'This ball is worth its weight in gold,' the tidy man speculates. 'And where do I get what's owing.'

'Gentleman Spendwell at Mansion House will be knocking. The ball is his. He'll see you right,' says Moe.

Seth Applegate has left his flock with fellow shepherd Ebb to care for. He has also pushed his way through the gathering to stands at the table next to the stranger.

'It's what you want lad,' the man says looking at him. 'Hold it. 'Tis three day's work.'

Seth holds the new ball.

'You're not from the village?' questions Seth.

'I'm not from anywhere round here. I was a boot maker, no more boots. I listened to the talk and make the balls now. Hyde Park every morning. They play with the balls I make. Many want to play, crickets coming,' he prophesies. 'Wagers are in London news sheets. Coffee houses talk of crickets, many folk are watching,' he pauses. 'I'll collect two crown from Spendwell for this ball.'

Moe moves into the throng of bodies in the parlour. He looks at faces, uttering occasional remarks. As he move he places a hand on the shoulder of the privileged selected. There is no name calling nor the writing of names, but he has only four. Seth looks at the tidy man, and feels he cannot trust him. His mind drifts far away, he thinks of Livy and feels a hand on his shoulder and jumps with fright. He turns to see who owns the hand.

'A friend of Gaunt's worth a try, so you're to be at Welcome Field to knock second after Gaunt. That what I've planned,' says Moe to Seth's surprise.

'Second to Gaunt it is,' replies Seth.

'First game got to show our worth to the turnip heads of Bourne.'

'That's there,' says Moe as he points to his smallest finger.'

He looks around. He remembers the crash of Reuben's new bat and looks for him. Moe's hand goes on his shoulder, and the final member of the Men of Meads first game 1740 is selected.

'That's my team,' says Moe. 'Farmer Spendwell is one more. You know who you are. Welcome Field, Saint Marks, Cuckoo Day,' Moe shouts out. 'Nine on the clock. Hefty wagers are out there. See we hit the most.'

The suspense is over, but the game is not, and the familiar shouting and chattering noise returns to the parlour. Nell and her helpers watch for empty tankards that are promptly filled and soon the men drift back to their furlongs and the inn parlour waits for their return when dusk is falling. The furtive mouse re-appears at its hole in the wall, looks out at its table and sees just four feet. Two on large legs disappearing next a three legged stool and two of the innkeeper's that it knows well.

Reuben returns to his barn and continues shaping his piece of willow for the important occasion. As his sharp blade shapes the bat he discovers to his horror dark marks in the grain of the wood that judder across the width of the bat. A defect he has never seen before.

'That's evil.' he mutters as his wandering eyes fix on the marks. He runs a finger across the discoloured wood. 'Feels evil. Some strange wickedness in the wood?' he asks himself.

His nervous temperament obliges him to seek an answer to this question.

'That could be an evil spirit, I'll see what Gendles can do. They will know if 'tis evil,' he says to himself after considering the myths of the gallows wood and its secrets.

The two Gendle sisters, Clarisse and Notelle live in the hanger wood that surrounds the slopes of the Warren. They are tall slim women whose slimness suggests want. Upright in posture, slow moving with conviction and rarely speaking has given them the appearance of serious authority. Their father had spent time in goal after being accused of having magical powers and dealing in spells. His daughters now have protection from the law against such accusations. But rumours and loose tittle-tattle still flourish and keeps them apart from the village folk who still fear magic and witchcraft.

Morning sunlight is filtering through the small green leaves of spring as Reuben enters the wood on his way to the Gendle's cottage. The air is crisp and still with a morning mist that lingers in this sheltered wood. He holds the willow tightly under his arm wrapped in a piece of linen. He treads the soft earth of the wood on a narrow path lined with the tongues of green ferns. Although aware of unseen spirits he is sure that they do not interfere with his emotional stability. He confidently approaches an area where myth, legend and mysticism may exist. He smells the smoke of a fire after a few minutes walking and sees the sister's cottage. One of the sisters is in a cultivated patch of ground in front of the cottage and when he sees her she is already looking at him. She has heard him approach and knows he is a stranger. She watches the slow shift of his body as he walks. The length of his stride, the features of his face. His clothes and movement as she gauges his integrity. She finishes her inspection and looks at the ground and the feeble root vegetables she is tending. He walks hesitatingly towards her.

'A noisy wood it is for heavy feet,' she says quietly still looking at the ground.

'Spirits are in these woods. Good or bad I know not,' he says.

'They never worry us. But they are here. You carry something for us, coffin maker?' she says straightening herself and looking at him. Her eyes look into his and he feels uneasy.

'It's for the honour of the village, our worth,' Reuben explains. 'I've seen you watching us at crickets, keeping apart but watching. We're not casting spells running up and down to sticks in the ground. 'Tis a game for winners and losers and what is under this linen is the village's instrument for the game. But it is disfigured and I need to know if 'tis an evil piece of willow.'

'You are here and not at your trade. A bad day for the Reaper?' she questions, looking up at a gathering of grey cloud.

'This willow has been marked with something never before seen by me. Is it a sign from a spirit? Is it good or no?' he asks as drops of rain begin to fall.

He looks around and sees the Gendle's goat looking at him between two goat skulls on posts.

'They are together. It is a good spirit,' says the sister 'They are his parents. People who visit us are wanters. People who bring their trouble and want relief. When I heard your footsteps, I knew. 'Tis another.'

Clarisse walks towards the cottage door then turns and beckons Reuben to follow. He follows her through the door feeling more anxious. The cottage has one large room on the ground floor with chimney, inglenook and staircase at one end. He stands looking at the smouldering embers in the inglenook as his eyes adjust from the sun to the dimness of the room. Clarissa sits at a table. He looks at the mantel of the inglenook and as his eyes adjust he sees the mantel is crowded with dozens of small objects piled on top of each other. As he contemplates what he is seeing he hears Clarissa speak.

'Coffin maker come and sit with me. Tell me what troubles you.'

Reuben turns towards her and sees the room behind her. It is like the mantel but with larger object; some he identifies but many more are in the jumbled heap. Farming tools, pottage pots, boots, swords, flagons, brooms and spinning wheels can be seen. Teapots, kettles, candlesticks, three cornered hats, several fleeces and a pair of pattens are in the heap. An open oak chest displays knives, trinkets, clocks, and stacks of pewter plates and drinking vessels. All covered in soot, dust and cobwebs. Reuben stands gazing at this mystifying heap of objects until he hears Clarissa's voice again.

'Sit with me poor coffin maker and I will tell you what you see,' she says in a soothing voice.

When they have sat quietly listening to the rain, she begins her story.

'What you see have been given to us, our father and his father. All by a long queue of mortals who needed something that no number of crowns would buy,' she looks at the smouldering embers in the hearth. 'Given for our mystical stories of what might be, people have given well to get their wish. My father was asked to make spells and magic for some while others cried witchcraft from their fear. No more does the hangman slip his rope around our necks and no more are we roped for burning. The law prevents such injustices. All that...,' she says raising her thin arm and pointing to the heap, 'given by the wanters for our parent's spells. It has not been touched since their day.'

The cottage door is open. Rain can be seen turning the green of the wood to shining silver. Reuben slides the bat out from the linen sheet and lays it across the table.

'Look,' he says,' pointing to the disfigured grain. 'Is it an evil spirit? What does it mean?'

She places her hands gently on the bat, closes her eyes and choosing her words carefully whispers to Reuben.

'I feel the willow wood is warm to my touch,' she says softly. 'The young willow is fresh, nothing is paining me. Nothing speaks of an evil spirit.' She slowly opens her eyes and looks at Reuben.

They sit in silence again listening as the raindrops spatter on the door stone. Reuben looks at the heap of piled gifts rising to the thatch.

'But I have nothing for you,' he says repentantly.

'Like all the others, you will have,' she replies in a quiet mocking voice, which she follows with a laugh. 'The willow is young, it is energetic, it is trying to find peace with itself. No evil spirit dwells in it,' she says as she looks at Reuben who believes his question has been answered.

'No evil spirit. Those are good words. Good for a man's heart,' he says.

As he says these words he sees Clarissa look disturbed.

'What do you mean? ''Good for a man's heart,'' she asks with alarm.

'It's nothing. Just that it's what I wanted to hear,' he replies.

'Your rolling eyes tell me coffin maker that you are looking for more?'

'For the worth of the village and our souls this bat needs to win the knock.'

A shadow falls across the open door and Notelle stoops under the low doorway and enters the room.

'This man seeks the meaning of this mark in the willow, nothing of a spirit is seen. But now coffin maker seeks more. A spell to be good at crickets,' Clarissa closes her eyes again, 'What will be, will be. Believe you will win. What will be, will be,' she prophesies.

'As sure as light will come on the morrow you will have a gift for your spell,' says Reuben glancing at the heap of strange objects and hoping to leave.

'But this willow does not want earthly objects like those,' Clarissa says pointing a long finger towards the heap again. 'We need to live,' both sisters look into Reuben's eyes. 'We need nourishment. We cannot live on the things that grow feebly from our soil. We need things that walk above the ground,' says Clarissa with a strange smile.

As he hears these words he feels confused, he feels a fast beating in his chest and sweat dampening his armpits.

'Walk above the ground!' he chokes out.

'Aye. Walk above the ground. We need nourishment not candlesticks, tables and iron tools.' Clarissa says with a serious look.

There is silence in the room as both sisters look at Reuben.

'It will be. It will be,' he says nervously.

'A heart and its meat is needed,' Clarissa says without feeling.

Reuben suddenly feels sick and dizzy as sweat gathers on his forehead. He feels guilt for his greed to cheat with a spell.

'Your need will be met,' he says disturbed by what he has said. He feels feeble and the need to hurry away.

'Good. Make it so coffin maker,' Clarissa mouths out in a strange voice.

The rain has passed and sunlight now shines on the wet surfaces of the wood as Reuben leaves the sisters' cottage. As he makes his way home his mind is spinning. The sisters know he is a coffin maker. How can they ask for a heart from a body? He couldn't do that! But perhaps he could! He sweats in fear and amazement at what has passed. He thinks of his funeral ledgers and whether it is possible to make a single exception. That night he does not sleep. His wife thinks he is thinking of honest crickets. All night he is in turmoil as he remembers the words 'a man's heart.' He sees the soft light of morning filter through the wooden shutter. He has not slept. He feels exhausted and sick.

'If I don't keep my promise to the Gendles what will become of me,' he whispers nervously to himself as he stumbles down his cottage's twisting stairs. He has agreed to meet Butcher at the inn. He ambles along The Street tired and haggard wondering if a spell has been placed on him already. He hangs for a minute on the door of the inn to steady himself.

'What ails you, Reuben?' shouts Butcher who sits with ale and pipe in the parlour. 'Have you seen the devil?' he jokes. Reuben hears the words and slowly slips towards the ground.

Butcher places pipe and tankard on the table and goes to assist the fainting man and supports him to his table.

'A strong nipperkin for this poor fellow,' he shouts across to Full.

The liquor is downed in one gulp. Reuben looks at Butcher through tired red eyes.

'You're still asleep. What has been?' asks Butcher. 'Did you meet the Gendles?' he asks.

'Aye. I met the Gendles alright!' Reuben chokes out. 'I'm for hell and damnation with flames. What can I do?'

'So what say they. The spell for the bat,' he reminds Reuben.

'A gift. They want a gift. They want a man's heart. But I am a good man. A gift. What can I do? I've said I will provide!' he says as his eyes widen and a look of horror creeps over his face. 'There's a spell on me to give them a heart. Something that walks above the ground,' he whispers.

'They always do. I know,' replies Butcher in a matter-of-fact tone.

'A heart from....a body,' Reuben whispers quietly looking round. 'A body. They know my trade. It could be an empty coffin to the cemetery.'

Butcher sits in silence thinking of what he has heard.

'What did they say?' he asks.

'Gift to be something that walks above the ground. Above the ground. They said a heart. A heart!' he screeches in horror.

Butcher is silent and looks puzzled but slowly his face signifies recognition and he chirps out a quiet laugh. Then laughs louder.

'They want a body.' laughs Butcher. 'Reuben, you are a great turnip head my friend. You misheard. What they want is meat. Many have come to my bloody yard and asked for meat for the Gendles. That's what they want. Meat. Pig's heart is a favourite, beef, pork, horse sometimes. Not bodies, my friend.'

Reuben looks up from staring at the table top. His face slowly moves from a frown, to puzzlement. His downturned lips move, his mouth opens and he releases a wobbling laugh that turns into a hysterical screech. The two good friends scream with laughter rocking from side to side. After much laughing, shouting and another nipperkin the laughter slowly subsides and the two begin to deal with practicalities.

'So it's meat. Just pig meat,' Reuben says with serious relief as all his fears have disappeared into thin air. 'And you can provide?' he says looking hopefully at Butcher who is a butcher.

'My cherry red yard has supplied meat for the Gendles many times. I know their taste of meat and can provide,' he replies with a look of some pride.

'The night was a bad one for me but I feel a free man again. What is the meat?'

'Pig heart is favoured, beef then lamb.'

'So pig or beef it is?'

'Aye, pig heart and meat with it. Good meat. No leg. A good prime slab top loin for slicings. Some suet for puddings will satisfy,' replies Butcher finishing his tankard.

Full is called over to bring more tankards and they discuss the business. Pennies change hands and the two men leave the inn.

The following day is wet. Grey cloud lingers with soft sticky drizzle coating every surface. The business continues as

Reuben calls at Butcher's yard and collects a straw basket for delivery to the Gendles. The damp slim tongues of the ferns wet his stockings and breeches as he walks again along the narrow path to their cottage through the hanger wood of the Warren. His curiosity stops him and he lifts the lid of the basket. Cherry red, white and black pieces of meat sit on a prime slab of darker meat all sitting on large dark green cabbage leaves that line the basket.

'Worthy victuals for penniless country mortals and a spell,' he mutters to himself.

The door of the cottage is open and he calls to within.

'Hey ho. Hey ho.'

'The coffin maker is here,' he hears.

Both sisters appear. The contents of the basket are inspected and their appetite produces mild smiles on their faces.

'A good gift,' says Clarissa looking to her sister who nods her head in agreement.

'Strong wood the willow. The bat will serve the village well,' says Notelle smiling at the basket. 'It will be salted and we'll remember your generosity.'

They disappear into their cottage and Reuben is left standing at the door.

'Good day to you,' he shouts into the cottage.

As he turns to retrace his steps he hears the clinking sound of cooking utensils. He has achieved more than he thought. He has been assured the disfigured grain in the willow is not an evil spirit and feels he has been given a spell to favour the Men of Meads. He makes his way to the inn and sits in the parlour with Butcher. Nell is serving ale at a nearby table.

'Those trotters made fine jelly for my kidney pies,' she says. 'You ready for some?' she asks looking at Butcher.

Nell is keen to provide a selection of victuals that are up to date and is proud to add.

'That's what they eat in London. If it's good for them it's good for you,' she says as she sits with Butcher and Reuben. 'Someone's due at the old Place,' she continues. 'All chimneys with smoke.'

'Aye. That place will need some drying out after that freezing bad winter. Nothing more sad than a wet bed when sleep's upon you,' says Butcher with a dismal face.

'That be true,' agrees Reuben.

'Wagon from the Wells was making a delivery. All under tarred sheets, large lump it looked. Waggoner said it had come from Westminster,' reveals the innkeeper.

Chapter Nine

A spring bud

A small hairy dog with black markings on ears and body is barking somewhere beyond Goodwin's barn. It barks at the closed door of a tumbled cottage as the morning sun lifts itself above the distant horizon. Gaunt is sleeping soundly within. The dog's tongue hangs and quivers, its water bowl is empty. It is thirsty and hungry and knows if it makes enough noise its master will appear.

'Jack, you noisy fellow,' says the sleepy-eyed man who opens the door.

Jack is in the cottage at the water bowl before the sleepy man can turn round. Gaunt yawns, rubs his head, looks out onto the breaking day and yawns again. He retrieves a wooden platter carrying a small pieces of bread and cheese and sits by the door with his dog Jack beside him. The sweet fragrance of blackthorn blossom is present in the air. A faint grey mist hangs over the downs as he looks towards Welcome Field where his services are needed. Abe is approaching in his new wagon drawn by a single fine horse.

You about then?' he shouts.

'Aye. I'm about and waiting to hit some. A king's transport for me today,' he says looking at the wagon for himself and Jack.

'Hittings needed,' says Abe. 'Aye, new wagon. Butcher wants the old oxen. You proper awake?'

'Awake as Jack here,' says Gaunt.

Abe waits in the wagon while Gaunt clears his platter.

'That's me set up,' he says as he consumes the last piece of cheese and climbs into the wagon. His dog leaps in beside him.

The wagon slowly moves up Prentiss Street, turns left at Kent Sheet then makes its way between the furlongs to Welcome Field where they see Moe pacing out a pitch. A tidy wigged man stands watching. It is a field that has seen many ancient sports and sits comfortable in an enclosed space surrounded by sweet chestnuts. They have been laid out in a semicircle along its western boundary while a line of the mature trees form its eastern boundary, and the whole space sits in a downland hollow.

'Watchers from the Wells. Right tidy and shaved,' says Abe nodding towards the wigged man.

They watch the man fix a pair of sticks into the ground and balance a third stick across the top.

'Here's the man that hits,' says Abe as his wagon stops beside Moe. 'Any more to collect?' asks Abe.

'All here except Spendwell. He's on his way,' says Moe pointing to a small cart where Spendwell and his Mistress are approaching the field. 'No more to get. All here.' concludes Moe.

A Bourne man comes over to Moe.

'We're having six bowls,' he says.

'We're doing eight. Six's too little,' says Moe, 'and we still use the popping hole.'

'Hyde Park there's always six,' says the Bourne man.

'We're not playing there. We're playing here,' replies Moe confidently. 'We make the rules on our pitch. You bowl six we'll bowl eight. No difference.'

As the spring sun creeps higher the players gather in their teams. With the pitch agreed Moe checks his responsibilities and eyes his team.

'Gaunt good. Seth good. The large man Full, he can hit sometimes, Reuben, the man whose seen the Gendles, the willow spirit better be good. Butcher, some muscle there, Spendwell knows the game and Acorn he can see and hit that's all that's needed.'

He is contented that he has achieved so much. He looks at the Bourne team who stand about looking vacant, he looks back at his team and is disheartened as they too stand about with vacant looks. A tidy watcher signals the teams. Gaunt and a Bourne man walk over to him, a shout comes from the Bourne man, a coin is tossed and falls into the grass.

'It's not good. It must lay flat. You must agree. Toss the coin again. It's not flat,' says Gaunt pushing his honest face towards the watcher. The coin is flipped again.

'It's not flat. Toss it again.' repeats Gaunt.

The watcher looks mystified and indicates to the two players to retreat and calls to the second watcher. They crouch down inspecting the coin lying in the grass then look seriously at Gaunt and award the opening choice to the Bourne team. They decide to bat after three turns of the hour glass. Gaunt's honest oval face has not influenced the decision of these independent watchers.

'We've got the wet grass,' Moe mutters to Seth, as he lobs the new ball to a Bourne man.

'Mists laying it thick,' replies Seth.

They watch as the ball is tossed between the Bourne team.

'Sun will be up drying the dew when glass is finished,' prophesies Moe.

They watch as a Bourne man runs for a catch. His feet move faster than his body, the dew has a victim; he falls to the ground uttering curses.

'Life's better on two feet,' says Gaunt. 'There's no need to crawl about like a sick goat.'

The man curses and blasphemes. The watcher points at Gaunt and then the sticks.

'Bat will tell what's to be. A good spell for the village?' questions Gaunt as Reuben slowly unwraps the bat from its cover and hands it to Gaunt.

'Aye. Use it well. It has no evil in it,' he says rubbing his hands lovingly over the face of the bat. Gaunt takes it in silence and moves to his stance in front of the sticks. His shaggy canine companion has moved around the field, and has attempted to herd catchers and spectators into a manageable group but they do not respond to being considered sheep. He concedes defeat and sits next to Gaunt at the sticks, panting for air with his hot dangling tongue. His master is practicing swinging the curved bat. A stick keeper, Gaunt and Jack are around the two sticks.

'This dog must be taken off the ground. Are you its master?' shouts the watcher looking at Gaunt and pointing to the dog.

'Aye, 'tis my dog Jack. He's just four summers and a good dog. Good at all things ...,' the watcher does not wish to hear and he interrupts.

'I'm decision maker. Take the dog away to the trees,' the watcher demands, pointing to the semicircle of chestnuts around Welcome Field.

The dog follows Gaunt to the shade of the trees, where his master points a governing finger at the dog.

'Wait. Wait. Jack, wait!' The dog is obedient and remains as Gaunt returns to the sticks.

'First ball of six,' shouts the watcher as he waves to the bowler to proceed. The ball bounces along the rough ground, Gaunt's quick eye swings the curved bat down. He is a strong man, the bat feels light, his muscular arms power the bat and with the solid sound of willow meeting leather the ball hastily changes direction. The resulting reassuring sound snaps into the silence of the downs, the ball rises, flashes across the sky and descends into the chestnuts. It bounces down between the branches to settle in the grass with all eyes upon it. The watcher nods his head. A precedent has been set on this pitch that this is a notch on the thick tally stick and the watcher dutifully lifts an arm to signal the event. Shouts go up from the crowd mingled with the ringing of the Ship's bell by the innkeeper. Nell has taken advantage of the gathering and arrived with an ale cart loaded with casks, tankards, pies, cheese and bread. With her rosy cheeked daughter Barley it is an easy day for her. Heavy slow Gaunt does not need to exert himself; he laughs and looks at the bat with interest.

Nell has only talked once with Gaunt since the snow. When he is at her inn she places pies on the table in front of him. She looks at him. She knows his body is young and strong. She does not like a cold winter bed alone. But a husband would own everything she has, her inn, daughters and adopted son, as laid down by the patriarchal social order of the day. But there may be a way to do things differently. The sides of the cart are lowered; it forms a flat table. She manoeuvres the platters and victuals as she likes to see them. She sits on a stool dividing her time between watching Barley slip coins into the leather purse round her waist and Gaunt sending the ball into the chestnuts.

'Put those in front love,' she says to Barley to finalise the arrangement of the produce of her inn.

She can see the Gendle sisters standing apart from the crowd. Tall and straight they stand watching the proceedings, their sharp eyes watching every stroke of the bat.

The sun has climbed higher when the attention of the gathering is drawn to a distant object that slowly moves up the track from South Dean. As it nears, two men are seen in coloured breeches and coats carefully evading uneven ground carrying a large box with a small window. They are large men with a determined manner, tidy and neat with silver buckles glinting on black polished leather and gold edging gleaming from three-cornered hats. They are carrying between them a blue velvet covered sedan chair. As the men arrive at the field a blind is raised at the small window and a face looks out, inspects the ground around the chair and nods to the two chairmen. The box is lowered to the ground, carrying poles are removed and a small door opens. The man within steps out, smiles and ambles about with the help of a stick. The crowd have their attention diverted from Gaunt's knock to this colourful event and there are whispers.

'It's old Fordingbrook from Westminster.'

The two chairmen stretch their backs and lean against the chestnuts as gentleman farmer Spendwell approaches them.

'There's good entertainment here for your passenger with a bat like that,' he says pointing to Gaunt at the sticks.

'I'm sure it is a good game, sir. He's arranged a cart of victuals,' says the chairman. 'That is the cart sir, coming across now,' he nods his head towards an approaching horse and cart loaded with various size barrels and baskets.

'We knew nought till we saw smoke from the chimneys. Seen the boxes in London but none down here,' says Spendwell thinking of brandy.

'My Lord Fordingbrook always has a chair to the Palace of Westminster to avoid the mud. Yes, some coal needed burning at the old Place down here, damp as a cottage,' says the chairman watching his passenger. 'He watches crickets in London whenever he can. Some big county matches been set up, slipped quietly away from Westminster for time here where he knew there was rumour of a knock.'

As he says this a cheer goes up from the spectators as Gaunt sends another ball high into the chestnuts for another notch on the fat tally stick. Fordingbrook stands beside his chair, smiles and twirls his stick in the air in appreciation of Gaunt's powerful and accurate stroke.

Gaunt has seen the Lord arrive and knows of him from previous summers and decides to share the event. He raises an arm to halt the bowler and walks over to the man and hands him the willow bat. He is not a young man and the situation resolves itself by Gaunt holding his walking stick as the man hesitatingly takes the bat and uses it to ambles to the sticks. The onlookers are silent with anticipation as the bowler pitches balls to the man but cheer loudly as he bats the balls towards the chestnuts. The cheering continues until he has returned the bat to Gaunt who continues the game.

'Whose he for?' Spendwell asks a chairman.

'He doesn't need to take sides.'

The dewy grass is drying. Warmed by the sun the moisture drifts slowly away in a thin white mist. Horses graze under budding chestnut trees. A woodpecker in a nearby hanger wood competes with the knocking of leather on willow while a distant cuckoo sings for a mate. Some lie on grass, some lounge against tree trunks. The sun filters between green leaves. There is rest from the physical effort of survival. Labouring, hoeing, spinning and ploughing are forgotten as a feeling of deep contentment and pleasure settles on the assembled throng. Taps are turned, tankards are filled, platters loaded and the enjoyment is complete. Fordingbrook signals to his chairmen. One slides out a small table while the other fills a glass from a small cask and places it on the table. He sits watching the sport on the green field as thoughts of tedious Westminster and the smell of the Thames are forgotten.

The hour glass is almost ready for its second turn and Gaunt has laughed a lot as the ball endlessly drifts into the trees. His dog's accurate keen eye has followed each ball's tempting trajectory and the obedient dog waits. The dog wants to run and his master knows. After a handsome number of knocks Gaunt decides to care for his dog. His last stroke powers the ball almost to the tree where his dog waits and he is expected to run and touch the far stick. But Gaunt is not interested in running. His dog's whole features are concentrated on the moving ball and he hears the command,

'Go Jack boy. Go!'

The dog leaps into the air and chases after the ball, chased also by two catchers. The dog reaches the ball and grabs it between his teeth as the two catchers collide. The dog turns and races to his master and drops the ball at his feet.

'Nice work, Jack,' says Gaunt as he stoops to pick up the ball. 'Good at all things my dog, even at crickets. That's my morning of it. My thirst calls for a drink and I'll leave the game now for others to do what they will,' he says to the stick watcher as he hands him the saliva damp ball and walks over to Seth.

'Knock well lad. Bat finds the ball with its magic so give it some liberty, but needs strength behind it,' advises Gaunt as he hands Seth the bat with no evil in it.

He watches Seth settle himself by the sticks then makes his way under the chestnuts towards Nell's wagon of victuals.

'Spells have never turned my head,' Seth says to a Bourne man. 'Don't work for me.'

He sees a Bourne man remove a waistcoat. He sees him look around at the catchers, stretch his arms and then proceed to a violent underarm throw. The bat is over Seth's shoulder, two crowns for a ball, easy work he thinks, his fingers tighten, the ball is in front of him, the bat swings down.

Nell watches Gaunt approach her cart.

'Take some ale,' she says from her stool as he arrives.

Barley turns a tap and a tankard is filled. Nell looks at Gaunt who looks at pies and cheese.

'Victuals need to be eaten,' advises Nell who gets contentment seeing the produce of her inn being consumed, especially by this muscular man. 'You need something after the knocking you gave,' she continues as she watches his thick arm delicately lift a wedge of cheese.

She would like that arm to help her with the heavy work of brewing. She wants him to see her. She stands up and flashes her arm across the cart, insects fly up. They hear a dull thump as the ball falls in the grass and Seth has to run to the distant stick.

'Good day to you innkeeper. The cuckoo is about with a song for us, but a stealer of nests some say. Should be in the pillory,' says Gaunt with his eyes still on the contents of the wagon.

He is aware of the attention Nell gives him. He values it. He would like to live at the inn. When his tithes have been paid he has a few coins remaining. Nell shakes her head as he offers one.

'A generous innkeeper you are, Nell,' he says returning the coin to his purse. 'Snow was worst ever. New year to think of now,' he says. 'Tom Hemming's evil thatch fell on him. Found him all broken and dead when the white had gone. Was inn waiting for him to test the ale?' he asks.

'He was the Constable and that's what they do,' Nell replies.

'Think he had more things to do than look at ale,' says Gaunt looking at the innkeeper.

'He never did. Your soul looks for things that aren't there. You've been bachelor too long. I've been told about your dreams. Innkeepers know all,' admits Nell with a glance into his eyes.

'Dreams. dreams. I didn't put them in my head,' he says with a slight frown showing on his honest face.

113

'As long as they stay there and my daughters don't go by your bed, apples or no,' she says lowering her voice as Barley comes close. 'My man's gone. But it doesn't mean I'm a helpless widow. But he never looked at me,' she says with another glance into Gaunt's eyes to emphasis the point.

'Rolling a barrel's a worthy pastime if you know it's yours. The worth's in the ale and when it's drunk the worth's somewhere else,' muses Gaunt.

'Barrels aren't the only thing that needs rolling at an inn,' offers Nell.

'But have they any worth in them? Some ales ferment slow and seek many days for their best,' adds Gaunt.

'That's not my kind of ale. My yeast is the freshest. Fast worthy ale it brews,' replies Nell. 'Ales not the only worthy thing at my inn, look at these,' she says nodding towards her wagon of victuals. 'They keep body and soul together. Plenty of worth in those.'

'Would you like a new Constable at your inn?'

'Not a new Constable but a worthy man who keeps a promise,' replies Nell.

After their verbal jousting Nell changes the subject.

'Thirst you have now,' observes Nell. 'Give him a drop more ale, love,' she says to Barley as she points to his tankard. She watches him as he finishes his ale and cheese and walks back to the Men of Meads who lie in the grass beneath the trees and she tries to think of a way to dispel his fear of amorous constables.

'They've come to see it work,' says Reuben to Gaunt, as he points to the Gendle sisters who watch. 'The spell is aiding our efforts,' he says quietly under his breath as he prepares for his knock.

The game continues. The tallyman is kept busy and it is when the sand has fallen through after the third turn the game is halted and the men of Meads take their places in the field. It happens when the fourth Bourne man strikes the ball. The bowl has come in high from Seth. The batter is a stout man and the ball is given a solid but strange sounding knock. It spins in the air, loses its togetherness and splits open. The wool in the ball floats down midway between batter and bowler, the leather quarters fall around the bowler and the musket balls are never found. The watcher slips a hand under his wig and scratches. The players gather around him looking for an answer.

'Give me the tally sticks,' he demands.

He is given eleven pieces of stick of differing sizes. His skill enables him to discover the score at each fourth man and he is surprised to find that the notches appear equal.

'At fourth man the Men of Bourne and the Men of Meads each have the same tallies,' he shouts. 'So the knock gives no winners.' he announces holding up the tally sticks.

At first the decision is agreed by both teams but after the Men of Bourne have studied the tally sticks and talked amongst themselves there are concerns.

'The tally sticks say we won,' shouts a Bourne man who turns to look at the watcher.

'So they do,' shouts another after he has seen the sticks.

The Bourne men gather round the watcher who looks anxious.

'Don't miss that,' shouts a man as he points to what he thinks is a notch.

'That's no notch,' says the watcher. 'It's just where a spring bud has been rubbed off and it's left a hole.'

'No. You've got that wrong. It's a notch,' shouts the man. 'It's a notch isn't it?' he shouts as he looks at his team who all agree and shout. 'It's a notch! It's a notch!'

The watcher takes the questionable tally stick to his companion where they look at it with concerned interest and look across at the vociferous complaining team.

'What is it?' the watcher asks his companion.

'It's a bud. Just a bud that's been stripped off to clean the stick.'

'I'm not going to say it's a notch if it isn't. We haven't come all this way to tell falsehoods. They're a rum lot. Are their heads empty? I don't want any bloodshed. Do you want to tell them?' whispers the anxious watcher.

'No, I don't want the work of telling. It was your idea to do this,' says his companion with a laughing smile.

The watcher walks towards the Bourne team with an anxious frown and at a distance shouts,

'The decision of the watchers' is that it is a spring bud. No notch.'

The Men of Bourne have their eyes on the two watchers who are walking hurriedly away.

'See them, hurrying away like that. That's a sure sign of the shame of guilt,' shouts a man.

As the afternoon drifts into evening the blue sedan chair with its occupant and the wagon of victuals have returned to old Bourne Place. The watchers have returned to their room at the Lamb Inn and bolted their door. But the Men of Bourne and the Men of Meads have not gone. The Bourne team look across at the Meads team with strong expressions of malice and grievance.

'It was no spring bud. Our winning has been stolen,' shouts a Bourne man.

'Stolen it was. I'm ready for the thieves,' says another who has slipped back to Bourne and returned with his mattock that he holds in the air.

The two groups face each other with dedicated hatred. Nell has seen this before. She takes a deep breath, smiles at Gaunt and stoically walks between them, looking at one side then the other.

'I know you!' she shouts out. 'I know you. We can all win!' she shouts. 'All win! Do you know what you're fighting about?' she shouts looking around.

'You're the innkeeper. What's it to you?' comes a voice.

'Don't let a spring bud lead you to a sore head. You're fighting over a spring bud. A spring bud!' she shouts followed by a deep throaty laugh. 'Yes. I'm innkeeper. What's it to you?' she shouts glaring at the player.

'We could all win,' she shouts again.

Gaunt sees the brave innkeeper and knows what he must do. He joins her between the two groups.

'A spring bud!' he shouts and laughs with her.

'If we don't fight, what do we do?' comes a warlike voice that has reasoned.

Gaunt does not know the answer.

'The innkeeper will tell you,' he says looking hopefully at Nell who laughs again.

'Come closer. Come closer,' she calls in a deep voice as she waves her large arms for them to come to her. As they stand around her she whispers,

'Let us all win. Nothing's been stolen. At my inn there is the dark stuff to drink. A large barrel of the finest from France.

Our enemy as you all know. It has been kept secretly in my cellar and it could be opened this day. There is no Constable to interfere with us. Burnt wine strong and rich,' she says. 'The best dark brandy for your dry throats. So leave fighting over a spring bud to some fools and come to my inn to see you merry.' She pauses and looks at the faces round her and knows she is winning. 'I'll give you all a tankard of the burnt stuff for the entertainment you have given us.'

'The best from France,' repeats Gaunt to the faces around him.

There is a confused silence as the teams look at each other. Some heads shake. Some heads nod and smile. It is not long before the smiles win and the heavy barrel is pulled from the cellar by many helping hands. Even before it is opened the rich aroma drifts through the parlour. It is tapped and tankards passed around.

'The best from France it is!' shouts Nell as she holds her tankard up. 'Let us all be winners!'

An immense roar of approval shakes the old timbers. The parlour of the Ship Inn throbs with shouts and laughter as the dark golden liquid slips down dry throats, slips into arteries and veins and fuddles the mind. The aroma of the spirit drifts up to the boards above where it squeezes between the shrunken timbers and rises into the rooms above the parlour. Up it goes into the deep thatch above where small insects and mice sniff the air with great satisfaction.

Blossom, Barley and Full are busy providing meat, cheeses, butter, bread and churdle pies to the celebrating noisy throng.

'T'was a game village will remember. Neither won nor lost,' says Butcher looking at Reuben.

'Aye, we'll never know who is the better.'

'We'll have to wait for the next knock,' replies Reuben.

The Gendle sisters are pleased with the result as it has confirmed their secret. A secret buried behind the Gendle's cottage deep in Warren Wood. The Gendle's parents had been refused a Christian burial. They lay side by side in a fold of the Downs close to an aged hawthorn tree. Their simple country lives had got them involved in spells, sorcery and witch magic as they tried to understand the miseries and joys of the nature around them. It was a business just like any other, to make potions with herbs to help the sick or a spell to settle a score. To deal with fear and dread where payments were made, egos satisfied and life in their mysterious world could continue. The consequences however went deep. They had to live apart from the normal life of the village where they were shunned, feared and abused. The sisters wept each night after the death of their parents. After the weeping they discussed their life and resolved to bring to an end all the activities of witchery that their parents had led them into. They decided to bury all the tools of witchery and spell making that their parents had used. This act of repudiation they did with great thoroughness in the dark of night feeling intense relief as the objects were buried deep in the earth. But there were more decisions for the sisters. They came in the form of more wanters who threaded their way along the path in the wood to their isolated cottage.

'My young boy is weak. He ails in his bed with pain and cries. We cannot help him but you can. He is our life,' the man says shaking with fear. 'Take this for your help.'

The man holds out a small purse.

'We take no money. Put the purse away,' says Clarissa pushing the purse away.

'I can bring bread,...meat or ale. Please....hear my plea,' the man stutters.

Clarissa is silent. She looks for her sister and at the feeble vegetables and herbs that just manage to survive in their shady patch of earth. She is resolute.

'Go man. Go to your son. Feed him to give him strength. Tend him and let the world be,' she says pointing for the man to return along the path he came on.

That night the sister considered their predicament.

'I gave the poor man nothing. Nothing. No spell to help his boy. I am a torturer, a murderer,' says Clarissa with quiet panic.

'We must not get back into those evil ways. We made a pact and it should not be broken.'

It was a few days later when Clarissa hears the sound of footsteps again in the wood on the narrow path. They sounded familiar. She is right. It is the man who had come about his ailing son and whom she had sent away. He looks lively.

'There is nothing here for you,' she shouts as he approaches.

'It is done. Bless you both,' he calls out.

'What is done?' she asks.

'These are for you,' the man places a basket on the ground. 'For you.' he repeats then turns and walks back along the path.

'What is done?' she asks eagerly.

'My boy. Your spell has worked. He is back with the plough and oxen tilling the furlong. Bless you,' he shouts back as he disappears along the narrow path.

That night the sisters have bread, cheese and salted meat to add to their frugal meal.

'But there was no spell made,' Clarissa says to her sister as she slices the meat. 'We buried the means. Nothing was acted. We have kept our pact like honest people and there is nothing to worry us. If talk is all that the wanters need, so be it.'

The sisters can have almost anything they want in exchange for a few carefully chosen words is the legacy from their parents.

Chapter Ten

Flash of a knife.

Martha twists her body as she sleeps. The mysterious visitor is close and large this night. The fully waxed orb hangs bright in the sky shedding a brighter light that floods through the shutter of her room and falls on her as she sleeps. Her dream images are in turmoil, unknown and threatening. She feels panic and tries to flee. She twists to escape. Her eyelids flicker, her eyes suddenly open, she stares at the orb that stares back at her. Her mind calms, she stretches and turns her head away and looks at the dry thatch of reeds above her. She knows this dream when she is awake. It is a regular visitor but when she is in the dream it is the first time all over again. Her eyelids slowly droop and shut and do not open until the first light of a day steals silently into the room. She rubs her face with a cold wet piece of cloth, plaits and pins her hair, slips her loose working gown over her bed shift, ties her apron and slips into shallow leather shoes. She takes her black widows cap, gently places it and ties it under her chin. She calls out as she descends the stairs.

'Maids. You're to be at the hay meadow. Get the early cut in.'

Today a scythed area of a hay meadow is ready to be loaded onto a cart for storage in a hay barn. An undemanding activity enjoyed by the young maids. Lizzie has placed buttered bread and lumps of cheese on the table next to a corked jar of small ale. The girls are talking sleepily.

'He'll lie-down and fall asleep watching us work,' says Beth rubbing sleep from her eyes.

'Well he can,' replies Livy as she packs the victuals in a straw basket. 'It's not his job. As long as the flock's safe with his dogs.'

'Did you dream?' asks Beth.

'No dream, Beth. But I wish I had. Some nights I feel free to let my mind wander wherever it wants to go, drifting over the downs to a sunset or the morning sun. It can fly. But after you told me of how you feel heartbroken and unhappy having no news of your Charles I began to feel your loneliness too. I think that's why I was dreamless.'

'I heard her say we are untutored,' whispers Beth. 'I don't want to be tutored if it makes me like her. I know my maid's work. Lizzie has shown me how to make rush candles. I spin, work in the fields and cook. The woman in the house is wrong. I hate her, Livy! She made me sad. If she hadn't said what she said he would have come for me. I know he would.'

Beth's eyes moisten with tears.

'Hate will give you bad blood, Beth. It's not good for anyone. Try and forget it. It was a long time ago,' says Livy.

'I know. But it keeps coming to my mind.'

'Away with you now.' Martha's loud voice shouts. 'Hay to the barn. Take a hay rake. Forks will be by the wagon.'

The girls leave with the basket of victuals and jar of ale and take it in turns to carry the hay rake. They reach the edge of the hay meadow and gaze at the prospect. An extensive random shape that is indicated by clumps of Blackthorn that lazily step down to a shallow valley then rise as a compact hedge to form a rough enclosure.

Soft green grasses with a myriad of coloured flowers stand upright enjoying the fresh morning air, their faces waiting to follow the path of the sun. Lady's mantle, cranesbills, buttercup, hay rattle, scabious and clover scent the air. Bush crickets add a scratchy voice to the song of a skylark as a female glow worm descends a grass stalk after her nights work and field mice sleep in their grass nests under thorn bushes. The girls feast their eyes on the captivating site of nature then lift their eyes from the meadow to a small figure of white that moves over the green downland towards them.

'Come on,' says Livy. 'Let's move some hay before he reaches us.'

The girls make their way to a scythed part of the meadow where the hay has been raked to dry in the sun and is now the colour of gold. A worn aged hay wagon of dry faded oak boards waits for its load and a horse to draw it. Large chalk stone markers are the only trace of officialdom. All the local farmers are aware of the importance of this meadow and diligently restrain their livestock from trespass until the allotted time. Beth holds the rake and pulls the scythed hay into piles. They find hayforks by the wagon and begin tossing the sweet-smelling grasses onto its old boards.

After the death of Barnabas Seth has taken over his father's flock and today has left it with a neighbouring shepherd and is making his way to the hay meadow.

'We've started. You can go back to your sheep,' says Livy as Seth arrives at the meadow.

'I've seen to the sheep. They've sent me to see their hay is good,' he says looking at Livy pulling the rake.

'You can tell them it's good but they have to wait till the snow's here,' she replies.

Seth goes over to the wagon, sits in the grass and pulls off a boot.

'I must get this out,' he says as he examines a boot.

He tries to locate a thorn and can just hear Livy's voice as it floats across the meadow.

'Rake, Rake. Rake it to the wagon for hungry sheep and goats,' she sings.

'How do you know if someone loves you?' reaches his ears.

'I don't know. It's many things. If you feel it, it will be there,

'I think it was there,' he hears.

'I don't think Martha thinks of Barnabas every day now. But be hopeful dear sister, he won't forget you.'

Martha Applegate has been attentive. She has watched the maids climb the Warren track with their victuals and hay rake and noticed the appearance of Fisher who stands in his usual spot in his heavy black tarred clothes. She knows that he also has watched the maids climb the track. She remains watching him as she begins spinning by the window. He leans against a wall, kicks some dust and looks restless. His manner reminds Martha of her disturbed dream and she wonders if the night's large silent orb has similarly disturbed him. After some time, he stands still, looks up the track, looks about then he too makes his way up the same track. Martha's intuition has told her that this man is a threat to her family. But she knows her intuition is sometimes at fault. She gets increasingly anxious about the man that watches her children almost every day and gives the girls presents. After sitting motionless as her mind tries to shape a judgement there comes a point where she can wait no longer. She leaves her spinning, looks around for something to take but realises this is very likely a pointless intuitive led journey and leaves the cottage. She can see Fisher far ahead pacing quickly up the hill as she furtively manoeuvres her position to be obscured behind bushes. She is soon high on the downs watching the black figure of the man descending into a valley in the direction of the hay meadow. She loses sight of him but continues towards the meadow. Soon she is hidden behind a thick bush watching Fisher as he approaches the young people. Livy and Beth see Fisher and wonder what he is doing. They stop their raking and watch with some alarm as the man strides deliberately towards them. He takes something from his pocket and takes it towards Livy, but she shies away. He moves quickly towards her. She walks quickly away from him but he runs after her, grabs her arm and pulls her to him. Livy's arm twists and she shrieks in pain. Seth has been watching, he has extracted the thorn and is slipping on his boot. He hears the man shout.

'Come he....here you!' the man drags Livy towards him. 'I've come for you at la....last. I want you. You're mine now!' he screams out.

Livy cannot escape his hot heavy hand that grips her wrist. She tries to pull away but the grip gets stronger. She looks towards Seth and screams. Horror and disbelief fills the onlookers faces. Martha watches from behind her bush some distance away. She sees Seth run across the meadow to Livy, then straight into Fisher. The blow stuns the man who releases Livy and falls to the ground. The man jumps to his feet, Martha sees him take something from his belt as he shouts curses at Seth. She sees the flash of a knife as the man moves towards Seth. It flashes bright in the sun as he slashes the air with the blade. Martha is rigid with fear. She gathers her strength, leaps out from her hiding place and stumbles as fast as she can towards the man. She is behind him, she is getting closer, she thinks she will just run into him like Seth has done, but something catches her eye. A hayfork is lying in the grass. She is now close behind the man, her shaking hand unconsciously drops and grabs the long handle. She is behind the man. She raises the long fork high above her head and with both hands swings it down with all her strength. The oak tines crash down and sink into the man's shoulder crushing and tearing skin and tissue. There is the cracking sound as the first oak tine breaks and the second goes deeper into flesh splintering bone. The man screams in pain and falls clutching his shoulder. The knife drops from his hand. Martha releases the handle of the hay fork. The handle drops. Its weight twists the tines upwards and the fork jerks and twists itself out of the man's shoulder as he screams in agony. The quiet of the hay meadow now has the screams of a torture chamber as the man's pain approaches a point where it almost consumes his consciousness.

'You mad, mad fool,' cries Seth looking at the man wriggling and screaming in pain on the ground.

'God preserve us!' exclaims Martha. 'Throw that knife away, son,' she says pointing to the fallen blade.

Beth has run to Livy who is sobbing.

'He won't touch you again. Look at him,' Beth says pointing at the man.

'I don't want to see him.' she shouts with tears running down her cheeks. 'Never see him again.'

They stand shocked and confused.

'You fool,' shouts Seth again looking at the man but he is now still as a corpse. 'What have we done Martha?' he asks in a nervous faltering voice. 'What shall we do?'

'I'll take the girls away. You return to your cover. He will not be any trouble now,' says Martha as she looks at Fisher's body in the grass.

'What about him?' asks Beth looking at the man.

'He's mad. Mad,' shouts Livy.

'He's swooned away. Leave him in the grass,' says Martha.

They gather their tools and walk away stunned at what has happened in such a short space of time.

'He won't bother us anymore. Martha has seen to that,' says Beth with her arm round Livy as they descend the track to their cottage.

'Why didn't he grab you. Why me? You were nearer to him,' sobs Livy. 'I don't want any more presents from him. Why did he say "you're mine," Will he be my master?' Livy asks with horror on her face.

'Never. Never. Never!' says Martha loudly. 'We'll soon be home. There's carding to do. We can talk about it another day. The weather's good,' she says looking skyward. 'The hay can wait.'

Chapter Eleven

I was born on Ludgate Hill

The weight of the lantern clock in the parlour has been lifted many times since the trouble in the hay meadow. A visitor is standing on the door stone hammering the open cottage door with a heavy stick.

'Jamie! Where's your mother?' the visitor demands. 'I have something for her.'

Nell, the innkeeper of the Ship Inn stops wielding her stick.

'Ma.' Jamie calls up the staircase. 'Nell's here for you.'

'Nell!' exclaims Martha cleaning her rough hands on her apron. 'What keeps you from your barrels?'

Nell takes a folded piece of paper from a pocket.

'It was given me yesterday. Abe's been to the Wells, asked me to pass it on. It's addressed to the Ship. Abe says you're the one it's for.'

Martha takes the paper and looks at the address.

The Ship Inn
The Street Meads
The cottage up the track to the Warren

She snaps a small piece of sealing wax and unfolds the paper.

Dear Friend,

It's a long time ago now but I feel I must get a message to you. I have a position in a house in London and we are now at The Wells. My mistress is writing this for me. We are going to Brighthelmstone, she wishes to visit family. We will be staying at the Ship for five days. I hope the little ones are well, please bring them; I would just love to see them so much. Come any day, I'll look out for you. I hope everything has been alright for you. You were so kind to me.

God Bless you all,

I call myself Cathy.

Martha feels tears forming in her eyes as she looks up at Nell after reading the message.

'Is that what reading does to you?' asks Nell as she sees the silver drops.

'It's from my friend, a very important good close friend,' says Martha rubbing her eyes with the back of her hand. 'I never thought I'd see her again, and now she's come to the sea. I must see her. Yes, she is an old friend of mine,' Martha says to reassure the innkeeper.

'Old friends are the best to find,' says Nell.

'It's been so long and she wants to see my girls. I understand how she feels. She's coming to Brightstone.'

'Carts from the Lamb some days. I hear you can be in Brighstone after four hours if the track's dry. Customers need tending at the inn,' explains Nell as she turns to go.

Martha reads the note several times before she returns to her kitchen where she had been helping Lizzie grinding herbs in a stone mortar.

'Livy and Beth,' she calls. 'You two go over to the Lamb, I need news of a cart to Brightstone, what time and what day does it travel. We'll be going to see a friend of mine I've known since you were babies?' she says testing the dried herbs between her fingers.

After some days of dry weather the carter has decided that a journey to Brighthelmstone would be possible over the chalk downland track by way of the Haven where passengers and horses would be fed and watered. They should arrive in Brighthelmstone at approximately noon.

The driver of the cart, or coach as it is now sometimes called, is a small man with a flat face that only manages a small stumpy nose. He has a large pair of hands that move as though he is using a hand brush. He has no philosophy for life and it has managed to preserve him from his young Redcoat army days at Reigate Garrison and then later at Reigate Prison. On release he happened to wander along a track that was to be one

131

of the first turnpike roads in the south of England and while he stared at the track, deep in thought, he heard the crack of a whip. Four horses pulling a painted wagon sped by him swerving from side to side with trunks and boxes on the roof and frightened faces peering from small openings. When he returned to his rural isolation, he spent much time at the inn talking and gesticulating with his hands about what he had seen.

The imagination of carpenters, blacksmiths, and cobblers at this inn had been inspired. With chisels, saws, anvil and skivers they created the answer to the increasing local demand for personal transport. Various parts of farm carts, wagons and cottage furniture had fused together and the synthesis of their dreams was a coach of preliminary design that now waits outside the Lamb Inn. Robustly constructed with a thick metal and leather springing arrangement and accommodation for six passengers inside, four in the open boot and one each side of the driver, who was proudly pleased with the result of his forethought.

'There are passengers already in the coach, Martha,' says Beth as they see it for the first time.

'Have not seen this afore now. We are not inside but have seats in the back that I'm told are better,' says Martha. 'We are for Brighstone at the back. All's paid,' she shouts to the driver as she looks for their seats at the back.

'My name is Enoch. This coach...,' he bangs the side of the coach with a large hand. 'This is maiden journey of Bourne coach. I am pleased to carry you all. To Brightstone it will be.'

They pass their small bags up to Enoch who stows them on the roof amongst trunks and cases.

'You're in the boot, good lady,' Enoch continues waving his hands brushing Martha and the girls to the back of the coach.

'Through the small gate there,' he says pointing.

The boot attached to the back of the coach is surrounded by a low wickerwork wall with a small wicker access gate; it has two benches. Beth and Livy sit on the rear bench looking forward while Martha sits on the bench looking back with an empty seat beside her.

Enoch checks his whip, picks up a battered brass hunting horn, puts it to his lips and his strong chest pumps air over the valve. The loud blast wakes the remaining passengers at the inn who rush out to find their seats. The last passenger finds the coach full except for the seat next to Martha in the boot and he climbs aboard and sits beside her. He is a well-fed portly man and the boot which is on a delicate cantilever arrangement sinks a few inches lower as he enters. Their travelling companion is Clergyman Wigmore, a visiting clergyman who they have been introduced to by way of the pulpit.

He looks at the two girls sitting opposite him.

'Good morning,' he says slightly nodding his head as he speaks. 'I am the visiting clergyman that....' he turns his head to look at who is sitting next to him and his eyes open with surprise as he looks at Martha's black widow's cap. 'Yes, I remember that cap from the Sabbath last when I gave my sermon,' he says smiling at Martha and looking about. 'The countryside here takes my heart away I would live here if I wasn't in the clutches of sinful London, and the poor souls I need to tend....'

But the coach has now started on its journey and with the jolting, dust and noise, conversation is difficult and soon they sit in silence with the girls trying to avoid the clergyman's eye. The Haven is reached without incident and after all are refreshed the four-horse team pulls them towards the village of Brighthelmstone. While travelling down a steep slope into a small village the coach jolts violently, the passengers find little to hold onto and become anxious. The passengers in the boot hear a loud cracking noise and stare in horror at the floor as a board breaks in two, falls out of the floor, and they are left staring at the ground racing by below them. They sit still and hope nothing else will happen but there is soon another cracking sound and the rear bench with Livy and Beth sinks dangerously down towards the rushing ground. Livy leaps over onto Martha's lap but Beth does not want to leap onto the clergyman's lap and she remains in her seat. The frightened passengers in the boot shout and hammer with their fists on the rear of the coach but those inside cannot hear them. Another loud crack is heard as one of the blacksmith shaped metal bars breaks and the rear bench swings up and down almost touching the racing ground below.

'Ma! Save me!' screams Beth.

Martha looks in horror at the perilous situation as the bench with Beth rises and falls almost touching the racing ground.

'Hold tight.' shouts Wigmore as he stands up, grabs Beth's arm, and swings her across the missing floorboard onto his seat while he remains standing on a small piece of floor feeling unsteady. He desperately tries to find a handhold by putting his arm around the side of the coach and manages to grab the edge of a window opening. An inside passenger sees his grabbing fingers, pokes his head through the opening and shouts, 'What's happening back there?'

The clergyman manages to twist his head round the corner of the coach and after a few hasty shouts the inside passengers manage to get the attention of the driver who pulls the horses to a halt. Enoch makes some temporary repairs but two seats are out of use and it is decided that Martha and the clergyman could now travel on the roof of the coach while Beth and Livy would have the safe remaining bench in the boot. This is Martha's first journey on a coach and her mental constitution is usually calm whatever the situation but the idea of travelling on the roof of the coach with a man of the cloth, who may wish to converse intimately is something she is not looking forward to. The clergyman is quickly on the roof and lowers a hand to assist Martha who looks up at him slightly bewildered as she floats quickly upwards with his strong pull. She crawls over the low roof rail and sits between the luggage while Wigmore fusses around her moving boxes and cases until they have built a comfortable space. The coach moves forward but this is not what she expected.

The wide green expanse of the downs is all around them. Overhead a blue sky with billowing brilliant white clouds. There is no noise from the crunching wheels, the dust does not reach them and a cooling breeze floats in their faces. They sit smiling and laughing as they fly high like a bird, through the chalk grassland as weasels, stoats, deer, bustards, and hares stare in amazement. The change of position from the cramped boot to this open scenic view makes them feel exhilarated and free. They can now converse without difficulty; Martha's inhibitions have disappeared and they chatter with interest.

'I was born on Ludgate Hill,' relates Wigmore when their initial excitement has passed. 'Where my father rents a bookshop selling bibles and religious tracts he gets from a press in Shoe Lane. It's near St. Pauls. He always has his nose buried in some book; he only follows the strict interpretation of the word and talks of little else.'

A gust of wind tugs at Martha's black widow's cap and it is nearly lifted off. She grabs it and reties the ribbon. Wigmore looks thoughtful. 'I only wear my black cap now. The black gown takes my spirit,' she reveals to Wigmore.

'I often give marriage ceremonies around Ludgate Hill but I'm not married,' he says.

He has grown up slightly apart and after his theology studies enjoys his position in the church that has given him some comradeship. When in the pulpit he looks down at the women in his congregation with some fascination and mystery as he has had little opportunity to discuss life with the child bearers of the world.

'I noticed when you arrived at St Mary's wearing a black cap,' he continues.

'The cold spirit of winter took him from me. He was a good man, but too good in winter when he went to save his flock. Clergy do not have to fight snow and ice for their flock,' she says looking at Wigmore.

'That is true, we are provided for,' he says wistfully. 'I hope to have a wife before Michaelmas to share my good fortune.'

'That will be good for the lucky lady. Is it a lady from Ludgate Hill who will be lucky?' she asks.

'There is no person yet but my eyes are open. I'm catching a coach to London but I return often to Bourne,' he says changing the subject. 'London is busy, I wait outside coffee houses and talk about my father's bookshop to help his trade.'

'I've never been to London. Is it as bad as people say?'

'The Fleet Prison is near and I try to get people to be God fearing and change their ways. Yes, it's bad for some, but we have the cathedral, shining in its white stone with statues on the roof to see,' suggests Wigmore. 'To live somewhere like this green spot of earth away from the horrors of London is a blessing for some. Gin is a terrible curse. I do apologise, I don't know your name.'

'My name is Martha Applegate,' and after a pause adds, 'I'll not wear this black cap more than is necessary.'

Wigmore looks thoughtful again.

'You have two fine daughters, Martha,' he says. 'They may need a father to help them find their way.'

'They are good maids of all work and help me so much,' says Martha looking towards the rear of the coach where Livy and Beth sit in the boot. She is surprised and impressed by the agility of Wigmore in saving her daughter but feels little attraction for this man of the cloth. She feels sorry for the dismal story of his life but that is the extent of her feeling for the man. But then she remembers her own dismal future which may include the workhouse and she looks at the man with added interest and thinks again of his heroic rescue of her daughter.

'My future is unknown. When my son is of age, he will have the cottage and I may need to work as a maid servant. All I know is how to be a mother, teaching my children,' she says looking at the clergyman.

'Mothers are foremost in the scheme of things,' he says, then quickly adds. 'Work with their husbands to bring children into the world. Baptised and with the faith will give a fine family.'

'That may be the life for some who are lucky.'

'I am sure you will be lucky, Martha. I would like to make you happy,' he says smiling. 'Had a fine stay at the Lamb; sweet ale, thick meats and good bed.'

Martha did not feel like discussing the comfort of her bed and was silent but after a while they talked freely of their separate lives and it is not long before Wigmore shouts down to the girls in the boot.

'We'll soon be there. Brightstone is in sight.'

The coach stops in the cobbled yard of the inn. Enoch is keen to get the passengers down from the roof and immediately goes to help Martha. This is much to the dismay of Wigmore, who has jumped down almost before the coach stopped in order to assist Martha, and has damaged himself on the cobbles. Enoch waves his hands brushing Martha and the girls towards the entrance of the inn.

'I will be open preaching at St. Mary's again soon and I hope you will be there. I'll give you good day,' he says politely as he nods his head to the Applegates.

'Some want wives. Some want husbands,' Martha muses to herself as they watch him leave the inn yard.

They enter the inn, are given directions to Cathy's room, but there is no answer when they knock on her door. They leave the inn and walk along the track just above the shingle and see the damage to boats and cottages from a recent storm. On returning to the inn they see three people in the parlour.

'That's Cathy!' Martha exclaims quietly pointing to a dark haired, slim woman dressed in maid's clothes. Martha without hesitating hurries over to her and they embrace each other tightly. Cathy turns her head and looks towards the two girls.

'Many summers,' says Martha.

Cathy, still looking towards the girls asks. 'What are their names?'

The girls are called over.

'This is Elizabeth and this is Olivia. Both good maids,' says Martha putting her hand on their heads in turn.

'Oh. I can see,' says Cathy looking at the maids. 'I have come with my mistress who wishes to visit family and may step in the sea.' she says to both girls.

'Rather her than me,' says Livy looking at Beth.

'You can't see the bottom and it tastes bad,' says Beth. 'Coach brought us from Bourne.'

'Was it a good coach ride?' Cathy asks Livy.

'Floor broke apart and we were close to falling off.'

Cathy introduces her mistress and her husband who leave to visit relations. The two mothers find seats and order ale. The deep experience of motherhood unites these two women who chatter with shared memories. The girls go out to the yard to see the horses.

'I really was so ....,' says Cathy.

'It was some summers...,' says Martha at the same time interrupting. 'You go first,' she says laughing.

'I was so lucky,' says Cathy.

'Well I was with child and my husband agreed. The vicar knew nothing. All names are in his book,' says Martha.

'I'll never tell you my name or his,' says Cathy quietly. 'He must never find me. I would fret if he knew.'

'I'll never tell anyone,' Martha says raising her eyes to Cathy's. 'It's all best left alone.'

'It was a sad time for me.'

'Everything is alright now,' says Martha watching the girls come in from the yard.

'Can we go out along the beach?' Beth asks.

'Yes. Be back soon.'

The sky is grey with only distant small blue openings and the calm sea reflects the greyness. The coastal air is salty and heavy. They walk along the beach watching bearded fishermen in black tarred clothes with grim faces busy repairing their broken boats.

'Hard work is needed for a sea harvest,' says Beth to Livy as they look at the working fishermen.

A fisherman hears her, looks up from his work but remains silent. A light rain interferes with their wishes and they return to the parlour of the inn where they find Cathy and Martha still in eager conversation.

'We should eat together,' says Martha in a gap of the exchange and it is not long before the four are served with a generous lobster meal.

'You are both fine girls. Are you with young men and thinking of babies?' asks Cathy looking at Livy who is pulling meat from a claw. The girls look at each other and remain silent.

'That means you are,' reasons Cathy.

'They are but they don't tell me everything,' says Martha.

They look into the courtyard of the inn and see clergyman Wigmore boarding a coach for the Wells.

'We travelled with him from Bourne,' says Martha. 'He's looking for a wife.'

They hear Enoch send a blast on the hunting horn and they gather at the inn yard. Emotional farewells are made and the passengers are pleased to find the good coachman has given them places inside to compensate for their earlier experience. They watch Cathy standing alone in the inn yard until they turn a corner and are soon watching the seaside village with its busy fishermen and fresh lobsters disappearing in the distance.

Chapter Twelve

Silver hoops

It is the third day in a procession of identical grey skies that stretch from horizon to horizon; interfering with the perception of days and time. Nevertheless, a large heavy wagon loaded with bundles of reeds, ladders, spars and thatcher's tools makes its way through shallow mud at Susans on the appointed day in the direction of Meads hamlet. A thatcher has harvested fifty bundles of fine, medium and coarse reed from his patch on Pemsey marshes and as he sits on the wooden seat with reins in one hand, a moving expression of anxiety and sympathy passes over his face in time with the creaks and groans of his overloaded wagon. It is time for this wagon to be left idle in some Pemsey marsh to let the dried timber soak up moisture to its shrunken parts. But the thatcher is a busy man with many calls on his time and he has more important things to attend to. The thatcher's name had been written in a well-thumbed parish register as Amos Reed or possibly Amos Deed. The vicar's quill pen had spluttered but the first name of Amos was decipherable. Cottages and hayricks were just two of the many features of the chalk downs that needed a watertight roof against the winter rains, sleets and snows. The reeds on his wagon were destined for repairs to the roof of a cottage close to the Warren track.

He had been told by the estate the name of the cottage where the thatch needed repair and the name was Applegate. His shoulder length dark black hair hangs down over his forehead and eyes; his free hand has the important occupation of parting it to a locality behind large silver hoop ear rings where he endeavoured to leave it. Occasionally it rests in place until jolts from the wagon release it and the parting hand is required again. Two heavy working horses lug the wagon slowly to its destination while the thatcher ponders his youth. He was the son of a thatcher and had spent his childhood around the Pemsey marshes where reed was harvested. He had married the mill owner's daughter whom he had courted and loved. She brought him a healthy son whom he began teaching the ways of thatching but their blissful life was cut short when a pox brought agony and death to his small family and the people of Pemsey. Some said 'We must not interfere with God's will.' Others said it was the work of spirits and his wife was left to die in agony with painful sores; a common occurrence at this time of scarce medical knowledge and misleading beliefs. Her small son died soon after. The lonely heartbroken thatcher now busied himself in his work. He had done well and prospered and now owned an acre of marshy ground, a box of silver coins and a sturdy cob named Furlong. He often contemplated the possibility of adding a new wife to share his life. He recalled a young girl, who assisted with the harvest when he had some sixteen summers. Dark haired with dark eyes, hardworking, the owner of a penny Chapbook. These facts were clear in his mind.

As the wagon rocks on its way, he is deep in thought. He tries to discover in his mind to which coin of prettiness the marsh girl belonged. As a youth he would attempt to judge maids in order of prettiness, he had some knowledge of coins so the system he chose was coins. It went, penny, thruppence, sixpence, shilling, crown. So, his vacant mind, as he rumbles along dwells on the prettiness of the maid and to which coin she belongs in the system. It gives him great pleasure in selecting one coin then changing it for another. His interest in this question is brought about by the knowledge that the girl from his youth had left to marry a shepherd with the name Applegate. His contemplation continues as the wagon rumbles along bumpy tracks and eventually comes to the cottages at the bottom of the hill that rises to the Warren. Here he wakes from his muse, jumps down, wedges blocks of wood behind the wheels and walks in through the open door of the nearest cottage. He looks round a parlour at the usual cottager's furniture and day to day objects but the room is silent.

'Thatcher.' he calls. The silence remains.

'Thatcher's here,' he repeats and hears a shuffling sound coming from a partly open door.

'I don't know that voice,' Lizzie says as she appears in the parlour and studies the man from head to toe.

His face is almost concealed by long thick black hair that hangs free. Around the waist of his grey smock is a large leather apron with a tool pouch worn smooth from generations of use. Short leather breeches hold muscular legs that descend without stockings into short leather boots. He looks about through the gaps in his hair. She wonders how he will work with such strange hair. He realises someone is there and his parting hand comes to his face and the hair is left behind a large silver hoop.

'You've been lucky to have some spare silver,' Lizzie remarks as she observes him.

'Aye. It's safest through my ears,' he replies.

Lizzie knows men. She has loved and lost and loved and won. Her love now is the smell of hay meadows and playing children. She tries to recognise thatcher amongst the men she has known but he remains an unknown quantity.

'I'll wish for some ale to slake my thirst. If my wish is heard, God's in heaven and the larks will sing,' he says almost to himself as he looks up at the rough boards above his head.

'Those who are too hasty may trip and fall. All in good time. We've had estate man to see thatch. Parlour floor runs with water, last winter it iced. No blaspheming in this place thatcher,' she says raising her voice.

'Never to blaspheme is hard with winters like that. I know about the winter, I was alive too, over at Pemsey. God's up to no good to give such a winter. If we get more like that then God's a devil,' he answers.

Lizzie is shocked and silent.

'No more on your floor if I have my way. Your feet will be dry,' he continues as he looks at Lizzie's small misshapen feet.

'Well, make it so thatcher,' she demands. 'Without more blaspheming from a loose tongue.'

'You must have picked many apples in the garden,' he says flippantly.

'You coxcomb! Never you mind my love life,' returns Lizzie fiercely.

'Words are sounds in the air I've been told. My tongue fashions my world. Such as it is.'

'The good bible fashions mine,' replies Lizzie with conviction.

'I've been told this is Applegate cottage?' he asks, and as he looks at Lizzie with a knowing wide smile, his right eye slowly closes, creases and opens. He has winked at her. She feels bewildered and tries to untangle the emotional meaning of being winked at by a blaspheming stranger.

'What's that for you shameless man. That's no respect for somebody who could be your grandmother's grandmother. It's not Christian,' she feels flustered. 'To work. There's much to do here.' she says raising her voice and trying to calm herself.

'No offence intended. A cupid never sleeps so let it play where it will,' he says looking through a shutter at his pair grazing on good grass at the side of the track. He pauses and looks at Lizzie. Her grey hair is neatly plaited, tied with ribbon under a starched clean linen cap around a wrinkled face that smiles or frowns with ease. Her gown and apron have marks from food, burns, ash, wax and soil and she frowns.

'I've been told that we provide the victuals for your labour?' she says with a frown, 'and aye, the Applegates live here, and don't tell me about cupid. My cupid days are over.'

'I've just pulled that load of thatch since sunrise. My throat is sore,' he says feeling his neck. 'Your goodness to a working man will be rewarded in the churchyard.'

'I won't be in the churchyard. My body will be in the yard but my soul in a better place. You should listen to the sermons,' Lizzie instructs him with a deeper frown.

'I'm pleased to hear it,' he replies.

She fills a wooden staved tankard, cuts bread, produces a dish of butter and the dissimilar mortals sit on wooden stools around a wooden table.

'Looks clouds for some days,' he says slicing the bread with a knife from around his waist.

'We need to know what you were christened. If you have been?' she asks.

'My name is Amos Reed some people call me Mossy.'

Lizzie's frown slightly lessens at the sound of this semi biblical name.

'All my thatch is good for years you'll have no worry. You will be dry all winter. Last winter saw much thatch thrown down, it busies my trade. Hayrick's thatch blown across the furlongs something terrible. We don't want him giving us another winter like that,' he says nodding skyward.

The conversation slows and ends as Lizzie finally decides in the thatcher's talk that he is definitely not a God-fearing person.

'I have a basket to attend to,' she says as she leaves the table.

'And I'll away to the roof.'

Amos returns to his wagon where he pitches a ladder to the roof, ascends and begins stripping moss, lichen, grass and ivy from the damaged thatch. Lizzie is curious as to how he can work with such long thick hair that falls over his eyes. She pokes her head through a shutter to observe him and sees him under what was once a felt cavalier's hat that has been beaten many times to accommodate different size heads. There is ample room within to accommodate his long hair that is tucked up inside while outside a white goose feather catches the eye.

As the various members of the Applegate family come and go he observes them closely from his ladder to see if he can recognise any traits or subtle mannerism that would enable him to identify the young girl he knew in his youth twenty summers ago. It is when the stripping has nearly finished that he sees a woman's figure approaching the cottage. As it approaches, he can see curls of dark hair below a tight black cap. He looks again but the distance keeps detail a mystery. After two more passes with the stripping tool, he looks again from the corner of his eye. The figure is closer, but just as he looks the figure changes direction and disappears behind a nearby cottage. He turns back to his work and watches myriads of disturbed insects frantically search for a new home as jackdaws and starlings descend on the homeless. He surveys the cleared roof, plans his method of repair and descends the ladder. He has anticipated working alone but Livy and Beth agree to pass him bundles of reed and save him many trips to the wagon. Lizzie, sitting in her chair just outside the cottage door is weaving a small straw basket. He descends the ladder and stops by Lizzie.

'It will be just two days and then the work will be finished,' he says. Amos has mentioned this fact as he wished to ensure his place at the evening table. He watches her withered bent fingers thread and pull with skill and speed. Her long nails have been picked clean with a sharpened twig but deeper soil shows black.

'Go in and see the girls if your throat is sore again. They'll give you ale.'

He goes into the parlour. Beth fills his tankard, he returns and sits on the door stone a few feet from Lizzie resting his back against the wall of the cottage. He looks at the pale-yellow liquid. The girls come into the garden with a scythe blade and gently push it against a spinning sharpening stone laughing as the sparks fly into the air. He turns his head and looks across the track through a gap between two ivy clad hovels of cottages. He can see the green downs and the brick walls of the Mansion House with its tall chimneys. He looks again at the remaining pale liquid and lets it trickle down his dry throat. He then ascends the ladder and continues his work.

'The wagon just spoke with a creak and a groan. A heavy load is in the bible but it's not about wagons.' says Lizzie looking up from the basket remembering a distant sermon.

Amos looks across at his wagon with its high load of bales that lean at a delicate angle.

After a while he hears Lizzie talking and he looks down. She is talking to the woman with the black cap. Amos watches from high on the thatch, his view is limited and he cannot see faces. He listens to their talk.

'Thatcher here for roof.'

'Look at this.'

'Seen a bigger one. Not one so feeble as that.'

'It's for the tea.'

'Won't get much in that. Whatever's for?'

'It's for the stirring. I promised the girls I'd get the tools for tea and this is important.'

'But it's small, Martha, so small.'

When the name is mentioned, Amos leans away from the roof for a better view. He sees the woman polishing the bowl of a small pewter spoon with her thumb. His mind races back to his childhood as he realises that this is surely the girl from the marshes and he tries to conclude his male question of prettiness. Her contours roll into comfortable valleys with rounded tops just like the downs. Her cottager's clothes have stains, sewn up splits and neatly stitched patches. Her fingers are rough and slender. Untidy dark hair curls out of the back of her cap and passes her shoulders. He studies her lips, nose and mouth and cannot make up his mind as he considers pennies, sixpences and crowns. As he is looking at her there is a flicker of movement in her eyes. Her face turns slightly towards him and her eyes focus on him. He forgets about his coins and looks at dark eyes, laughing and smiling. Eyes that beam happiness. He feels warmth and comfort. There is a moment looking into her deep warm eyes and then they are gone and he looks again at the roof that needs new thatch. His mind is confused, the bank is empty the coins have vanished, the system has failed. This is not the right place for coin and he realises how foolish he has been. He hears Lizzie's voice.

'I don't know about tea. Vicar should say in sermons about it. If he doesn't say I'll not take it.'

When he looks again Lizzie is there on her own. The woman has gone. He thinks about the momentary glimpse into the dark eyes then brings his mind back to sombre reality and continues his work. Fresh bales are passed up by Beth and Livy. The reed is folded and held with pointed spars sunk deep into good thatch. The grey sky has cleared and the remaining clouds have turned pink and golden as the sun sinks. Dusk is fast approaching and the thatcher ends his days toil, checks his pair, stores his tools in a wooden chest on the side of the wagon and finds himself in the parlour looking at a small glow in the hearth as he draws on the short stem of a clay pipe. The wet nose of Halfpenny has identified him as an ally and now lies on the floor beside him. Lizzie is loading a table with butter, jam, freshly baked loaf, earthenware jug of milk, cheese and cold mutton. A pottage of peas, turnips, onions, oats and herbs steams in an iron pot on a hanger over the fire. A fresh barrel of ale has been delivered and is on tap in a corner of the parlour. Livy, Beth and Jamie sit on a bench along one side of the table looking towards the fire where Amos ponders the day.

'Come and eat thatcher,' calls Beth.

He recalls himself to the present moment and seats himself on a three-legged stool at the table. The dim room has a flickering light from rush candles that add to the warm red glow of embers in the hearth that have brought the pottage to the boil. The room smells of wood and tobacco smoke along with the smell of herbs and the heavy body odour of the thatcher together with the sweet smell of freshly baked bread. The rush candles add to the parlour's aroma with the smell of burning mutton fat.

''Tis a treat to eat with you maids,' he says smiling. 'You were busy making sparks with that blade.'

As he speaks there is the sound of footsteps descending the stairs and Martha comes into the parlour holding one of her small babies.

'She's my youngest. One summer and now heavy as a cask,' she says as she gently lowers her burden to the floor where it crawls about. She looks at the thatcher as she walks over to the hearth where she stirs the pottage with a wooden spoon then raises it to her lips. He watches her lips as she sips and tastes.

'Good for the king if he were here,' she says looking towards the table.

'I'd talk with him if he was,' says the thatcher.

'I'd ask him about tea and pots,' says Beth.

'I'd want no tax!' demands the thatcher banging his tankard.

He sees Martha is looking at him, their eyes meet. She sees him begin to wink but he changes his mind and smiles. Lizzie has told her of his discourteous wink and Martha had pondered her own fate. After they have each come to the steaming pot and ladled themselves generous portions into various types of bowls Martha serves herself and sits on a high-backed settle facing the fire. Amos tries to look at her face but she has not come close to a candle where features are discernible. She has moved about in the dim light from the embers. He feels a stranger at the table, feels obliged to explain himself in some way and he searches his memory for a possible subject, but he doesn't get far and stays with the warm presence of the family.

'The babes are something to be thankful for. They learn right enough and are soon on the harvest. If there is a harvest,' he says with a knowledgeable tone as he slices a large piece of turnip in his wooden bowl with his knife. He understands the meaning of the black cap.

'I'll put my head down by the wagon for the night. All the loads from the Pemsey marshes where I grew and harvested reed,' he says hoping to get Martha's attention, but there is no response from the widow sitting in the dim light of the fading embers. But a moment later she suddenly turns and looks at the thatcher whose face she can just see in the rush candle light.

'Mossy Reed from the marshes!' she exclaims loudly. He turns to look towards her but in the dim light he cannot see what he is looking for.

'That's my name. Some summers passed now since we were reed harvesting on marshes. You did as maids do and went off to marry a husband,' he says as he takes his stool to the hearth, places it at a modest distance from the widow and sits down. He looks towards her and at the eyes that he has waited to see.

'My family,' she says proudly nodding to the children at the table. 'There is another in the bedchamber and Seth my eldest boy is shepherding.'

'Great help today your two maids. The day's work has gone well,' he says as he looks over to the table where they sit. Beth is fitting a new reed candle while Livy cleans her bowl with a piece of bread and Jamie is scrawling chalk letters on the table.

'It was easy work,' says Livy as she puts the bread in her mouth, 'and good work if it keeps rain off our bed.'

'This is thatcher Reed,' says Martha. 'I worked with him when I lived by the marshes twenty summers ago,' then turning to the thatcher continues. 'I have a widows cap now, since the spirit of snow and ice took my husband. It was a killing whiteness that fell,' her features show her horror of that night. 'It was bad for the seasons. The following spring was late. The next snow won't be so bad if this thatch is sealed up. It was rain, snow and wind that came into this parlour.'

Having heard Martha talk about her husband Amos relates his own sad story glancing between the eyes and dwindling embers. He holds up a silver chain around his neck that carries his wife's wedding ring.

Lizzie appears from the kitchen, clears the table, lifts the clock weight and waters the dog bowl. She then disappears again into the kitchen. Martha looks across at Jamie who is still scribbling marks on the table.

'Come here, Jamie,' she says. 'Bring the chalk pebble,' Jamie arrives beside her and holds the chalk out to her.

'No, I don't want it, Jamie. I want you to show thatcher Reed the letters you know. Write your letters for me.'

Jamie sinks down cross legged on the floor. His small face goes into contortions, his small hand squeezes the chalk and he slowly writes his letters. A B C D E F G appear on the stone floor of the hearth.

The thatcher looks with fascination at the small boy and thinks of his own son.

'There are more.' says Martha looking into Jamie's small face.

'I know these,' he says pointing at the letters.

'You will soon be reading and writing. Then you can read to me,' prophesies Martha.

Amos looks on with some bewilderment at the small boy as he knows nothing of letters.

'What do you know of this thatcher?' Martha asks in a formal tone.

''Tis not for me. Some say 'tis sinful to know such. From bad spirits,' he replies.

'No sin. Everyone is learning. Out of this village all read papers and books of knowledge. You should learn,' advises Martha.

'Get the cards Jamie.'

The cards are collected from the table.

'Show thatcher the letter M.'

After some sorting and more facial contortions the small boy holds up the correct letter.

'And what sound does it make?'

'MMMMMMMmmmmmmm...,' he hums looking at Martha for any advice on his noise.

'Where do people get the learning?' asks the thatcher.

Martha is not sure how to reply. Her experience teaching men has sometimes been difficult. She feels thatcher may be difficult as he seems slightly unexpected.

'In Bourne there are people who will tell you everything about letters.'

'You taught Ena words and letters, Ma,' shouts Jamie.

'Yes. Yes. I did. She lives just in the next cottage.'

The rush candles splutter and begin to fade, the parlour gets dim. The girls and Jamie are soon heard overhead. Dust falls through the floorboards as they settle for the night. Talk continues around the fire until Amos says his goodnight and slips out to his wagon. Martha closes the shutters, slides the wooden bolt to the door and makes her way to bed. Lizzie has lost her frown. Her wrinkled face smiles as she remembers the wink from the thatcher as she rocks herself to sleep. Amos is on his wagon. His head rests on a pillow of hay and like many who labour on the downs his night time gaze is upwards towards the moon and stars. Black creatures silently flutter and dance in the air above him as they search for echoes in the darkness. He thinks of the letters Jamie has written on the stones and his eyes slowly close.

At first light he is again on his ladder. He labours through the morning, the girls pass him bundles of reed and leave him a platter of cheese and bread and fill his wooden tankard. At noon he uses the soil privy and looks at the marks on the back of the door. He moves his pair to fresh grass. The soft glow of an evening sun creeps silently over the downs. Their sculptural forms gradually emerging as the valleys slip into deep shadow and the soft rounded tops glow gold. Amos has completed his labouring at the Applegate cottage.

Grown, harvested, sun dried, bundled and laid; the reed forms a thick coat of nature protecting the cottagers from the vicissitudes of the weather. The inherited thatching skills of generations have enabled him to weatherproof the Applegate's home. His leather mittens are torn. His hands are sore and his arms ache. He sits at the table with the Applegates as rush candles are lit and the evening meal is laid out on the boards.

'We won't see snow in here anymore now the work is done. Will we Thatcher?' asks Lizzie as she stands at the table.

'No snow. No rain and no wind. That's why I learnt my trade,' he replies.

Livy, Beth and Jamie are again seated at the table opposite Amos as the Applegates eat their last evening meal with their thatcher guest.

'There are no bad spirits in my thatch. Isn't that so, Martha?' asks Amos. 'They are from the same spot where we harvested twenty summers ago.'

'Never known any,' replies Martha.

'My life is my bond,' he says as he looks across at Martha placing small cuts of cheese on waiting platters. He looks at her black bonnet.

'Your blaspheming tongue has left you?' questions Lizzie. But there is no reply.

Practical matters need attention and he feels into a pocket and withdraws a short hazel stick. He takes a knife from his belt and begins to incise a small notch into the tally stick.

'What's that for?' asks Jamie.

'This one is for the last....' he holds up an open hand to indicate five, 'bundles that went round the chimney,' he says as a tiny notch of wood pops out from the hazel stick and lands on the table.

'I am on numbers and I know some,' says the small boy proudly.

'She has taught us numbers and letters,' says Livy nodding towards Martha.

Amos had noticed letter cards on the cottage table when he first arrived and had thought about who was teaching who and as a slightly enlightened thatcher had speculated on his own abilities to read and write. Now he knew who it was, would she teach him? He knew she would think up a good excuse if she didn't want to see any more of him. There were many ways to turn him down. If he could learn, it would be good for his business. These thoughts are in his mind as he sits at the hearth on the last evening in the Applegate's cottage. He decides to ask Martha to teach him. He sits with his last tankard of ale, Martha sits in the high back settle, the girls are gossiping around the table and little Jamie is again playing with the chalk pebble. Livy gets up from the table and takes a pile of small papers from a shelf, places them on the table, holds one up and begins to proudly read a short poem.

'We have a Chapbook,' she says after the last line of the poem. She holds up a book which has been opened so many times that the binding is split and a few pages escape and fall onto the table. Beth takes up a page and they both read different tracks loudly, shouting each other down then dissolve into laughter.

'They are good with that book. They read it every day, so they know it off by heart. But there are many more words for them to learn,' says Martha. 'What about you thatcher Reed, have you learnt any words?'

Martha is pleased to renew their old acquaintance and feels some motivation to maintain their friendship. She waits for his reply then continues. 'Let me teach you to read letters, I have other books for you to learn from.'

Amos is startled; he did not expect the offer and Martha is surprised she made it.

'But I live way over on the other side of the marshy levels,' he replies as a matter of fact and with some regret. 'It's some walk. But I've heard it's dabbling with magic.'

'Magic it is not. Vicar Lod reads on Sabbath. The distance is the evil. I was forgetting, it was a while ago.' she says.

Amos regrets his practical reply and tries to recover the situation.

'I have Furlong a fine cob,' he says. 'But it's a good trot or more. She's not keen on gallops but she can.'

He searches her face for her reaction before she speaks.

'It's a long way,' she replies, leaving him adrift in a fragile boat. 'Yes a long ride,' she murmurs looking at the fire.

The thatcher thinks his fragile boat is about to sink.

'You have a cob?' asks Livy excitedly.

'Yes.'

'Your cob, is it an easy rider?' asks Martha looking up from the fire.

'Furlong. She's a fine cob. Good hocks, head calm and tranquil. Gets you where you want to go.'

'I would dearly love to have a horse,' yells Livy.

'I could visit family that live on the levels,' says Martha.

Amos can see land from his fragile boat.

'I will trade Furlong with you when you teach me,' he says with some enthusiasm. As he says this his thick hair escapes from behind his silver hoops.

Martha smiles at this idea and looks across at his long straight hair almost hiding his eyes, but says nothing.

'I will send the cob to you. Abe will be over at the levels on the morrow. I'll hitch Furlong to his wagon.'

'I don't know about a horse. I don't think so. Cold seasons coming. It will need stabling and hay,' Martha speculates.

They sit in silence; Martha tends the fire and looks into the flames.

'A horse, Ma! A horse! We can graze her at the bottom of the Warren. It's good grass, better than the levels and there's Nell's stable!' Beth squeals out.

'Can we ride her sometimes?' asks Livy.

'While I'm learning you can ride and feed her. But it depends on Martha.'

There is a patient silence in the parlour as a decision is awaited.

'When the teaching is over, what then?' Martha adds. 'Can we have her sometime?'

'What then?' murmurs the thatcher. 'After learning she will be back to the levels. I don't want to lose her.'

'She will go back to you thatcher but it will be sad,' says Beth.

'I will teach you over on the levels for the loan of Furlong,' says Martha. 'But I decide when you've learnt proper,' she says firmly.

159

Amos's fragile boat appears to have arrived safely at a sandy beach.

'So it's settled and done,' he says. 'It's a contract. Teaching to be at my cottage at an agreed time, for the use of my cob Furlong, till I know to read and numbers.'

'I decide when you do,' states Martha.

She knows it gives her a free hand to have the cob as long as she wants.

'Abe will bring Furlong. There are more ditches in the marshes now, so let her be your guide. It's settled!' says the thatcher with a satisfied smile behind his thick hair.

He parts it to behind his silver hoops and looks at Martha with the hope of some mutual affection with her in view of their childhood friendship. But she is looking into the fire.

'She's a good cob. Good manner, Roman nose and steady,' he says as he remembers something he always shows his customers, 'I'll get my fox,' he says and goes to his wagon and returns to the parlour. 'Best for the top,' he says, 'very top.'

He holds up a perfectly shaped fox with a bushy tail made from reeds of different thickness.

'It's almost real,' says Beth as she holds it.

The rush candles splutter, the parlour grows dim and the thatcher feels it is time to look at the stars. He leaves the Applegate's fireside to sleep by his wagon and before sunrise he is gone. The question of the name Applegate and the marsh girl of his youth has been settled. It was her.

Since the loss of his wife and child he has felt emotionally starved, empty and miserable. He has devoted his time to his trade and worked through the years. His sleepless nights have been spent working by rush candle light preparing bundles of spars. On moonlit nights he would venture onto the marshes with his tools and work at extending a ditch into his new piece of land. This was the life he would soon be returning to. But he felt his life may be changing and as he looked across to the Pemsey marshes from the high hamlet the day seemed clearer. He could see across the flat marshes to where his cottage stood in the distance, and onto the wooded ridge on the horizon, clearer than he had seen it for a long time.

Chapter Thirteen

The alphabet song

Next morning, true to his word the thatcher hitches the cob to Abe's wagon for her journey to the Applegate cottage. The wagon halts outside the cottage as dusk is falling.

'He'll be ditch digging on the morrow. Says be there for lesson sunrise day after,' calls the wagoner to Martha with the thatcher's short message.

Martha takes the halter and leads Furlong to the waste where there is good grass.

'He'll have to learn,' she mutters to herself. 'I'll not be there for sunrise.'

She examines the horse's low back and considers the prospect of bare back riding as she does not have the purse for a saddle. She rubs her hand over Furlong's back and feels the warmth of the animal's body.

'I will ride her on morrow to see how she is,' she says to herself as she considers her legs each side of the warm barrel.

The next day after her spinning she mounts Furlong, trots around the cottage, feels easy and relaxed and is pleased with the arrangement. The day for the first lesson has arrived. She waters Furlong and loads her teaching tools into a shoulder bag ready for the morning's ride. She has a loose gown, short boots and her widow's cap with a tight extra knot. A sea mist is wet on her lips. She unhitches Furlong's tethering rope, ties a leather rein and stands beside her. She strokes her cheek, gives a gently puff of air toward her nose and strokes her neck. She holds the hairy tufts on her mane, steps back, swings a leg, pulls herself up and she is on Furlong's back. She straightens the bag and she is ready for the ride. She gently pulls the heels of her boots together, flicks the rein, clicks her tongue twice and Furlong walks forward. They trot down Prentiss Street, pass Sea Houses and onto the Langney Road and head for the marshes. The air is still. The mist is thick and she soon feels Furlong's stride labour in the softer damp earth of the marshes.

The thatcher has lived the whole of his life in his cottage making it so familiar to him that he rarely notices it. This has made it invisible to him and it has been left to rest in peace through many summers. It has stood since before his father's time and has become blended into the landscape. The only indication that a craftsman lives here is a thatched hazel hurdle proudly displaying a reed fox that trots across it. The cottage foundations have succumbed to the rise and fall of ground water and have withdrawn their support to the old crucks above. One of which has tumbled outwards allowing part of the thatch to be at ground level. An eaves window is now at marsh level partly buried in the earth. This window now forms a grand entrance for any flying or walking marsh wildlife that needs shelter. The sodden fallen thatch is covered in tall thick grasses and marshland plants that grow freely as it decomposes. The remaining walls and chimney drift slightly from the vertical and appear to wander aimlessly about but their curves follow the need for space for activities within the cottage; straight lines are not a requirement of this hand-made structure. Their great thickness of earth, lime and straw packed between old timbers, now generations old, is still wind proof, rain proof and presents a comfortable snug space around a winter fire.

The Lamb Inn at Wartling is the nearest inn to the thatcher's cottage. He would get his meals and meet his friends in the small smoke-filled rooms that reverberate to laughter and song at the first opportunity. Loud cheery laughter had shaken the walls for several minutes when he mentioned that he was learning letters and numbers. It was considered one step away from sorcery and an ungodly pursuit. But later quiet enquiries were made and serious talk flowed between the tankards. He considered cottages as simply places to satisfy only the basics requirements of human existence. The cottage status quo at that time was that there was no place for decoration to ease idle moments. Visual pleasures were nature's creations of the world. The sight of a wild meadow before haymaking or sunsets painting the earth shades of crimson. But in his mind, he was hoping that the tutor on the way to his cottage would become a close friend, a sweetheart or possibly a practical wife who would share the work of reed harvesting. He remembers his previous family life when his wife disregarded the cottage status quo and filled all the ledges, shelves and mantelpiece with meadow sweet to scent the cottage when a visitor was expected. On returning to his cottage on the previous day, he had loaded his wagon with meadow sweet and had laid the white flowers on the surfaces as she had done. On this morning although the air is warm a small fire has been lit. He sits on a log in the quiet morning watching the path that leads to the main track through the marshes.

He hears Furlong before he sees her as the cob knows she is home and her snorty neigh reaches his ears from a distance. He watches Furlong lead Martha between the maze of drainage channels and then to her stabling where she waits and Martha slides to the ground.

'Noblest ride this side of heaven?' he asks.

'I'll be the judge of that. Thatcher Reed.' she says as she tries to assess the tutor pupil relationship running her eye over the remains of the cottage and the thatcher.

'The good cob has brought me here in a good spirit for a worthy cause. The lesson I hope will go the same way, thatcher,' she says in a slightly vigorous manner. 'I teach at a table.'

'So be it,' he says. 'Table's in the parlour.'

'A table and two stools are part of good teaching,' she says. 'And I teach better on the grass here,' she says pointing down to the grass beneath her feet.

'Let me get the table,' he says looking at her with a surprised expression.

'Yes. Get the table.'

The table is awkward and heavy and it is not without difficulty that Amos arranges the teaching furniture on the grass.

'Sit there,' she points.

When they are both seated across the table she lays her bag on the table between them.

'The bag of magic spirits,' he mutters.

'You will learn,' she says as she looks and rummages in the bag and brings forth a handful of alphabet letters and numbers painted on small pieces of wood.

'We'll start with these,' she selects the alphabet and sets it in two rows across the table facing the thatcher.

'Look at them and repeat after me.'

She taps the first square, sings out the letter and waits for his response. As she waits she looks over the marshland with its sheep and cattle on the firm ground and reed beds edging stretches of clear water. It's not as she remembers. She looks at his cottage with a mystified expression as a waterfowl creeps through the fallen eaves window to a nest.

'This cottage hasn't taken much of your time,' she says as she smiles at the accommodating ruin.

'She has just walked into my larder. She is happy with her home. Perhaps there will be others,' he says raising his voice and eyebrows.

'Perhaps there will not be,' she says firmly.

He tries to see her eyes but they flash away to the marshes.

'It's not as I remember it,' she says shielding her eyes and looking at the sun on the water and the many colourful shining dragon flies. 'Not so much water now.'

'Channels have been dug to take it away. The space between those is my land and it will soon be good for sheep,' he proudly announces.

'It's not magic. Say after me,' Martha resumes calling out the letter 'A' and this time there is a reply. Amos follows Martha's lead and for the first time he hears the twenty-six sounds,

'There are so many! If God reads, he's made too many,' he says after the first round.

'If you want to read and write these are what you need,' she says trying to allay his dismay.

He looks at Furlong, the bargaining chip. He looks at the row of letters and realises he won't have the cob for some time. He looks at his tutor's brown smiling eyes and wonders if he has made the right decision.

'Now like this,' she says encouragingly after seeing subdued panic on his face. She sings through the alphabet pointing at each letter in turn. The thatcher, a reasonably prudent man, starts singing this strange magic song quietly along with her, and as it slips into his memory he gains in confidence and sings it with a loud jovial voice. The duet drifts across the marshes on the still morning air and after several trips through the alphabet Martha raises her hand.

'Now say the sound as I point,' She randomly points to letters. He sings to the letter then voices the sound.

The tutoring continues as waterfowl enter and leave via the eaves window. The thatcher feels he is mastering the alphabet, he sings and laughs. She knows there will be more lessons when questions can be tactfully posed, if tact is required as her first thoughts of the thatcher were that here is a strange uncouth man. But as the lesson progressed she thought her first judgement had been too harsh and hasty and he is perhaps just a strange man. She has set her mind on a surprise visit to the cottage of a sister and as the sun passes noon decides to bring the lesson to a close.

'One more pass through the letters,' she says with some finality. He looks up at her.

'One more pass!' he exclaims looking into her eyes.

One more pass,' she repeats. 'Then I am to my sister's cottage.'

She looks at him.

'I wish to be tutored for the day, Martha,' their unblinking eyes meet. 'For the day as God's in his heaven!' he exclaims raising his voice.

She sees his eyes widen. She feels his anger. She has born a family. She smiles at his eyes.

'There will be more tutoring. Remember what you have sung out today. There is more to be tutored. You will not learn with anger,' she says as her emotions flicker but she speaks firmly as she begins to collect the letters into her bag.

He is not used to being ordered what to do by anyone. He knows he is strong. He grabs her wrist.

'There will be more tutoring. Now I visit my sister,' she says managing to smile as she looks at his rough hand on her wrist. He releases her hand.

'But I want to learn, Martha. I want to learn,' he pleads with her.

'Remember all twenty-six. Seven days today I will be back,' she reassures him as she continues picking the remaining letters off the table and placing them in her bag.

He silently watches her and does not hear her deep sigh of relief as she mounts the waiting cob. He watches her retrace the path between the new ditches until she trots out of sight towards her sister's cottage. He feels dismal and works until dusk cutting spars. He eats a simple meal, snuffs out the rush candle and lies on his mattress in the darkness considering his day. Tutored by a widow with a family. A small boy for a new son, a daughter, a wife, a new family. He fondly remembers the family he lost and pictures himself recreating a family life with

Martha. Her words come back to him, 'Remember all twenty-six.' arrives in his consciousness and he laughs. He laughs again. Then in the darkness sings out the alphabet song, louder and louder. His powerful voice disturbs the marsh wildlife that inhabit part of his tumbled cottage and they join his loud jovial singing as the strange alphabet song drifts across the dark marshes.

Chapter Fourteen

My blood is in this sack

Seth is tending his flock and Martha busies herself with the routines of life. Each morning as she ties her black widow's cap the memory of the killing spirit of winter comes into her mind and she remembers Lizzie's wise words. Her husband had not been the only person to lose his life during the snow of winter. The weight of snow had proved too much for one cottage where the roof had collapsed killing the occupant who died in the freezing darkness. It was the cottage of Constable Hemmings.

The administration of Collstocks Manor has undergone continual adjustment since earlier medieval times. Geography, climate, tradition and the people themselves have all played a part in the development of their particular customary manorial system. Changes were made to enhance the common good within the spirit of the original ruling and the duties of manorial officers and their titles have also changed over time.

'Gentleman farmer coming up the track,' says Lizzie one summer morning with surprise as she peers through a shutter and sees Spendwell approaching.

'What's he doing here?'

He has seen Lizzie watching him and he waits on the door stone till the door is opened.

'Martha Applegate,' he says directly to Lizzie as she opens the door.

'Martha.' shouts Lizzie. She does not take kindly to Spendwell, her face carries a frown. Spendwell stands and looks around at the small garden.

'Bailiff Spendwell. What brings you to this cottage?' asks Martha.

The important medieval Bailiff's duties are now carried out by others but the villagers use it as a sign of their belief in Spendwell's upward aspirations to secure some goodwill. He is only a gentleman farmer.

'Business of the mansion needs to be done. Your garden would be better if the onions were under ashes in winter,' he says still looking at the small patch of soil. 'Yes, the mansion,' he continues. 'You may know that Constable Hemmings is not with us this year after the bad weather. The parish have put a man forward to keep him off their roll call. He will be at the Court seven days from now and you are one of the jurors as proposed. You will be there?' he questions in the affirmative looking at her, as she submissively nods her acceptance of the task. 'So seven days noon.' he says as he turns to go.

On the morning of the seventh day a heavy rainfall had soaked the green downs. Shepherds had smiled as they watched their dew ponds filling with the fresh water. By noon the sky is blue with a hot sun bringing a mist from the drying surface of

The Street. A hunt had gathered earlier in the morning outside the mansion and this was followed by a team of eight oxen that were being led to ploughing on the furlongs. The soft chalky mud and puddles had then been further stirred and augmented by a further selection of passing beasts. As Martha makes her way to the mansion her patten shoes lift her feet just above the level of the fetid mud. The court is held in the hall of the mansion, a substantial space with polished marble floor, wainscoting to the walls with hangings above. Large oak chairs line the walls for the use of the jury. A wide staircase at the back of the hall leads to an upper storey corridor. The old original medieval courtroom has been converted by the gentleman farmer into a library for his personal use. But it still waits for its first book. When Martha reaches the mansion the large entrance doors are open, she is ushered into the hall and takes a seat along with six other seated jurors. At some point a signal is made, a footman places a candelabra on a table and the large doors are slammed shut and bolted. The footman leaves through a door below the staircase. Loud voices are heard from behind this door which eventually opens and two tidy men with tailored clothes and wigs appear, stroll through the door and stand in the middle of the hall.

'It grieves me to think of our Constable Hemmings suffering the horrors of those winter days and nights. We all regret his passing,' the man slightly lowers his head, the seven jurors follow his example. 'God rest his soul,' he requests to the Almighty.

He is a large portly man with a large powdered bob wig that almost surrounds a rouged face with tight curls. A dusting of powder lies fresh on the shoulders of his bright blue coat. The second man's wig is smaller, not straight and tufts of hair have escaped. There is no powder on his coat. He is a thin boned man with pale cheeks, but is taller.

'The Steward has words for us,' says the bigger wig as he nods towards the tall thin man.

'We have a fellow who seeks to be our Constable,' says the Steward looking towards the door below the staircase.

'A fine fellow,' interrupts the bigger wig.

'His work is finished at old Bourne Place where he has been waged,' says the Steward.

As he speaks a man with a sack over his shoulder noisily enters and stands by the door.

'Will Cheer,' the tall thin man reads. 'You are here to be examined as to your Godliness, honesty, duty and allegiance to the customs and laws of this manor. To arrest vagabonds, night walkers and others, to preserve the peace for king and country. Do you understand what I say?'

Will Cheer's chest rises, fills, rests and then slowly throws vibrations into the air.

'Aye, Aye. English men are in my nation and the speaking of it is known,' is returned in a deep rich resonant bell like voice that rings round the hall.

The jurors look at him with added interest after the entertainment of their ears.

'To ensure the assizes of ale and assizes of bread are forthcoming and have the required purity and strength,' continues the tall thin man.

'Tell him to enter. Tell him to enter.' orders the bigger wigged man impatiently.

The tall thin man holds a piece of paper, his hand is shaking, he looks at the paper then at the man with the sack.

'Will Cheer enter this hall,' he says as he points to the centre of the hall floor. 'Step forward to speak to the jury.'

There is silence as the two wigged men settle themselves in their chairs and Will Cheer carries his sack towards the centre of the hall as the juror's eyes follow him. As he reaches the prescribed spot, he lets the sack fall to the floor with a loud metallic crash. He is not a tall man or a short man. His main distinguishing feature is the prominence and generosity of his chest which pushes itself forward in a worn leather waistcoat. Over this is a coat that opens as it descends with buttons at an ever-increasing distance from their respective holes. Breeches, stockings and short leather boots descend to the marble floor. He smiles at the jurors with a face that speaks of worldly wisdom and shows a crooked tooth. He has eaten little over the past few days. He is fatigued, miserable and hungry.

'We are told your name is Will Cheer. Is that so?' asks a juror leaning forward to observe him.

Will Cheer's chest fills, rests and then slowly throws more vibrations into the air.

'Aye. That is so. If it not be so there's no God-fearing man in this place, look you. I'm no villain to be to be pricked with your questions,' is returned in the deep resonant bell like voice.

Martha has some questions for him, the most important of which may involve her. She sees him looking at her.

'Will Cheer,' she begins, 'The Constable before you could neither read nor write. There would be gain in your work if you have the wit to do both. Would the gain be your wish?' she asks.

'Have heard of such things. If I am Constable will look to both. My life has many wishes and I will tell you all if the world will wait,' he replies.

'You are away from your nation and may wish to return there before your term as Constable ends. We will need you to swear an oath on the terms of four full seasons,' advises a juror.

Will Cheer looks at the marble floor and his sack.

'All men of my nation honour and discharge any spoken oaths. An oath is my bond. We are not knaves and coxcombs,' he sings out in his resonant voice as he looks along the line of jurors.

'Your voice,' says the bigger wig. 'Do all the men in your nation have such a voice.'

'My voice sire, is my voice. The men of my nation have their own voices. We have what God gave us.'

A juror who sits upright holding a small book looks at Will Cheer and asks,

'You have dwelt here sometime working at the old Place. Some Sabbaths in that time. To have the Godliness that is asked for you must be in the church on the Sabbath. I am dutiful and attend on the Sabbath but where are you? My eyes have never seen you in the holy place.'

'On the Sabbath I am forever in the church of the God. I have my place. I am one of the earliest to the church and I never leave till all my prayers have been said and that is when the church has been emptied and I am alone in the holy place. That is why I am never seen,' he says in a convincing voice that rings around the hall.

The jurors look at each other; some shake their heads, some nod.

175

'We have seen you in the village here, but we do not know you. We need to know the course of your life. Of whose blood are you?' asks another.

Will Cheer points at the rough sack on the floor.

'My blood is in this sack, God rest their souls. It's my blood! My blood!' he shouts as he lifts the sack and lets it drop again on the marble floor.

A profound clattering noise emanates from inside the sack. His blood has a voice. The voice screams and shouts as the sack hits the floor. Screams and fearful cries fill the old hall. Screeches of pain, the clash of sword on sword. Musket balls tearing through flesh and bone. Blood and death as men and horses die screaming side by side in fields of blood. The cries and screams of widowed women. The sack crumples down on its contents and the hall is silent. The man's face under the bigger wig is disturbed.

'But what does your sack carry?' he asks. 'What is its meaning?'

The bottom seam of the sack is grabbed by Will Cheer and he jerks it upward. The days and years of generations, rusty and now meaningless in themselves tumble out of the sack and noisily clatter about the marble floor. The hall becomes silent again as the objects come to rest.

'But what things are these?' the bigger wigged man asks again fearing he is being played with.

The candidate with a certain solemnity steps between the objects then moves two slightly with the tip of his leather boot.

'Naseby. Great grandfather. Bless his soul,' he sighs.

One object is a broken and bent royalist sword with inscriptions under a rusting blade the other a short length of a pike shaft. His boot moves a rusty spherical object with flaps and bars. 'Then the commander gave them these iron pots to wear over their cropped locks,' he looks at the faces of the jurors but no questions are asked. He points a finger at a group of small lead musket balls. 'A gallant man I've been told but these things took his life away,' his voice rises and he shouts, 'That's the blood of my nation. My blood!' The old hall is silent. 'My grandfather and a son then meet the new King's army at the War Castle,' his foot points to a rusty bayonet. 'But musket balls give them death from the King.'

There is another silence as the man waits and calms himself.

'But some peace comes to my nation and thus it is that with my father I worked with the stucco on big houses, palaces and churches and with foreigners at the old Place.'

A door creaks open, a footman looks into the hall then retreats.

'And what is your contribution to the many objects that lie on this floor,' asks the Steward.

'My contribution, sire. Is this, sire,' he moves a group of objects together with the tips of his boots.

They are metal and wood trowels of various sizes, sculptors' callipers and strips of metal all stamped with a sign.

'But my labour there 'tis finished now. Marble dust and burnt chalk shaped the smooth bodies, columns, and scrolls, to the walls and ceilings of the old Place. 'Twas my task to repair some old and shape some new,' says Will Cheer looking at the objects on the floor with compassion.

'I am told you are honest and true,' the man with the big wig discloses as he stares at the objects on the floor. 'But the devil can find proverbs for his cause, but what I am told weighs more than proverbs. Is there any more to hear?' he asks.

'My boy, Wilkin. Apprentice he is in my care, will be by my side to keep the peace of this place. If 'tis to be,' is answered.

'Your boy Wilkin and where is he?'

'He is without,' replies Will Cheer nodding to the under stairs door.

'Get him in here, Steward. I want to see him too,' says the bigger wig as he sits back in his chair.

'Call your boy,' directs the Steward.

From Will Cheer's lips comes a tuneful rippling stream of unknown words and sounds that again entertains the jurors' ears. The door below the stairs opens, a youth enters and stands by his father.

'You both will soon be known in the village here,' says the larger wig.

'He is quick and sharp,' explains the father.

The bigger wig stands, adjusts his coat, nods to his Steward, and leaves the hall. The Steward stands and speaks.

'On this coast there is avoidance of excise from the seafarers who ply illicit trade. There is piracy for you and the Riding Officer to defeat with Dragoons to help. The owling and shipwrecking that has been going on along this coast must be stopped. We need to keep the peace in this small hamlet. That is what the people here, law abiding people, church going people, all wish to see,' the jurors nod their agreement.

'You can leave now for the jury to consider all they have seen and heard.'

'Keep you well,' sings the candidate as he gathers the objects of his blood into his sack, lifts it over his shoulder and leaves through the under stairs door with his son close behind.

'He's not our man for a Constable. He's a rogue with a quick tongue and a sack full of rusty useless things for his story. A rogue I call him. Who else is there to be our Constable?' voices one juror.

'There are none! None want it. They receive nothing, and live by other means that come their way by good fortune. Thatch over their head is all they are given. We need a Constable more than not needing such,' the Steward replies dismally as he considers the simple administration he can delegate to the man.

The footman reappears, attends to flickering flames in the candelabra and stands by the door. The jurors gather in quiet whispering groups. After laughter, argument, nodding and shaking of heads a verdict is reached. The Steward smiles with relief, the footman slides the bolts and the mansion doors are thrown open and daylight fills the old hall.

As Martha makes her way back along The Street the successful candidate appears from the servant's door of the mansion. He is not alone but with his son who now carries the sack. Martha and Will Cheer are unaware of each other and they both head for their destinations. Martha looks at the ground to avoid the mud and Constable Cheer looks at the ground while thinking of his future. These thoughts resolved themselves into the fact that Martha steps slowly along, choosing her footsteps carefully while Constable Cheer, keen to begin his work hurries along with great haste with his son. The projection of their paths is a collision but the young apprentice is vigilant and Martha hears a loud shout in a tuneful language.

Will Cheer sees the back of Martha's muddy pattens and looks up but his velocity is such that he cannot stop himself and he pushes himself against Martha's gown. Fortunately both remain upright but there is much embarrassment as Martha turns to see what has hit her and looks at the close face of Will Cheer that is turning a light crimson.

'May God preserve me!' he exclaims. 'What have I done. Please accept my most utmost apology for my beast of a behaviour,' he feels sorrow to its full extent for treating a widow to this embarrassing humiliation.

Martha feels a flush of heat, her cheeks are a warm pink. She is annoyed.

'That's no way to preserve the peace! Your first task as a Constable to go about molesting widows. Are all fools constables?' she says loudly glaring at her assailant.

'No fools are Constables my good lady nor Constables fools. We are to preserve the peace and I think rightly that the peace between us is preserved. I do but hope for it,' he tries to smile. Martha looks at the crooked tooth.

'What do you mean by doing such a thing?' she asks, ignorant of the circumstances.

'Am I guilty of all. I was hurrying across this street looking at God's earth and not knowing where I was going. My son here warned me just in time. Am I guilty for looking at God's earth?' he explains in his resonant voice.

'Where you look is no matter to me,' says Martha looking at the ground endeavouring to proceed across a large puddle.

'My boy here Wilkin saved the day,' he says nodding to his son. 'Although the circumstances are dismal the meeting has some fortune for a Constable who also has fresh lost a spouse. We are similar travellers.'

'The world has many travellers, and some will travel alone and therefore.... Good day to you, Constable!'

Martha looks away and tries to concentrate on the immediate task before her but her mind is unsettled. She steps forward, a patten slips and her body sways. Will Cheer stretches out and takes holds of her wavering hand. She feels the rough hand as she steadies herself and feels hooked in an emotional trap.

'And so we meet again dear widow under more pleasant and friendly terms. It seems we cannot part. There is some good fortune for the Constable to be holding the hand of someone who has known the same sadness. We can share our histories together. Let not this chance encounter lead to nothing but back to lonely lives and dark nights.'

Martha is not listening to the words flowing out of the Constables lips. Her total endeavour is to be released from the rough hand that still clutches hers.

'A chance encounter that does not happen perhaps by chance. But are fortune's forces at work,' continues the Constable.

Martha looks about the street for a solution and then she sees the answer. The innkeeper's two daughters are emerging into The Street leading a heavy horse.

'Blossom,' she calls loudly. 'Blossom, where is your Ma? I wish to speak with her.'

Will Cheer's intimate conversation is brought to a sudden end. Martha's hand is released and she raises it to attract the attention of Nell's daughters.

'Keep you well. I'll leave you to your business with the maids. But we will meet again I'm sure as heaven is for the good,' he says as his eager face becomes crestfallen and he trudges off through the fetid mud with his son.

'Nell is yeasting the ale, Martha,' Blossom calls back. 'Martha's here and wants to talk,' the young girl yells back at the top of her voice towards the open door of the inn.

Martha makes her way safely to the hard surface outside the inn.

'He's our new Constable,' she tells Nell as she points to the receding figures. 'Jury settled on him this morning. Measures and ale tasting so you'll have him in your parlour before long. He's lost a wife and is looking for another with his tongue. An innkeeper would make him a good wife.'

'Not this innkeeper. But a man gave me those. The best present I have,' she nods towards her two daughters, 'and that's enough. But what did you want to talk about, Martha?'

'It was nothing, Nell. He was holding my hand as I almost slipped in the mud and he wouldn't let go. He kept talking of things and I wasn't listening and didn't know what to do till I saw Barley and Blossom.'

'Hey Ho! Dear Martha. He was holding your hand and wouldn't let go,' laughs Nell. 'He's on your tail to be his wife. He won't want to meddle with an innkeeper when there are better things,' laughs Nell as she watches her daughters progress along the street. 'And he wouldn't let go. It's a desperate man that's coming to the village. We'll have to find him a wife. A Constable who has a cold miserable bed will load his misery onto us and treat us all like felons.'

'I don't want him!' says Martha abruptly. 'Marry him! You've got worms in your head Nell to think of such things. He needs a maid who'll cook and patch for him.'

'I'll find him a maid and get him married,' says Nell confidently. 'Tell no one Martha. If the vicar hears he'll send him a God fearing soul who'll lock him up in religion.'

'Aye, that's true. He has a smooth tongue for being in the church when he isn't so a churchly maid will blemish him.'

Martha has recovered herself. She leaves Nell to return to her yeasting and plots her way carefully back to her cottage. In the dark of night, she relives her meeting with the Constable and tries to choose a maid from Meads hamlet to be his bride but without success.

'I'll leave it up to Nell to be Cupid,' she whispers to herself as her eyelids gently close.

It is only a few days later when Constable Cheer arrives at the Ship Inn to carry out his first duties with regard to ale excise. Barrels are tapped with a small hammer, measured with callipers and searched with gauging rods for secret compartments and to ascertain volumes. This technical and manual work is performed by Wilkin and an assistant while Constable Cheer stands and watches.

'Good day to you, Gentlemen,' says Nell as she finds them amongst the barrels in her yard. 'You are always welcome at this inn to search and tally for your ale and victuals,' she says generously as she knows she will not ask for something for her purse. 'When your work today is done sit in the parlour for meat.'

'They are words that comfort my soul, innkeeper. To eat well is what we were made for. I will visit the parlour,' says the Constable beaming with anticipation.

Nell talks with Full and instructs him to set mutton by the fire and stoke the fire under the fresh pies while she busies herself in the kitchen. She looks in at the parlour sometime later and sees the Constable sitting alone at a table.

'Constable Cheer. I am pleased to see you in my parlour. Your belly must be sad after such work. What do you call for this day to put victuals where they belong,' she asks as Full turns the spit at the fire.

'I feel your welcome outshines others. To have a good inn is what we are for as I say. I have been told your name is Nell Broad and keep this inn with your two daughters and a man and am told much brewing comes from your efforts.' The Constable's resonant voice rings loudly round the parlour. Full looks up at the speaker. Nell pleasantly listens.

'And good brewing it is,' she replies.

'Good innkeeper. The taste of ale, its quality and its worth are the reason I am here. I have been chosen by the cottagers to judge the ale and your opinion of the ale, is appreciated for what it is, but it may be that I may not agree. You are the brewer. But fear not I'm no villain,' he elucidates in a friendly manner.

'Your judgement is of great importance to this inn. None complain of bad ale any season of the year,' says Nell as she sits opposite him at the table and they talk of victuals and inns until Nell begins her strategy.

'All men are hungry. I know that from my work. Especially lonely men, widowers and such.'

'But I am a widower and lonely it is,' says the Constable with surprise.

'All widowers need attention. You need a woman to cook for your needs. Mutton is ready,' she says looking at the fire. 'Mutton and kidney pies with raspberry sauce are hot and ready. They are as they are cooked in London,' she says proudly.

Pie and ale are consumed and the Constable compliments Nell almost to excess. He is invited to return in a few days when fresh pies will be ready. Nell delivers her ale to the imposing white building old Bourne Place where she is always invited into the kitchen. Although the cook never discusses her recipes with outsiders, Daisy, one of the kitchen pastry maids, does not keep secrets well and Nell gently turns their conversation to recipes when cook is out of the kitchen. This is where she has obtained the recipe for her London kidney pies.

The Constable arrives on the appointed pie day. The parlour shutters are closed. It looks dim and Nell coaxes him to a dim and gloomy corner table and his hot pie is delivered. Nell has arranged to meet Daisy at the inn for one of their gossips and they sit together in another dim corner of the parlour and talk of recipes. Nell has occasional furtive looks at the Constable and as he finishes his pie and wipes his lips, she stands and opens the nearest shutter to Daisy's table. Bright sunlight streams into the dull parlour and falls on Daisy; whose bright eyes and fair curls make best use of the golden light. She then excuses herself from Daisy and sits at the Constable's table.

'I trust the victuals have satisfied your hunger,' she says. 'A widower man needs a cook or he will be weak in his duties.'

'It is good to have an inn with such food. We are in Hemmings' derelict cottage, living as best we can, but there is no fire to cook until it is repaired. Bread, ale, cold salt meat and fish is our fare, and that's no meal,' the Constable replies to Nell with concern on his face.

'But as she is here it is for me to tell you that the maid you see in front of you is the maid that gave me the recipe. She can cook the pie even better than the one you have just eaten,' she explains.

'The maid there?' he asks looking over Nell's shoulder towards Daisy.

'That is so. She is the pastry maid from old Bourne Place. A maid who knows the best methods for cooking,' says Nell as the Constable peers over her shoulder to look at the maid, squinting his eyes in fascination, 'A maid that may interest a Constable?'

He looks from his dim corner table to the maid whose fair curls are lit by a shining beam of bright sunlight. He sees her bright eyes and smooth cheek. His mind wanders as he looks at the saintly vision.

'Will she be here next pie day?' he asks with enthusiasm.

Chapter Fifteen

The secret

The invisible threads of emotion grow like colourful gossamer between the physical boundaries of beings. Their generation and manipulation are beyond the conscious control of the host as they tie kith and kin with bonds of little substance but latent potency. The colours of these gossamer threads stretch from shades of loving to shades of rejection to shades of nothingness. People live their lives in a web of these varying and silent invisible threads weaving hidden colourful abstractions that would be astonishing to witness. The threads encircle their host, catch them and defy them to escape or hold them in comfort within a secure wall. A mother's love for her children is a deep strong loving colour, but there are many shades and Martha looks anxious.

There is a secret that only she knows and the time has arrived to share it. She knows that gossamer threads may break and their colours change or fade, but the warm golden rays of a setting sun fills the downs and cottage gardens with a comforting magical presence. The evening air is still and full of the late scents of the many herbs. Plump sparrows are gathering on the thatch after a busy day while moths search for night nectar in wild honeysuckle. Livy sits alone in the garden tying a ribbon into small circles and putting them round her fingers. The memory of the struggle with Fisher at haymaking and his strange oaths had not faded. She had asked Martha for their meaning several times and Martha's reluctance to talk about it had made her feel that she was being devious. Herb beds line the narrow path that leads from the cottage door to the orchard. As Martha walks along this path for her talk with Livy she takes a sprig of lavender in her hand for its calming medicinal qualities. She closes her eyes, raises the scent to her nose and slowly breathes the air. When she reaches Livy she divides the small bouquet and hands her a share.

'Come with me,' she whispers.

The girl looks up and follows Martha onto the downs through the orchard to the fallen tree.

'I will tell you now,' Martha says quietly as they sit on the old tree trunk. She feels pain herself at the thought of what she will say.

'I have often wondered what it meant. I was so frightened of him,' says Livy, not in her usual tuneful manner. 'He had a knife at Seth and said he wanted me.'

'Barnabas and I had agreed never to tell anyone except you, if you ever asked the question. I am the only person now and I have kept my word. The secret will always be safe with me,' she says sincerely.

'Many summers ago,' starts Martha. 'One night when I was full with child. Beth was in me. A stranger came in the night and banged on the cottage door. I took a candle to the door and when I opened it a woman was standing there. In the candlelight I could see a young woman crying and sobbing. I asked her to come into the cottage but she said she would not. ''I know you. Please help me,'' she cried out, ''He will kill it if you don't help me,'' Martha pauses, her throat is dry and her eyes are moist with approaching tears.

Livy has pulled bark from the trunk and is watching the revealed insects scurrying for shelter. Martha is surprised that Livy now appears to have little interest in what she is about to say.

'So I'll continue. It's important,' Martha adds looking sadly at the girl.

'The young woman at the door then asked for my help ''Please help me,'' she begged, ''I have been hiding in a hayrick, he has found me. He doesn't want it and told me to leave it out for creatures of the night,'' The woman then brought out a bundle from under her cape and handed it to me, ''Look after it as your own,'' she cried and then turned and ran back into the dark night. Before I closed the door I heard a man's voice shouting after her.' Martha's tears were filling her eyes.

'Martha, are you alright?' Livy asks surprised at Martha's tears.

'We took the bundle. It was a bundle wrapped in a sheet. We opened it and there, looking up at us was a tiny newborn baby.' Martha's tears were falling on her lap.

'A baby, Ma! A baby!' shouts Livy in excitement, 'Where is it now. What has happened to it?'

As Martha sits on the log her tears fall like drops of warm rain that soak into her clothes.

Livy is now eager to listen.

'It was the summer when Beth was born,' Martha continues through her sobs.

'But what about the baby. Was it a boy or a girl?' asks Livy still puzzled at Martha's tears.

'It was a beautiful girl. A beautiful baby girl. I must tell you Livy do not cry like me,' there is a short silence then she says through her tears, 'The little baby girl .....was....' she says as she turns and hugs the young girl beside her, who could not understand Martha's silence.

'What was she, Martha?'

Martha finds it easier to answer the question.

'The little baby girl was you.'

'Was me?' laughs Livy. 'Who was it really, Ma?'

'It really was you.' Martha says quietly.

'Me! What do you mean, Martha?' asks Livy with an innocent smile.

There is silence as both try to realise what has been said. Gossamer threads are trembling.

'The little baby was you, Livy. We loved you. We took you in and brought you up as one of the family. I had my baby Beth born the next day. We told everybody that you and Beth were born together. It was the natural thing to do. If we told what had happened you may have been taken from us and we didn't want that.'

There is another period of silence. Livy's face is perfectly still, her eyes look at nothing around her. Her eyes look in at her thoughts as pathways break, reassemble and send new messages.

'Oh no! No! That's not true!' her voice trembles out.

There is more silence. Martha feels relief that her burden of a secret has been told, but she now feels the loss. She has nurtured Livy from a baby as her daughter, believing to herself it was true, but now the reality has been spoken and she is not her daughter any more. A gossamer bond was getting fragile.

'Oh, it's not true, Martha, is it? It can't be.' her mind told her it was not true, it couldn't be. 'It can't be true, I can't believe it.'

'It is true child. It hurts me to say it but these things happened on that dark night,' whispers Martha through her tears.

But something whispers in Livy's thoughts that it might be true and she trembles.

'You are my family, Livy. Nothing will change. We love you just the same,' Martha says reassuringly. 'We have no secrets. I am pleased now that you know. I didn't like to deceive you.'

'Perhaps we will keep it a secret between us, and nothing else will happen. Oh, but why are you telling me this now? We can keep it a secret can't we, Ma?' asks Livy.

'I will never, never tell. But there is more to tell my child and it is cruel. The man, Fisher who grabbed you is...,' Martha's throat is dry. She finds it difficult to say. She doesn't want to say it, she waits....

'He is your father,' she whispers.

They sit silently on the log. Tears run down Martha's cheeks. Livy feels numb and looks vacantly out at the dusk of evening. This revelation is worse than the first. She shakes and throws her arms around Martha then suddenly pulls away.

'But you are not my mother and the man is my father,' she chokes out in panic. 'It can't be, Martha. It can't. What can be done,' she screeches out in fear and disbelief.

'He is a poor man. Poor in soul. I believe he came for you to live with him and care for him. But we are your family. You will never live with him, I promise you, Livy.'

Martha has told the secret. She is relieved. Her warm tears flow like a river. She fears for the young girl who once was her daughter.

'Your name will always be Livy Applegate,' she says.

The sun's light is no longer on the cottages of this small hamlet. The shadow from the high Warren Hill behind them has moved past them, moving slowly eastwards it quietly envelopes the rural buildings in the dark of night. The sun's light still touches the underside of the placid drifting clouds high above them, turning them into golden masses of vapour. The air now takes on a strange coolness as the warmth now radiates from the bare earth to the infinity of space. It was the close of day. Looking down at her cottage Martha could see that the other children had returned home. She stands and calms herself. She wanted to disclose all the facts of the secret adoption to Livy without the family being aware of it, and it is nearly achieved.

'There is more to tell and I will answer your questions tomorrow. Come when I am at the wheel,' she tells Livy.

As they are returning to their cottage a fox trots across their path and disappears into the wooded steep side of the Warren as their minds fill with sickening thoughts. Livy tries to sleep as she lies on her bed, but the knowledge that Fisher is her father frightens her, keeps her awake and she cries silently while her bed companion asks unanswered questions.

The following afternoon Livy sits placing teased out locks of wool on her carding paddle, slowly rasping the teeth of the paddles to align the fibres and rolling them to form rolages which she places in a rush basket. Martha has come and sat by the wheel. She has set Beth and Jamie to work in the garden, Lizzie sleeps in her chair in the store and they are alone. But she does not spin. She looks out the window to where Fisher often stood and continues the telling.

'There's more I must tell you,' says Martha. They watch as an empty hay wagon descends the track and passes their window. 'It is something you may be pleased to hear.'

'If he is my father do I have to go and live with him?' asks Livy in a faltering voice wanting answers to the fears that have kept her awake.

'Never!' exclaims Martha. 'Barnabas, bless his soul, is more your father than him. Nobody knows Fisher is your first father, except Cathy the lady you met at Brightstone that time. But she will say nothing about it.'

'But why does she know, Martha?'

'She wanted you to live. She was the lady at the door on that dark night. She is your mother.'

Martha's gossamer threads tremble again as she mentions the word mother. Her head tells her she has lost a daughter but her heart tells her that love will always be there.

'When you and Beth were born Vicar Lod visited. He even used my ink with his scratchy quill to enter your names in his book. Baptised too you are. So the world has you as my daughter, only heaven knows different. When I was with Cathy she told me how she had lived below the cliffs with Fisher. How she had to hide she was with child and when she knew it was time she ran and hid in a hayrick. You were born the night

193

she woke us, and we took you in,' Martha pauses, takes wool from the basket, carefully drafts a fibre away, links it to her spun wool thread and the wheel turns with a woody hum.

'Cathy told me about him, 'she continues. 'They lived down on the beach, happily at first, he fished with his brothers, but there was a bad loss at sea. He was found clinging to his upturned boat. He would not go back to the sea, they had no money, the parish would not help, he was violent and wretched.'

Livy has stopped carding the wool and listens intently to Martha as the last secret is told.

That night Martha's mind is sad but calm. Her gossamer mother daughter threads had trembled and changed colour but not broken. Livy had felt loneliness and fear until she was told that Cathy is her mother who she felt would shelter her if she ever got lost in the world. Life at the cottage continues as before and the shock of the revelations diminish day by day in Livy's young mind. She decides to tell her bed companion of her talk with Martha and the revelations of the dark night long ago and they lie side by side in the darkness.

'You are not mother's baby!' squeals Beth as she looks at Livy in amazement.

'I am not Martha's baby. But I know my real mother,' Livy whispers to Beth's close face, 'I could search for her.'

'What does it mean?' asks Beth.

'It may mean nothing. Everything will be the same. Martha will never tell others.'

'But what about Fisher? He might come again, grab you, takes you away and treat you cruel,' asks Beth.

'No. No, he's hurt bad. If he did Seth would save me.'

There is silence as the girls think. Martha turns in her bed. Night hawks screech.

'Oh no.' whispers Livy. 'I've just realised he's not my brother anymore,' the powerful silence returns.

'Seth's not your brother.' says Beth in amazement.

'No. He's not my brother,' repeats Livy in disbelief.

'He will still look at you. I'm sure there's love in his heart for you,' whispers Beth in the darkness. 'He's not your brother,' she repeats with wide open eyes. 'He's not your brother but you can marry him now. He will be a man, a proper man husband.'

'We could be proper married,' says Livy excitedly.

'Will I ever be married?' Beth whispers sadly.

'You have much time to go before you're seven and twenty. You will have someone if it's not Charles.'

'Yes. Yes. Let it be so,' squeals Beth.

The girls cannot control their whispers and it wakes Martha who whispers across the darkness.

'You will always be a daughter to me Livy, always an Applegate. Now rest your heads and sleep.'

'We will. We will,' replies Livy.

The girls wait for Martha's sleeping breath.

'He's not your brother. You don't have to tell him. I won't tell him. You have lost a brother but gained a man,' whispers Beth.

'I don't have to tell. I can tell him when I choose. It's my secret,' Livy whispers almost to herself.

'When you tell him his love may change,' Beth advises in a whisper,

'He will be a real lover for me. I'm sure he will. But I am sad Beth, very sad, scared and lost. I feel familiar things are strange,' Livy says softly.

'You must not fret. You will always be my dear sister. Always together,' Says Beth as she lays close to Livy and holds her hand.

'I will never tell the other maids of the village,' whispers Livy as small tears fill her eyes.

Beth catches a tear and presses her body against the girl who is still a sister in her heart. High above them the friendless lonely grey orb watches and slowly drifts silently over the hamlet as the entwined girls fall into their dreams.

Chapter Sixteen

The stair

The white chalk of the downs has many enemies who disturb its quiet slumber; the rain that falls is one of them. It knows its path well. Rushing off the curving slopes it gathers in the valleys where it seeps down through old crevices and channels deepening and widening them until the fissures split wide and the cliff face trembles. One night a close full moon was accompanied by continual rain and a howling wind that built the sea into a monster. It charged over the beaches damaged the shacks of the Fisher people and spent its remaining energy devouring the base of the white chalk cliff. Much had fallen.

After a day and night of rescue a tired man from the Fisher village negotiates his way between fallen rocks as he makes his way along the Hollywell track beneath the cliff. He passes below Beacon Furlong and climbs the track to the top of the cliff and with wide strides makes his way to the Ship Inn.

He is a tall man who has little time for the unnecessary or trivial. He wears the fisherman's garb of black tarred clothes but sets himself apart with a tall wide brimmed hat that rises almost to a point. The only relief to this dark figure is a large white neckerchief and a leather bangle around a wrist. The parlour of the inn is noisy with laughter and talk as he enters. He sits by the door looking earnestly at all in the room. As people become aware of his presence the laughter stops and there is silence as he needs no introduction. All in the parlour know him and know he is not here to try the ale. He is Strapper, the leader of the Hollywell Fisher people.

He begins talking slowly as he makes his speech.

'The storm has shaken the mighty chalk,' he says as he looks around the room. 'Fisher Nathan has lived at Hollywell with us for many summers with wife and seven children and often, as you know, delivered good herring to many of you in all weathers. On the night of the storm, that God sent, delivering to the hamlet here,' he pauses and looks at the attentive faces. 'He was caught in the cliff fall and is badly sick. A surgeon has been called. Nathan is in much pain, his body is bent, and we fear for him. His wife Leah sobs and Hollywell will provide for her if the parish does not. We hope you will provide for her also if she needs victuals. He has been carried to his place at Hollywell where he lies with Leah tending him.'

He pauses again. The room is silent.

'His pain has been caused by a fall of the chalk that has taken the stair away. The stair that you and I have used many times and Fisher Nathan was on the stair at the time of its fall. Much has fallen to the beach below and needs clearing and the stair needs to be worked on. I am here to tell you that we need many to assist in the cutting of the chalk to fit new stair timbers. There will be a cart in The Street sunrise to take some the long way down to the beach and some will meet at sunrise at the top where the old stair descended,' he pauses and looks at Nell who has come into the parlour.

'Much of our harvest comes to this inn as the innkeeper will tell you. We need the stair rebuilt so we can trade as before, I trust you will understand. It is good for both of us to barter our harvest of the sea for your tables. I have spoken to the house and they agree that the work is of serious need. If you work for them, they understand. Bring any tools you have and we can put this evil thing to right,' he stands and addressing all in the parlour concludes.

'On the morrow. That is all. On the morrow,' he says and leaves the room.

'There will be ale on the wagon,' shouts Nell as the noise in the parlour begins again. 'Those stairs get many victuals to this inn.'

'God save the man. I've served him ale many a time and his poor wife,' says Barley with anguish in her voice.

'A tankard was all he downed when I served him and he left herring for coin,' replies Blossom.

'The cats will like him if you don't,' quips Barley.

'Over there. See to them,' orders Nell to her two daughters as she points to a busy table. 'Pin on wagon at sunup and a couple of the wooden tankards,' she says to Full. 'A surgeon will help him pass away, and a vicar will save his soul for better or worse. He has brought oysters and herring for us here,' she says to the drinkers around her, 'many victuals come to this inn as Strapper says. There's much to be done here on morrow. No need for you to go cutting chalk for stair,' she says looking at Full. 'Brewing to be done,' she concludes asserting her priorities.

It was not long after Strapper's visit to the inn that Jamie Applegate was instructed to hurry up to Seth at his cover and inform him of the storm damage to the stair. Seth finds himself at sunrise carrying a mattock and spade walking down a narrow path between strip farms to joins a group of silent men peering over a sharp new cliff edge where the stair once descended. Strapper arrives with a wagon and more men.

'Sling it over, anchor it well,' he shouts to a man carrying a rope ladder. 'Cut yourselves a ledge to work on then following the markers cut your slots for the timbers.'

Farm labourers, shepherds and fishermen now work with a brilliant white medium that yields easily to their tools. Spatial thinking is an easy challenge for these practical persevering people who are still discovering the alphabet and numbers. Seth climbs down the ladder and reaches a spot where a wide ledge of fresh white chalk gives a space where he can stand and work. With ropes, plumb lines, pegs and shouted directions from above and below the markers soon show the outline for the new stair. They select their tools and the group activity commences as the old seabed of calcite shells and flints now yields to this collective group.

An early sea mist has drifted away revealing a brilliant sun sitting in an azure blue sky. The freshly cut chalk is brilliant white and below are ripples of silver from a sea that follows a gentle wind. Seth enjoys the opportunity to engage every muscle of his body. He looks out from his white space at the magnificence of the view and his heart is light and happy. It is generally agreed that this activity, working from sunrise to sunset, will take two days and Martha has arranged for Seth's victuals to be delivered at noon. White chalk dust floats in the air as he cuts deep slots for the timbers and after the sun has climbed higher he hears Strapper's commanding voice.

'Seth Applegate, victuals being lowered.'

He grabs a wicker basket that has appeared above his head. Pushes loose chalk with his boot to set a place for his table and places the contents of the basket on the white floor. He lays out a corked flagon of ale, thick slices of bread, cubes of slipcote cheese, a wheaten biscuit and a pickled onion. He slakes his dry throat and eats gazing out from his shimmering white space to the enormity of the sea stretching out before him. He listens to the rhythm of the waves breaking on the beach below. He rests then labours again in the white chalk till dusk tells him the day is ending. He does not return to his cover on the downs but returns to his cottage, falls on his bed, basks in the feeling of his stretched aching body and is lost in deep sleep. His mind rests and no fantasies trouble him as the grey moon drifts again over the hamlet and the night passes.

The eastern light silently appears and as if a waking alarm it lifts him out of his sleep. He sits up rubbing his eyes. Chalk dust still lingers on his hair and shoulders as he silently dresses and slips out of the cottage to his last day of labouring on the giant white cliff face. He descends the ladder, inspects the timbers he has fixed, picks up his mattock and continues his labouring. He expects to hear a voice telling him that his midday victuals are being lowered but the voice doesn't come. He waits and is surprised to see the rope ladder shaking and drifting from side to side as if a person is descending. He looks up and sees a small foot carefully searching for the next rung of the ladder, then another small foot, then an apron, a white shift and then a face looks at him through the rungs of the ladder.

'Seth. Seth. A surprise for you,' a voice sings through the ladder.

He hears the voice that delights and arouses him and sees Livy struggling with a basket. He stretches out, takes it from her and she hops delicately onto the floor of the shining white space.

'I've come to see your labours,' she says as she lands. 'and to see you dusted in chalk like a ghost.'

He lays the mattock aside, raises his arms and clenches his muscles for display.

'No ghost can do this work,' he says quietly to the girl who has descended into his white realm.

'I am eating with you, so use your manliness to clear a space for a table,' she says looking round at the lumps of chalk strewn over the ground. Seth clears a space, they sit on the white floor. The wicker basket is opened and Livy arranges the contents neatly on the floor beside them.

'I don't like that ladder,' she says. 'The steps are too far apart and it swings. It's evil.'

Seth does not reply as he has no feelings or opinions on ladders. They sit in silence.

He looks out at the sparkling sea while she looks at him with fascination. The age old white dust has drifted like thin snow to lie on the top of his curling hair, on his ponytail and small peaks on the top of his ears. It's on his eyelashes, on his nose and his bare shoulders. Rivulets of his body moisture form channels down his dust covered chest. Below his breeches, stockings and short leather boots are equally dusted. She ponders the secret Martha has recently told her.

'Seth,' she says suddenly, then changes her mind. 'Pass me ale, the sun's hot. Oh! You're so chalky!' she exclaims.

'I can hear the shouts but no-one can see me here,' he says peering over the ledge.

'No-body can see us,' she says correcting him as she brushes her hand across his shoulders to clear the white dust. 'Are you pleased I've come?'

'Yes, I'm pleased. I'm always pleased to see you. You know that,' he says looking at her.

'Why do you like me?' she asks inquisitively.

Seth searches his mind. His river of emotions is not deep. He casts his hook but catches little and replies,

'I wish I knew. A spirit may be at work.'

There is silence as they select from cheese, bread, meat, pickles and fruit.

'You like the cheese and ale I've brought.'

'But I can eat and drink those.'

'But you can't eat me,' she replies. 'Would you like me if you could eat me?'

'If you had been pickled like this onion, I might eat you.'

'That's evil talk, Seth,' she says slightly hurt at the thought of being pickled. 'What if I was a fresh apple?'

'I would love you in a pie,' he laughs.

'It's important, Seth. Don't laugh.'

'If you were an apple in a pie I would eat you and ask for more.'

Livy tries to think of herself as an apple in a pie but she cannot manage it and she laughs with him.

They laugh and smile, drop into silence and continue their meal until their appetites are satisfied and the table cleared. They look out over the blue sea and sky from their glistening white space. The sun shines on freshly cut pieces of white chalk that glow like solidified light. They peep down at the beach below where the blue waves rise, arch and fall through the air turning translucent then crash onto the golden sand. Glistening white foam races with eagerness up the sand until it slowly rolls back and disappears into the next wave. The pulsing rhythm of the crashing water, the noise of washed sand and rolling pebbles. The beauty of nature holds them until Livy asks.

'Do you remember the rain? When we threw off our clothes and rolled in the grass?' she asks.

'I have never forgotten it. Sometimes I think of it and think of you.'

'That was when it was so hot,' she says looking into Seth's eyes. 'You would be cool if you threw off your clothes,' she raises her hand again and brushes the white dust off his hair. It forms a small cloud that drifts off in the air.

'I need to be cutting the steps,' he says dismally but reasons with himself and says energetically. 'Without clothes no-one can see me here, I can work without clothes.'

They sit in silence each considering the proposal.

'What about you?' he eventually says looking at Livy.

'I might. But I might not. I haven't labouring to do.'

There is another silence. Seth stand, slips out of his boots and begins to untie his belt.

'Do you care for me, Seth?' she asks.

'I care for you. You are my sister and all brothers love their sisters. You know that. Mine will be off before yours.'

He struggles out of his clothes longing for the coolness of the air that drifts in from the sea. His clothes drop on the chalk floor and he stands gazing out at the sea.

'I can work like this, cool and free,' he says, picking up his mattock.

Livy looks at his body, brushes chalk off his chest and kisses his lips

'It'll be like in the rain,' she says untying the bow of her cap. She lifts the cap off then lifts her clothes over her head. 'We're free as the wind, Seth. Free as the wind.'

Seth looks at her white body and the memory of their rolling in the damp grass together floods into his mind. The restless nights, dreams and sweats. He feels hot. He feels he needs to hold the person that has charmed him.

'Why are you looking at me like that?' she asks. 'It doesn't matter,' she says when no reply is heard. As she speaks, he steps in front of her. She feels his hands around her waist. She throws her arms around his neck.

'You're white chalk, Seth,' she says laughing as she feels the rough chalk dust pressing against her.

'I know why you were looking at me like that, because I've looked at you like that,' she whispers in his ear as they tightly press their bodies together.

'I've wanted to hold you like this since that day,' he whispers.

'Oh, Seth. There are things I must tell you. But I love you Seth and that's all that matters.'

'We can live together. You can be my wife,' he says eagerly.

Touching and caressing they explore the valleys and peaks of their bodies. Kissing, squealing and laughing they pound themselves together until they are exhausted; their bodies bruised and white with chalk.

'It may not be right. I am your sister. But what if I wasn't your sister. Would you still love me?' Livy asks in a quiet serious voice.

'That can't be. We've been together since small babes, playing, running, skipping and now we're grown. Why do you think of such things?' he asks.

But Livy does not reply. She silently runs her hand along Seth's arm and feels the sweat and chalk that sticks to it. Then suddenly realises that she too is covered in the white dust.

'We are both white angels made of chalk,' she says smiling and laughing.

They sit in silence in their glistening space until a loud voice breaks their dream.

'Applegate. Get on with your labour,' Strapper's voice booms down to them.

'It's time for me to go. The white dust of loving,' says Livy as she tries to rub the chalk off her arms and struggle into her clothes. She collects the remains of their victuals and loads them in her basket. Seth steadies the ladder as he watches her tiny feet swing about to find the rungs.

Seth labours through the rest of the day till dusk then makes his way homeward. At the well he tips water over his dry dusty body. He lies on his bed, his body is weary but his mind tirelessly rambles through his dreams and fancies of the day. He knows of families that have flourished from love bonded siblings where the church has neither married them nor censured them.

'This room will be where my son will grow up. Where he will sleep and I will be here with Livy when away from my flock. Perhaps that what she meant when she said she had so much to tell me,'

He sees the grey moon watching him as it silently crosses the heavens on its cold journey as thoughts of a miracle, fatherhood and a son fill his mind. 'My boy will watch you one day,' he murmurs as his eyes close and he sleeps.

Chapter Seventeen

Oyster girl

There is news at the Ship Inn that the London lady and her son had been seen arriving at the Mansion House. It was only a few days after their arrival that Full from the inn is seen in the Applegate's small garden looking with interest at the medicinal herbs.

'Nell has sweats that ail her. Looking for the leaves of the groundsel she is,' he says as he sees Beth approaching.

'It's on the bank there. Plenty for taking,' says Beth pointing across the Warren track. 'Are her sweats bad?'

'Ague of sweats she has,' he replies as he puts a hand in a deep pocket of his breeches. 'Told to take this to you,' he says as he draws a small piece of paper from the pocket. 'Not to be known about. Maid from the house gave it to Nell.'

He hands Beth the paper. It is a small folded anonymous piece of paper. A rough piece of sealing wax holds the fold.

'For me!' exclaims Beth in surprise.

'Yes. No marking but told it was for thee,' says Full. Beth begins to slip a finger under the seal but changes her mind and hurries to where Livy is collecting lavender.

'Look!' she exclaims. 'It must be from Charles.' she says holding the note excitedly for Livy to see. 'We can read it together,' she says as her finger slips below the seal and the small note is opened.

The girls look at flowing writing.

'You read it to me,' says Beth.

'I will try,' says Livy.

After carefully looking at the markings and juggling words in her mind she begins to read.

'It says, "I must right a wrong. Come to South Dean track Saint Giles Day. Will get you into mansion for the tea I promised," that's all there is.'

'My young man from London. Oh Livy I'm so happy he hasn't forgotten me,' says Beth smiling as she takes the note and studies the words.

The excitement stays with her as she lies on her bed in the darkness. Something bright like cool rain on a long hot dry summer's day or the sight of the first white blossoms of spring. Something fresh and shining has jumped into her routine of slow cottage life.

She is the oyster girl for the cottage and always collects on Saint Giles Day. On the morning of the day she leaves the cottage early, turns into The Street and heads for South Dean Lane. It is a fresh dry morning with a gentle breeze that pushes wisps of thin cloud. She passes the house and turns into the lane where a row of laden Pippins mark the house boundary. A breeze rustles their green leaves as she finds an area of grass where the morning dew has dried and sits beside her oyster basket studying the Mansion House. It sits contentedly in the morning sun with its baked clay, stone, timber and iron skilfully assembled. She imagines the rooms, passages and staircases behind its brick walls. Dazzling sunlight reflects from the windows where she imagines Charles' room to be. She waits. The sunlight drifts away no longer on the windows. She waits till the sun is high. She contemplates going to the beach for the oysters and coming to the house when she returns, but she hears a voice calling. An earthy gardener is beckoning to her from a small back entrance to the house. After she has hurried over to him he ushers her inside where she finds a narrow steep servants' staircase. The gardener nods his head towards the staircase and places an earthy finger over his lips. She slides her feet out of her wooden pattens and begins to climb the stair as silently as she can. She is soon at a door and can hear voices.

'You are not good. You must work harder,' she hears. 'On the morrow I'll expect better. Till the morrow.'

She looks at the door and sees the keyhole. She goes down on one knee and peeps through. She sees Jollyboy looking in her direction. She sees a man pick up his hat as Jollyboy sniffs the air. The dog comes over and scratches the door, the man looks over to the dog, looks away then walks out of sight. She hears a door close. Jollyboy barks and Charles' face appears as he looks round from his chair.

'He stayed longer than expected. He's my tutor,' he explains as Beth comes into the room.

'Michelle is out with the horses,' says Charles. 'But Mirken is here somewhere. But we can take tea as I promised.'

Beth looks around the long narrow room that she remembers, and enjoys again the cherry wood smoke.

'Let us sit by the window,' he says as he closes a book on the table.

They sit in the high backed carved walnut chairs. She runs the sole of her thin leather shoe over the stretcher of her chair and feels the shape of the carved wood.

'Can you ride and walk now?' she asks.

'My leg is good and fit now. It was a bad day but by winter I was riding. Jollyboy is fit too,' he says watching the dog chew the corner of a decorative oriental rug of colours that captivate Beth's eyes. 'Michelle said we were to leave quickly for some reason of a meeting she had in London so I had to go. No tea then but there will be tea today.' he says.

'My father froze in the snow!' exclaims Beth. 'Snow spirit froze him solid.'

'The shepherd that brought the wheatears?' he asks.

'That was him,' she replies. 'I should be collecting oysters this day. It's the season.'

'Tea first and then off for the oysters,' says Charles as he stands and opens a rusty window frame and peers down into the garden below. 'Hortus,' he calls down quietly. 'Get Binty to bring the tea.'

The window squeaks as he closes it.

'Glass is so clear,' whispers Beth to herself as she studies the valuable material.

'He's the gardener of the old lord, he knows all about the soil. He dug up the lawn for turnips. Nearly got whipped.'

'Seth, my brother, has father's flock at Crapham Down.' says Beth.

They talk until their attention is drawn to an opening door. An elderly house maid enters, crosses the room and carefully places the contents of her tray on the table. Two small handleless cups with bowl saucers, a pot with spout and handle, sugar bowl with large lumps of sugar chipped from a block in the kitchen with their accompanying tongs and a slops bowl; all these items with matching decoration on thin white porcelain. The stranger amongst this delicate assembly is a terra cotta pitcher, the replacement for the milk jug which had disintegrated on the kitchen floor in a previous year.

'Twill balance the humours and remove ailments so I's be' told,' whispers the housemaid as she drops dented pewter spoons into the cups that ring like small bells.

Her appearance speaks of the garden and the kitchen at the same time.

'Do you have hot tea every day to balance the humours?' Beth asks as he looks into the milk jug and noses its contents.

'My drink is ale. It's always in the kitchen. When in London I go to the Fleet coffee house with Mirken. He goes every day to read the Courant and use a pipe. They live together but he is not my father. My father had land of five hundred odd acres with a stone quarry, woodland, some small farms. We went shooting. Are the leaves well soaked, Binty?'

'They are well soaked and ready, sir,' she replies

'Large lumps,' exclaims Beth eyeing the sugar bowl. 'We are getting a kettle and teapot and will be balancing our humours whenever we wish. Ma will get the leaves.'

She watches Charles intently as he pours the brown liquid into the cups. The housemaid remarks that she has turnips and pastry to attend to and makes her way back to the kitchen.

'I'll sweeten it,' says Charles as he uses the sugar nippers to drop a small lump of sugar into Beth's cup. She watches as his hand squeeze the nippers and a small piece of sugar drops into her cup.

'Stir it round,' he says demonstrating as his cup chimes.

Beth had often considered young men as she watched them toiling in the fields, eating, drinking and set in a different way to the girls. With her brothers it was family business but today it isn't. To her disbelief she is with a young man drinking tea. The first Applegate to drink tea. She had told Martha nothing of this rendezvous. She feels independent and in charge of her life.

'Where do the doors lead?' she asks after looking round the room.

'That one is where I dress and that one's where I sleep,' he replies as he indicates the doors. 'Oooh! It's hot,' he winces as he sips the tea.

He then picks up the bowl saucer and tips the hot tea into it. Beth copies this cooling method and they sit in silence for a short while as they sip tea from the saucers.

'What about the oysters?' Beth asks when the sipping has ceased. 'I need to go to the sea. But I don't think we can go together,' she says looking at him.

'Oh, the oysters. I don't think I can come with you. I didn't know about going for oysters.'

All Charles' young life he has been with people who have tailors. Men who pay for other people's skills. How can they go oystering together and he looks at Beth more carefully as she sits silently watching a bee bouncing against the glass.

'I could wear my best gown. My Sabbath gown has some ribbon,' she says.

'I get coats and breeches. All my clothes are to fashion, but I don't always wear them. My new coat is in there. It's the newest,' he says cheerily as he put his empty bowl on the table and opens the door to his dressing room.

In a minute he returns clad in his new clothes. A tightly fitting coat of glistening indigo with wide gold embroidered edges and lapels. A waistcoat buttoned to the waist, high pockets and decorated cuffs. 'Oh,... there's more!,' he exclaims and returns with a black three cornered hat with gold trim to complete the top view and flat heeled soft black leather shoes with bright buckles to complete the lower view.

'Ooooh.' comes from Beth's surprised face as the colours hit her eyes. Jollyboy has inspecting Beth's oyster basket, jumped inside and curled himself round. He sits watching as he rests his chin on the side of the basket.

'He can come for the oysters with me. He is dressed as a dog with no fine clothes, just his natural fleece as he came into the world,' she says as she looks at the dog.

'No you cannot take Jollyboy. If he goes I go. You must know he is always with me,' says Charles

Beth inspects his new coat, feels the fabric and pushes a small finger through an unused button hole. Jollyboy has left the basket and is now chewing the corner of an oriental rug and tries to throw it into the air. She laughs and points to the playful dog. Charles sees the dog and they laugh together.

'We can laugh together even if we can't collect oysters together,' says Beth when the laughter has stopped. After inspecting his coat, she glances into the dressing room and shouts, 'Look....Look at all that. Look, so many!'

The dressing room is a mass of fabrics and colours. The open doors of a wardrobe show shelves piled with folded shirts, neckerchiefs, breeches and stockings. Brightly coloured coats and waistcoats hang from the walls, with polished boots aligned below. On the floor a crumpled pile of shirts, breeches and under shirts. A shelf running the length of the room has a row of black felt tri-cornered hats, some with wigs sitting sedately on head shaped stands. Leather shoes with various heels and buckles are laid out neatly along one wall. Earlier generations of this old mansion had travelled to Europe and the Orient returning with objects that were now scattered throughout its rooms. One of these objects now stands in this dressing room. A graceful aged Venetian mirror stands close to a high window. Its glass has been etched with flowing foliage and buds that curve alongside a richly carved dark wooden frame. It returns a view transformed by the impurities in its old secret glass that have coalesced over time. Now in its forgotten retirement it gives colour back to the viewer by mixing light with the earth colours reminiscent of the works of a great master. Golds, ochres, sepias, umbers and vermilions are now added to its reflected light. Her eyes look at the colours as she delicately enters the room.

'A glass. A glass. It's as tall as me,' she shouts as she stands in front of it and her spirits rise. The light from her gown, apron, neckerchief and cap have been adjusted by the old glass which now returns a myriad of faint colours. Charles in his new coat comes into the room and stands beside her.

'What do you see?' he asks.

'My clothes have colours.'

'Yes. But what else do you see?'

'I don't know.'

He takes off his hat, puts it under his arm and says again.

'What do you see now?'

Beth shakes her head, 'If only I had some fine clothes,' she says.

'Take off your cap,' he says.

She slides out the wooden pin and her long dark hair curls down her back.

'There you have some high fashion,' he says as he drops his three-cornered hat on her head. 'We are both the same height.'

They gaze into the mirror.

'If I was dressed with....' her voice suddenly stops and she looks at Charles' smiling face in the mirror. 'We are the same height. What does that mean. No, No. I can't do that!'

'Of course we can. Yes.....Yes. If you can fit into these clothes we can go oystering together. No one will know.'

'But is it blasphemy? Is it evil?' asks Beth. Jollyboy has come into the room and is sniffing the soles of neatly set out pairs of shiny black boots.

'I'm not going to ask the vicar,' answers Charles as he looks at the thick curls of dark hair that fall from beneath the black velvet hat. 'Help yourself to anything in here. Some are stored in the camphor wood chest. We can get them out if you need more,' he offers.

She walks slowly about the room, filling her arms with a selection of clothes then drops them on the floor in front of the mirror.

'Oh what a dream this is,' she takes off the three-cornered hat and shakes her hair. 'I am modest and need to be alone.'

'Yes, I'll leave you to your dressing. Come, Jollyboy,' he says returning to the main room.

The dressing proves more difficult than expected. Undressing to her shift she selects the breeches and pulls them up her legs but they meet the bottom of her shift at her knees.

She decided to pull them to her waist under her shift. She realises her impossible situation and lifts the shift over her head. On reaching for a stocking the breeches begin to descend from her waist to her ankles and as she reaches she loses her balance and collapses on the floor. She is a bold but modest maid and refuses to let the young man in the next room know of her plight. She manages to stand and attempts to repeat the procedure. But the breeches will not stay round her waist. She waddles to the door and opens it a crack and calls in an imploring voice.

'Oh Charles, these breeches. How do I get them to stay up? Oh, but you can't come in!'

'There are strings at the back, pull them and tie them tight, if you can,' he replies from his chair at the table where he sits looking at the bee that has now stopped bumping against the glass and is walking along the rusty frame.

After much effort the dressing is complete, the door opens and Beth stands in her new suit of clothes holding a three-cornered hat, a wide smile, and a small white wig with her own hair still hanging down in curls. Her close-fitting coat and stockings are a light blue the waistcoat dark blue. The coat has plain edgings and flares out at the waist. Low heeled black shoes with small buckles sit awkwardly on her small feet. 'Oh, look,' she says adjusting her muslin hanging cravat, 'What do I look like?'

Charles's mind was dealing with the view of the girl before him and he could not get a sound of any sort past his lips. Was he going courting? Of course not. She's not a maid.

'What do I look like?' she repeats as she looks at his startled face.

His mind eventually resolves this new relationship and he finds his voice.

'You look like a new person but where has my maid gone?' he says with excitement.

'It's still your maid in these clothes?' she says looking down at her shiny buckles. 'Who am I going to be if I'm seen?'

'I'll say you're my friend from London. We'll have to avoid Mirken.'

She twists up her hair, pins it and slips on the three-cornered hat.

Charles stands up and carefully adjusts the hat saying, 'Front corner always above the nose. Are you comfortable in these?'

'They are a little loose and heavier than my cottage clothes,' she says, thrusting her thumbs into the waistcoat pockets. 'The stockings are a bit baggy. Oh, what's this,' she says as her fingers find a small object in one of the pockets. 'Here's something, look.'

She brings out a small circular silver snuff box and lifts it close to her eyes as she studies an engraving on the lid. Portraits of a female and a male character surrounded by playful cherubs in a secret flowering garden.

'Oh....how I like to look at it.'

'I had forgotten about that,' he says.

Beth places it on the table and Charles picks it up.

'It might still have some,' he says as he shakes it by his ear and hears the powdered dry leaf quietly rustle in the box.

'Yes, there is some in it.'

Beth has heard of snuff and being inquisitive she comes and stands next to Charles as his fingers tighten on the lid and gently attempt to open it.

'No. It won't open,' he says after a short pause.

'Try once more for me.'

He gives a twist one way then a gentle twist the other and then a more forceful pull. The small silver article divides in two and flies into the air. The old dry snuff is free and airborne. It rises in a thick cloud around their heads as the silver lid and base land noisily on the wooden floor. Their terrified nasal passages explode as the old powder does its work. They screw up their faces, close crying eyes, sneeze, sneeze and stagger about.

'Oh, my nose!' cries Charles when he thinks he has recovered. But immediately bends forward and sneezes again and waves his hands to attempt to disperse the snuff laden air. Jollyboy has immediately bolted to the furthest corner of the room and watches them with his head leaning to the right and then the left as they bend themselves to sneeze and then recover. A door opens silently. Binty has returned.

'Oh you poor souls!' she exclaims, as she watches them jerk about the room. She looks at Beth with compassion and says. 'You young masters don't need snuff. The old lord used it. Said it was for his gout. It smells like his old stuff,' she says as she sniffs the air. 'Doesn't worry me.'

'We found....a....a....,' was all Charles could say before he sneezes again.

After Binty has loaded her tray and left the room their sneezing changes to laughter and eventually the laughter changes to silence. Charles changes from his formal set of clothes into his day-to-day wear and begins to search the room for the lid of the snuff box.

'Oh. The oysters. We must go or they'll be under the water. We need to go when the sea is away,' she says.

Charles leads the way down the main stairs, and into the hall where Beth remembers she heard the mystical music. They pass two fashionable house people who give Charles a 'Good day.' and he introduces Beth as his friend from London. They leave the hall by a small side door and are in the wide courtyard that opens onto The Street. He pushes open the creaking wrought iron gate and they turn along the main street towards the white chalk cliffs. Pass Gore Way on the left and reach the open stretch of ground between the ploughed furrows of strip farms. They pass close to a plough boy who is half way along his furrow steering a heavy plough pulled by a slow ox. The boy attempts to encourage the ox to move along the furrow with the aid of his ox goad but the ox has stopped to stare at Jollyboy who has started barking fiercely at the stationary beast.

'It's only an ox, Jollyboy,' says Charles as he picks up the dog and carries him in his arms until they reach a path that leads to the top of the staircase where he is returned to the ground.

'So these are the Fisher people,' he says as he gazes at the village below trapped between the enormity of the sea and the steep white cliff. He sees black clad figures hurrying about or sitting absorbed in their work attending to sails, ropes, nets, spars and ensnaring lobster pots. Their small boats hauled above high-water mark receiving their care from busy hammers caulking with tarred hemp. Away out in the shimmering distance are the triangular russet-coloured sails of their fishing luggers, drifting about hopefully in a calm sea.

Huddled along the base of the cliff are their fragile dwellings. Curling smoke drifts up from brick chimneys where the harvest of herring is cured. They see black figures here with white aprons and caps busying themselves around tables, where sharp knives slice along spines and bones and guts are tossed away. Others hang washing or nurse babies as children play around them. The hard-won harvest of the sea sustains this isolated village which is disregarded by the parish.

'Those are the stairs,' says Beth pointing to the timber staircase that descends the cliff face to the village below.

'Down there!' shouts Charles, with anguish as he looks down at the perilous timber stair wedged into the chalk.

'They're narrow. Not wide enough for two. My brother has laboured on them,' she says as she lands on the first step. She feels slightly uncomfortable as she has much to do. Her hat feels as if it is going to slip off, she has to crunch her toes together to keep her shoes on her feet and she carries the wicker basket on her arm. She hobbles down to the first landing.

'Let me take the basket. It will make it much easier for you,' he says gallantly as he stands on the step above the landing.

'Oh, that will be so good. You have rescued me twice now. Once with the clothes to borrow so we can go oystering and now on my way to the beach,' she says as she passes the basket to the young man and feels mildly pleasant at these rescues. He takes the basket and tries to carry it with outstretched arm and then with his arm straight down and then over his arm with the handle at his elbow but he cannot do it without great discomfort and fear of losing his balance.

'I've never carried a basket before,' he admits.

'You poor thing,' Beth sympathises. 'Let me have it back. I think I can manage a little better than you can.'

But Charles resists and they proceed down to the next flight but half way down she feels unsafe.

'Oh, Charles. I'm wobbling. My hat's slipping off,' she says as she attempts to hold one of its corners.

'Give me your hand,' he says.

Beth raises her hand behind her over her shoulder where Charles' hand swiftly grabs it. This simple solution of hand holding as Charles follows Beth one step behind leads to substantial bonding and a form of entertainment for both parties. The steps will only allow passing at the landings and they wait at various times to let people pass who skilfully glide past with baskets of herring, mackerel and other sea foods. It isn't until they reach the foot of the staircase that she realises her heart is in a flutter. Her hand is in his. What will he do? Will he keep holding it? I'm dressed as a man.

'Which way?' he asks still holding it.

'I'm steady now,' she says with a touch of disappointment. 'We go past the pool,' she says nodding towards the Hollywell pool of clear water. He has never held a girl's hand like this before and wonders how to leave it? What to do with it? Just drop it or somehow give it back to her?

'I'm steady now,' she repeats watching Jollyboy run about excitedly on the beach. 'It's these shiny buckled shoes that are too big for my feet.'

He opens his hand wide, splays out his fingers and lets her hand drop. She looks at him with a puzzled expression then a rough voice calls to them.

'Ho. Ho there, Gentlemen Lords.'

They turn and see a figure dressed in the black garb. Beth knows the man and looks away. He eyes their clothes and basket and says with great esteem and gravitas.

'I might be correct with the idea that you will be intending to collect an amount of sea victuals from hereabouts. If I am correct, I say with all good will and faith that there is duty to be paid for all victuals so taken from the sea, rocks and beach hereabouts. As is written in this fishing village's regulations. We are without the area of the good parish and we support our own.'

Throughout his instruction his raggedly shaved face moves from one to the other looking with almost hidden eyes from under thick bushy eyebrows at their faces. Beth knows this man as the Gateman. She has met him many times, she tries to avoid his direct looks and says nothing.

'My friend and I are here for oysters. We are from London,' Charles says loudly.

The Gateman looks at Charles then at Beth.

'If it pleases you, Gentlemen Lords. It would be fitting to visit me when you wish to leave the village with the duty for your oysters.'

'That we will do good man. We are honest and know the bible.'

They walk along the track at the base of the cliff and make their way to below Whitebread Hollow passing nets, piled lobster pots, barrels, hauling ropes and stacks of driftwood. They reach the end of the track and sit on a chalk boulder where a solitary shack stands with a stool by its door. It is a small dwelling built of driftwood and tarred weather boarding with a roof of tarred black sail. The sound of a crying baby comes from an opening. There is a noise as the door opens and a Fisher woman appears and sits with the crying baby on the stool. She moves the baby inside her loose clothing to her bosom and the crying stops. A minute later a fisherman comes out dressed in his black clothing. He is on the younger side of midway and carries a small black fisherman's cap. He comes to the seated woman and child, bends down on a knee and kisses them both. His quiet goodbye is lost from their hearing. He stands, pulls on the cap, hurries along the beach and disappears between the boats and shacks. The woman knows they are watching, she turns to them and says in a melancholy voice.

'Sometimes they don't come back,' and points far out to the horizon where the tiny sails drift in the immense hazy distance. The baby is silent and the woman returns to her meagre living space. Beth and Charles sit in silence as they think of this short glimpse of life.

'You may have a wife and a baby to kiss soon,' says Beth. She has no idea why she has said this but once said she feels it's important. She has no idea of Charles' London life and wonders what he will say but before he can reply she asks; 'Is your heart with a London lady?' She felt she needed to know.

'The ladies I know in London are all Michelle's lady friends. Older, motherly aunties,' he says dispassionately. 'I don't think I will soon be kissing babies. When my father died the land became mine but a settlement meant it remained with others until I'm older. When I have the land I may marry,' he looks at Beth and adds. 'But you may be married soon with a baby on your lap?'

'I am sure you will marry soon. A house of your own to live in and these fine clothes,' she pauses for a moment and then reveals. 'I once dreamt you would marry me. But dreams are dreams,' she says, as her face flushes pink.

The door of the small shack opens again, the woman reappears and raises her hand to shelter her eyes as she searches the vast blue expanse of sea.

'In London I'm kept away from young ladies. You are the first person I've been alone with for a long time, Michelle or Mirken are always with me. But today I'm away from them.' he says turning and looking at Beth. 'They may try to trick me to release my inheritance. I know they want to emigrate to the New World. They talk about it often, They told me they're going to Brightstone to sign papers. I don't know what for but it's important, they have a purse of guineas,' he looks at the approaching foaming white of the waves glistening in the sunlight. 'I like doing what I want to do. It's good to come to the sea. In London we just have the smelly river.'

'So you will come again,' Beth says coaxingly. 'You must let me know or I may be away with the sheep.'

'We could meet every year.'

'Every year!' she exclaims with disappointment. 'That's not very often. We may forget each other and never meet again.'

They look at each other then look at the sea. Charles leans across and kisses her cheek. She looks at the sea and feels emotions run like tickling feathers over her body.

'The water! It's getting deeper over the rocks!' she shouts 'It's just over there,' she stretches out her arm and points to a featureless area of low rocks where the water just laps their surface. They move along the beach, slip off shoes and stockings and walk along a sandy area between the oyster covered rocks. Beth puts on canvas mittens and lifts clusters of oysters into her basket. Charlie lifts some but is soon shouting,

'Oh Lord, save my fingers.'

'They cut and the sea stings. Don't pick any more, Charles,' she calls to him. 'I almost have enough.'

Beth picks a few more until the rising water threatens their breeches. They retreat from the incoming tide to a stretch of beach where Beth giggles as she tries to pull baggy stockings up her ladies' legs. She pulls on her shiny shoes and they set off back to the narrow staircase where they find the Gateman sitting in the shade beneath a sail.

'Gentlemen Lords, duty to be paid,' he announces standing by a set of weights and a scale. Beth hands over the basket and he tips the contents onto the scales and rubs his chin as he studies the scales with intense concentration. He then selects a counter weight and lowers it on the balance.

'Fat oysters this time o'year,' he says looking at the swaying scale. 'been feeding all summer. Balancing now. That there weight is right for sixpenny. That be the duty,' he continues. 'Blessed chalk it will be here Epiphany, after Vicar Lod's been,' he concludes staring at Beth's face with a puzzled expression.

She searches for a coin she has put in her new coat, presents it to Gateman and they begin to ascend the staircase. But ascending the staircase is more difficult. The basket is heavy. Charles goes one step ahead and holds Beth's hand. Jollyboy bounds up the steps in front of them. Bonding and entertainment continue, they reach the top where their hand parting uneasiness continues. They follow the track to the mansion and enter through the small back entrance door. The basket is left at the bottom of the staircase.

'You'll be gone soon. Back to your London,' she says as they climb the stair.

'I don't know what Mirken's plans are. He's always up to something pulling Michelle along. I'll send another message.'

Beth finds herself in front of the old Venetian mirror again. She sadly removes her hat, discards her expensive fabrics and watches the colours changing in the glass as she settles into her familiar simple maid's clothes.

'Here's the maid you met on the green slopes,' she says as she leaves the dressing room, 'My spirit was lost in those clothes. I didn't know who I was.'

'I know who you are now,' replies Charles. He stands looking out of his windows towards the sea where the setting sun has turned the clouds and sea into gold. Beth kisses him on the cheek and hurries down the staircase, picks up the basket of oysters and pushes her feet into her wooden pattens. She is back to her maid's way of life and walks along The Street, her head in a whirl. He has gone. A happy time that's now finished. Perhaps there will be a message. All that remains is the feeling that she is still wearing the three-cornered hat. Her hand quickly leaps to her forehead, but she feels her familiar maids cap and wonders what she will say to her bed companion.

Chapter Eighteen

A cabin in steerage

Wisps of silver fog thread their way between the cottages. They drift over the curves of the downs and collect in the hollows like pools of grey water. The air is cool and damp. A faint orange moon has given way to a sun that rises concealed behind banks of cloud. Beth has slept fitfully. Her mind has looked at remembrances of her enchanting day dressed in tailored clothes. She lies on her bed watching the light of day filter into the room between the oak bars of the shutter that could not keep out the early bird song.

'Are you awake?' whispers Livy.

'I'm sleepy and would like to sleep more but the day is here.'

Noises from the kitchen below rise through the cracks in the floorboards accompanied by the faint smell of wood smoke.

'You didn't come back till late from the oysters yesterday, was the water wrong? Tides this time of season aren't religious.' she asks as she sits up on the bed.

Her female intuition has signalled a change in her bed companion's demeanour. She wants to know what has happened at the oyster harvest below the white cliffs.

'I haven't told anyone and you must keep it secret if I tell you. It was a day I'll never forget.'

Beth recalls the events of the previous day in great detail as she watches Livy's eyes widened in amazement. At the conclusion of her tale they lie in silence.

'Is....is that really what happened?' she asks looking into Beth's face and eyes for the truth.

'Yes. Yes. It is. Of course,' replies Beth looking back at her.

The morning starts with a heavy sea fog but by mid-morning the fog has gone leaving the cottages and downs in bright sunlight. Beth and Livy are busy at the oven. A wild yeast sponge has been used to prepare a dough that has been kneaded, shaped and left to rise on wooden shelves.

'So you really had a set of clothes for oystering?' Livy asks again.

'They almost fitted. A bit loose but the breeches stayed up with a tight knot. He may not be back till next summer,' says Beth sadly. 'He'll forget all about me when he's in London.'

She looks up and sees Halfpenny raise his head from its sleepy resting place on his front paws, look into the distance, leave his customary seat on the door stone, come into the parlour and sit looking at the two girls.

'Someone's coming,' says Beth as she picks dough off her fingers.

They wait patiently and hear the dull clang of pewter. A shadow crosses the threshold and Full steps into the parlour bringing with him the smell of fermentation and ale. He has the appearance of an hour glass. An apron marked with the colours of ales and malts sits over his loose clothing and all are pinched at the waist by a tight thick leather belt where his pewter measures hang.

'Here be another paper from the house,' he says lifting a piece of folded paper from a pocket. He passes it to Beth and watches as she opens the folds. She reads it silently to herself then screeches excitedly.

'It's a message from Charles.'

Livy smiles but says nothing.

'Nothing to go back,' Beth advises Full as he looks around their parlour.

'Has the groundsel been good for Nell's sweats?' asks Livy.

'She may be wanting more.' he concludes as he turns and leaves the cottage with the dull sound of jingling pewter following him. Beth spreads the paper out flat on the table.

The girls read the note and both look at the single hand of the clock which is almost vertical. Livy has not been so diverted as Beth and she remembers the dough slowly rising on the shelves.

'I'll attend to the baking. You go now and be there for him. The loaves may not be ready for baking till sunset, I'll tell Martha you are gone to the beach for driftwood when she returns.'

'Oh, I'm so wanting to see him again,' says Beth.

She hastily picks up a shawl, slips her leather shoes into her wooden pattens and hurries to the place she remembers. She hurries down The Street pleased to be in the cool air and out of the smoky air of the cottage with its baking fire. She reaches the head of the steps and carefully descends. Below the cliffs the fog still lingers. It is thick and salty covering everything it touches in a cold dampness. The gateman is nowhere to be seen. Her pattens crunch noisily on the pebbles as she passes the ramshackle abode with the crying baby and arrives at the chalk rock where she had sat with Charles. She sits listening to the quiet slow lapping of the waves and the calls of the seabirds. Gradually another sound drifts around her in the fog, the sound of men chanting together.

'Ho ye heave ho....ho ye heave ho....ho ye heave ho.'

She can just distinguish through the fog a line of men, leaning forward, leaning back, leaning forward, leaning back, hauling on a heavy tarred rope. She listens and watches the strange spectacle of men and rope until the fog closes around them and all that remains are their lusty voices. She hears a scraping sound and the door of the nearby shanty opens, the fisherwoman emerges and stands staring anxiously towards the sound of the chanting men. She catches sight of Beth.

'He's been gone since sunrise. This mist's bad as a storm. I fret so. I must see whose boat they have?' she says as she hurries off towards the chanting men.

Beth watches her fade into the fog as another figure begins to emerge. She sees the outline of a three cornered hat and knows it is the person she is waiting for. The fog is not lifting or thinning. It drifts around slowly in patches of denseness that display distance then conceal it from view.

'I'm pleased to see you are here and not lost in this fog,' he says as he comes up to her. He leans forward to kiss her cheek but she moves to give him sitting room and he almost loses his balance.

'There has been so much talking and whispering about the journey that my ears are tired,' he says as he looks back along the beach and shouts for Jollyboy.

'Where are you going?' asks Beth earnestly.

'Michelle and Mirken have heard of it in the London coffee houses. Notices in the Evening Post say it's open land for all,' he says slightly excited.

'But where is it, Charles?' pleads Beth.

'It's called The New World,' says Charles. 'They're in charge of the estate till I'm twenty-one so they've sold it and say we will get land in America.'

She has heard the word America mentioned at the inn as a distant land but that is all she knows.

'America,' she repeats to herself. 'But when will you go?' she asks him dismally.

'We travel back to London at sunrise. A boat has been arranged,' he explains.

'Do you have to go?'

'Michelle agreed to Mirken making all the arrangements. She is excited and wishes to see how much land she can get and as she's my mother I need to go. If I stay I may miss the possibility of inheriting what remains of my estate.'

'We've only seen each other a few times. I fear you won't come back,' she says.

There is silence for a moment and they look through the lifting fog towards a narrow slipway where the fishermen have hauled a boat ashore and are rolling the lateen sail around its spar. A man and a woman are walking towards them, Beth recognises the anxious fisherwoman.

'A boat from Rotterdam calls at Dover in about seven days and we board it there. Mirken says he has paid for a cabin and it will be easy when we get to Philadelphia,' says Charles with hopeful anticipation.

'You will forget your shepherd's daughter, our dressing up and oystering. But I won't forget you,' she says in a sincere tone.

'No, no. I won't forget you,' he frowns. 'Yesterday we shared something I'm sure we will never forget,' he says, as his hand goes into a pocket. 'I've brought it with me.'

His fingers feel the smooth silver snuff box. He put it on the rock between them.

'The snuff!' she exclaims looking down at the small round silver object.

'You can keep it to remember yesterday.'

'But I can't have such a thing. It's not a law-abiding thing for you to do. I'm a shepherd's daughter and it's a silver snuff box.'

There is silence for a moment as the surprise of this rejection is resolved.

'It's a gift for you. Mirken often gives presents to Michelle, he calls them tokens, she smiles laughs and takes them,' says Charles trying to settle the impasse. Beth picks up the object and looks again into the secret garden.

'I like looking at it. Is this a token for me then?' she asks looking at Charles. 'A love token for me?' she repeats. Her eyes opening a little wider.

'Yes, I think it must be,' he says with a look of surprise at the revelation. 'Will you keep it to remember me?'

'If you give me this, I must give you something to remember me. I felt like an angel in the soft velvet clothes. I'll never forget it so I'll find you a keepsake to take on your travels. A love token for you.'

She stands and wanders off along the beach. Charles watches her and listens to the click, click, of her wooden pattens on the pebbles. She bends over and picks up a number of small objects, straightens herself, eyes them intently then throws them away into the lapping waves. She turns and looks back at him and holds her hand above her head with one of the objects.

'This is the best on the beach. There are others but this is the shiniest and best and it's for you to remember our days.'

She passes the object to him and he carefully takes it in the palm of his hand.

'It's so beautiful,' he murmurs in amazement as he looks at something he had never really looked at before. It has taken several years to make, but there is no secret garden, its creator was more interested in survival. It has been smoothed by waves and time, almost flat but slightly dished, its outline an irregular oval, wavy concentric arcs terrace its top. Its lower surface a complete abstraction of silver grey pearlescence. He moves it

234

slightly in his hand and a myriad of the colours of light are reflected from it.

'It's only an oyster shell but it shines sometimes,' she says with a slight tone of apology.

'But I like it so much. So very much,' he says turning it over and over in his hand.

'When you have gone to the New World you will be so busy with fences and cattle you may remember me....the oyster girl,' she fancies.

'I will remember you, I promise,' he says in the manner of a pledge. She looks at her silver token and carefully lifts the lid.

'Hold your nose.' she shouts as she shakes any remains of the old snuff over her shoulder. They laugh and sit in silence each examining their tokens. Beth looks closely at the characters in the garden wondering if they are meeting or parting.

'Before you gave me this it was just a shell on the beach. But now it has importance,' he says looking at it.

They sit together on the rock, talking and listening to the sounds of the foreshore and the sound of the Fisher people working their harvest. He holds the oyster shell as he stands, they say their goodbyes. He kisses her on both cheeks and walks away towards the stairs in the white cliff. She watches him slowly disappear behind the fishing shanties and laid up boats. She looks at the cherubs once more then puts the small object in a pocket of her gown. She makes her way to the Hollywell pool where she writes both their names on a beach pebble with a piece of chalk and leaves it by the water. She feels the snuff box as she makes her way back to her cottage and decides to tell Livy.

'He's given me a token,' she says quietly to Livy in the parlour. 'It's a secret I don't think Ma would approve of. She doesn't need to know about it.'

'A token,' replies Livy with surprise.

'A special token to remember him. He's going with his mother to The New World, where they hope to get land and become farmers.'

Beth points to a shutter and the girls walk out of the cottage and sit together in the grass by the old fallen tree.

'What did he give you that is so important?' Livy asks with curiosity.

'It's something cottage girls will never get. It's no piece of ribbon. It's for people who live in a city,' says Beth as she lays the shiny object on the grass and the two girls stare at it in silence.

'I've never seen one of those before. It must be worth many crowns,' Livy says in a hushed voice as she picks it up to have a better look. 'Ma will have something to say if she sees it.'

'I'm not to tell her. I'll hide it and just look at it sometimes when she is not here. Wouldn't look right under our thatch. It belongs in a city.'

'Don't let the Constable see it, he might ask questions,' advises Livy as Beth frowns at the idea.

'It'll always be hidden away. I might bury it and I'll not tell you where.'

The display of the token ends as Beth holds it securely in her pocket and they return to their cottage.

The exciting time dressing as a man and being with Charles is now over, she feels empty and spiritless, her only consolation is the knowledge that she can hold something that they played with together.

ooo000ooo

The trio of Charles, Michelle and Mirken are on the Dover Road. They are opportunist travellers; choosing the method of transport that presents itself to them. By carrier and stagecoach they make their way along the old Roman road stopping at inns for victuals and bed for the night. They slowly approach the port of Dover, find a room at the White Horse Inn and anxiously consider the next part of their journey. Mirken has paid for slips of parchment in London that give him access to the ship where he is to pay the captain the remaining monies for their voyage. This is achieved on a dull overcast day when both sea and clouds show nothing but a sad expanse of grey. Herring gulls cackle as they descend on the unloading fishing smacks. They look for their boat that has the name of 'Redeemer,' and carefully clamber aboard with their luggage.

'We're set for The New World now. There's no going back,' says Mirken after he has seen the captain.

They are shown down a short flight of steps to their small cabin where they look around slightly dazed with disbelief. It is a makeshift cabin in steerage with two walls. The two remainder boundaries being a rough waist high wooden fence one with a gate for entry into their private space. In this space are two bunk beds, the lower is a size for two sleepers, all constructed from timber showing signs of a previous maritime use. A square wooden table, a bench against a wall and a stool all fixed securely to the floor. This will be their home for six, eight or ten weeks depending on the temperament of Mother nature. Immigrants had boarded the ship earlier at Rotterdam and these now pace aimlessly about or sit in huddles covered with blankets as they mutter with sleepy blank faces watching the trio come to terms with their steerage cabin. The dim dark space has little daylight. Flickering hanging lamps swing gently from side to side in time with the calm water of the harbour and the sound of the creaking and bending the wooden hull. A rusty metal stove with a pipe chimney occupies the middle of this communal space. Its glowing embers drop onto a metal plate in the floor creating wisps of grey smoke that float up and spread into the dark space. A youth appears in the dimness, mounts a short flight of steps and opens a hatch. Daylight filters round the edges of the hatch as the youth tips the contents of a chamber pot over the side into the murky water. He lets the hatch slam shut behind him then disappears amongst the huddled travellers. They stand for a few moments looking around their private space then look at each other with various expressions of confusion and unease and eventually begin to open their wooden trunks. Reading the small print is an activity that Mirken rarely exercises and the large type, 'CABIN', was boldly above the much smaller print of, 'In steerage', and for this omission he is regularly chastised. They optimistically place items on shelves, ledges and various hooks then stack their trunks in a corner and sit in idleness in the dark cramped space.

Printed advertisements for The New World and published letters of paradise from immigrants who had made the crossing had been discussed in detail at the inns. There was no way of knowing where the truth lay in the letters or in the many anecdotes of hardship and misery. With no knowledge of what the next day or the distant future would bring them, they sit in their open cabin looking at the grim assemblage of humanity around them. They have fortunately been able to pay for their passage but many on board this wooden vessel had sold themselves to future masters.

'I'm dry as a summer,' says Mirken taking a wooden tankard from a shelf.

'This is a grim place for a voyage,' says Charles as he watches a shiny beetle cross the wide boards beneath his feet.

'We are going to be thirsty. I hear all the meat is heavily salted and dry,' he says pouring a liquid from a small stoneware flagon. 'And this won't last more than a day. Shall we play?' he asks looking at Charles.

'There's not much else to do.'

Charles opens the oak lid of the top trunk and takes out a wooden board that he places on the table. They place their fifteen chequers and for the next hour shake out the dice and are lost in an age old game of chance and skill. Michelle watches them until she hears shouting from the deck above but the players are oblivious to the noise and do not look up. The lamps begin to swing in greater arcs, the wooden hull creaks louder and the whole dim space rocks gently from side to side as their carefully placed items on the shelves roll about and soon crash to the floor. The boat leaves the harbour and sails west towards the Atlantic as the New World waits patiently for their arrival.

'What about Cowes,' asks Charles as he shakes his two dice onto the board.

'First mate didn't know. He said it depended on the captain whether we stop for provisions or not. We will have to wait,' Mirken replies, studying the dots on the dice.

'Three!' exclaims Charles as he moves his chequers.

As they sail west through the narrow sea their gaming table remains between normal horizontal limits and some relief from idleness can be achieved by hours of gaming with chequers and dice. But there is no relief from the dim fetid space below deck except when weather permits access to the top deck involving the temporary opening of the hatch at the top of the flight of stairs. The emptying of chamber pots with various contents continues as a regular distraction. As they enter the open sea the continual deep swell of the waves, the heaving from side to side, the lifting and dropping and occasional sideways slip all combine to remove any feeling of wellbeing in the travellers.

After a week the food is stale. It is free from worms and maggots but is frequently forcefully and uncontrollably vomited. The acrid stench of vomit adds to their wretchedness. The faith of some overcomes their weakness and they search through trunks for their bibles which they read aloud amongst the crying babies and sobbing mothers. The trio have their private space but this is little comfort as they eat the same food and drink the same murky water and share the same serious discomfort with all the travellers in steerage as they are daily tossed about. Sleep is impossible in bunks that leave bruises. One day the hatch opens bringing fresh air and daylight into their dismal space.

'The fire must go out.' the second mate shouts as he descends into steerage. 'The clouds tell of storm, rain and mountains of sea,' he says poking the burning embers out of the stove. 'Look,' he says as he returns to the open hatch. 'Look at that,' he says pointing through the opening. A few travellers crane their necks and see through the opening a dark mass of threatening cloud.

'That weather is two leagues away,' he shouts anxiously. 'Wind and mountains of sea.'

The travellers are hushed with fear.

'Can it really get worse?' Charles asks in desperation.

He has been sick from the food and his clothes bear testimony. Fleas bite him, he is thin, hungry and frightened. His hand is in a pocket of his stained coat. He feels an object and rubs his fingers over it. As the last two leagues are sailed the fearful travellers try preparing themselves but there is little they can do. Mothers hold their babies tighter, men sense the end, children cry and hug their elders. A man of the cloth continues to defy the elements and shouts tracts from the bible until he can shout no more. Death is approaching. After two leagues the boat's timbers are groaning in agony. Twisting, bending and shuddering they attempt to protect against the onslaught from the mountainous sea. Vicious waves relentlessly batter the oak timbers as the travellers are tossed violently about, are knocked to the floor and lie defeated.

'Take me, Oh Lord,' screams a man as he falls to the floor dropping his heavy bible.

Fallen bodies try to stop themselves rolling across the floor as the boat pitches madly from side to side. Freezing water has found the gaps around the hatch; it cascades into the dark space soaking the semi conscious travellers who are ready for their graves.

Half a century earlier, in a hunting forest, a healthy oak was surrounded by its small green fruits that littering the forest floor. The wild boar that remained in this forest frequently feasted on these fresh green acorns. But one morning men's voices were heard around its sturdy trunk and the feasting for the wild boar had come to an end. This old oak now forms the keel and deck beams of the Redemmer. English oak is a strong hard wood and with its strength and the knowledge of distant shipwrights the mountains of sea could not claim this ship.

Close to death the lives of these weary travellers are saved. After the horrors and endless days of fear the storm eventually blows itself away, the clouds clear and the reliable sun rises in the east. The travellers look at a calm sea in disbelief and hastily return to their bibles with prayers of thanksgiving. It is not long before the Redeemer is two miles from land with the tired travellers crowding its deck. Excitement and a future now fills their minds as they breathe fresh sea air and peer at The New World appearing through the fog.

Chapter Nineteen

Wigmore is willing

L ivy feels detached and distant from the other young maids who are her friends.

'They don't know Martha is not my mother. If I tell them will I be taken away?' These thoughts trouble her mind.
'The little baby girl was you,' is the one she hears most. They echo in her mind as she recalls what Martha had told her. There must be some mistake. But Martha is honest. Fisher was her father, it's impossible. A mistake! But Martha would never give a falsehood. Why would she say it if it wasn't a truth. Endless reasoning gives no peace to Livy as she tries to sleep through the nights. But slowly, as the days pass, she begins to accept the strange truth. She feels emotionally adrift, threads have broken and she looks at her new world. A new mother, a new father, no brothers or sisters, she longs for a bond and Seth is there. But a brother no longer.

'I want to marry my, Seth,' she tells Martha. 'In church with goodness and paper. If I don't marry I'll be locked in service with a master. I want to marry, Seth,' she repeats earnestly.

'I'll speak to Vicar Lod. It can be done. Don't fret and I'll never let you into service,' her mother says reassuringly.

'But you are a widow, Ma. They'll not listen.'

Martha finds this reply disturbing but soon finds herself on her way to St. Mary's church to discover if the vicar will listen to the happy news. The girls watch for her return over the downs, they see her appear as she climbs the slope behind old Bourne Place.

Livy raises her arm to let Martha know they are watching her, but she doesn't signal back.

'She is sad,' says Livy.

As she reaches the attentive girls, she relates what the vicar had told her.

'I told him and he listened. Then he went for his little book and opened it at the page with my ink on it, there was your name.'

'Vicar Lod said ''No! They are brother and sister. That's bad.'' I told him what had happened but he said it was my untruth and if I wanted he would come to me to confess to my untruth. His mind is fixed,' she says feeling disappointed and concerned for Livy for bringing the sad news. 'He will not marry you and Seth.'

It is not long before Martha remembers her rooftop ride over the downs with the visiting clergyman. She feels he will be more compassionate regarding Livy's predicament. He has been seen in Bourne and Martha decides to talk to him.

On the downs with his flock Seth's eyes are on a thick mist. Generated by the damp earth of autumn and the lingering heat of summer the air carries a mist with the odour of the soil. Fruiting bodies in the warm moist soil thrust colourful spore filled caps into the night as the moon looks on. Knowledge of such things is scarce and tainted with a belief in evil spirits of the night. He watches the mist in the moonlight creeping around the low ground like a ghost. But he has seen it before and knows it like an old friend come to tell him the season. Livy has visited him and told him that Fisher is her father and of the strange manner of her arrival into the Applegate family but he had said little about it. At first it puzzled him, but away in his quiet downland such a tale did not appear to have much relevance for him. After taking his father's place as shepherd the quiet tranquil life with his sheep has let his mind become a place of untroubled harmony, no petty discords can be found. The sole visitor to this mindful harmony is the memory of the seasons that colour his small world and rolling in the grass and rain and loving the girl he has always loved. His ambition to enlist in the navy to seek the status of a hero with prize money to spend has deserted him as the realities of life have thrown themselves upon him. The unexpected death of his father has given him much sorrow and has thrust him quickly into the adult world as he takes his father's place. He had learnt much during the occasional days spent assisting his father. Now the decisions are his alone and he feels a deep accomplishment. There is nothing else he wants in his life.

He lies on straw outside his cover looking at the stars, listening to the night. His two dogs sleep with their noses flat on the earth and at silent sounds raise their heads and look into the darkness. The sheep are motionless and silent as the mist drifts around them. The shepherd sleeps. The shepherd wakes. A yellow glow appears in the east to tell him a new day has begun. He drinks, eats, calls his dogs and wanders between his flock, his vacant mind living with his animals and the peaceful space of nature that surrounds him.

Martha also knows the thick mist that drifts across the downs and through the open shutter close to her bed. Her white cap, starched and pressed, waits for her on the table in the parlour. She contemplates her meeting with the visiting clergyman Wigmore.

'He must believe me and marry the girl,' she thinks to herself. 'It's true as God's in heaven, but people are strange. I've seen him look at me, he may want to marry me, but that's not what I want today. Perhaps another day.'

The thick mist is lifting from a weak sun as she makes her way again across the downs to St. Mary's church where she sits behind the named high backed pews but with a good view towards the pulpit. The small gathering of holy souls does not wait long and Wigmore is soon standing in the lower pulpit; his allotted space for preaching designated by the incumbent who is wary of this visiting man of the cloth. She remembers his advances and politeness during their ride to Brighthelmstone and has often pondered life as a clergyman's wife but today she seeks another marriage.

'Brothers and sisters, let us rejoice in the name of the Lord who has brought us together on this day,' he says looking at his flock. His gaze lingers for a brief moment as he sees Martha.

'We are children of the Lord who need guidance for our salvation.' His eyes meet Martha's, he sees her white cap, he remembers the cheerful wagon ride with her, his mind stumbles as he attempts to continue. 'Do....do not abandon your faith but see the church as the refuge for your soul,' he looks about the congregation. 'Bring your life into the church for your salvation.'

Martha looks away from Wigmore. She looks at her hands, at the soil behind her nails, at the cracks in the cold stone floor and listens to his voice as it reverberates around the old stone church.

'The church will give succour to all who belong,' she hears and senses he is looking at her but she does not look up. She feels she is deceiving him. Eventually the moralising ends and he stands holding a small prayer book in the church porch as the congregation file past.

'Martha Applegate my travelling companion from the year past,' he says smiling as she arrives in the porch.

'Clergyman Wigmore,' she says with a slight bow.

'I'm glad to know that sorrow is leaving you as I see a pleasant cap. A cap that speaks to me,' he says smiling.

'There is a matter I wish to speak of,' she says quietly.

'We can talk my dear lady. Please wait for me by the yew,' he says with bright eyes as he points to the tree amongst the gravestones.

The remains of the congregation slowly file out of the church. Wigmore stands alone looking at Martha as she stands under the thick boughs of the old tree. Her white cap his beacon of hope. He had often thought of her as he discussed biblical tracts with customers on muddy Ludgate Hill. He approaches her in high spirits.

'The church can be a saviour for all who want,' he continues in his preaching way as he stands by her under the yew.

'I wish to seek your services to marry a young maid,' says Martha.

'Marry a young maid,' he repeats with a smile.

'I have brought her up as my own. She was left with me when born,' she says as emotional feelings are revived in her heart. 'Vicar has her in his book as Olivia Applegate. But she is not of my family. She wishes to marry one that was her brother according to his book. But the book is wrong,' she feels gossamer threads breaking.

'Marriage ceremonies are performed by me in London close to Ludgate Hill but here in Bourne you will need to speak to Vicar Lod of the church here. Shall I speak for you?' he asks.

'He will not marry them,' continues Martha. 'In his register she is an Applegate child.'

'The ecclesiastical canons of the church say it should not be. That is how some vicars see the word. Although the bible is not clear and it is open to interpretation.'

Wigmore wishes to support and help her and his mind quickly hunts for possibilities.

'It would not be a marriage in this church then,' he says looking at the heavy stones of St. Mary's. 'Some other holy place is needed. Perhaps outside this parish, I do not wish to disturb the resident vicar. I have a visit here after the winter. After Lent, May Day, spring, it may be possible then. God willing we have survived another winter. I'll give you a licence for the marriage, but find a holy spot to join the two in wedlock.'

They remain under the yew tree, exchanging lives and thoughts. Martha returns to her cottage with the good news for Livy while Wigmore returns with a dismal heart to his room.

He feels disappointed but pleased to know he will assist a woman he thinks of and will see her again on his next visit to Bourne. Livy is waiting and watching for Martha's return. She sees her figure amongst the green. She raises her arm and Martha signals back. She looks happy.

'He will marry you both. Wigmore is willing,' she says as she enters their small cottage garden. The damp autumn mist has gone. She strokes Halfpenny's coat and looks at Livy's smile.

'Wigmore. He will marry us?' asks Livy for assurance as she looks at Martha who nods her head.

'He will marry you when he returns after Lent, Be patient and all will be well.'

Martha has achieved her wish; she takes off her white cap, steps into the parlour, takes her black cap from the table and ties it under her chin.

The green downs stretch away to the horizon under a warm sun. Birds sing high on the wing in still air and sheep bells sound following the barking of dogs. The peace seeps into the shepherd's mind as he sits and looks at nature. Slip and Bell his dogs lie with their noses toward the flock. He sees their ears prick up and their noses turn to another direction. He follows their gaze. A small figure is moving in his direction, he looks again and knows it is her. He feels his heart beat. He hears a faint distant voice drift across the downs towards him.

'We can be married. We can be married.'

He watches her approach, she is running, she descends a hollow and he sees her, but she stumbles and falls out of sight. The sharp black field flints that lie hidden in the grass appear in his imagination. He shouts to his dogs and with wide quick paces hurries towards the spot where he saw her fall. He expects to see her reappear as he hurries but she remains out of sight and his wide paces turn into a hurried scamper. He is hot as he hurries up the grassy slope that hides her. At last he can see her stretched out in the grass, her simple clothes scattered about.

'Hold me Seth, as you did before,' she says quietly with a contented smile. 'I knew you would come. The grass is cool and the sun is warm.'

He looks away from her white body in the grass towards his flock. He sees his dogs as he had left them intent on their charge.

'So a wife you will be,' he laughs out as he throws his straw hat into the grass and slips off his smock and every piece of clothing he can find until he too lets his whole body feel the warmth of the sun.

'We can be together married.' she joyfully whispers as he lies down beside her. 'Martha has spoken to Wigmore. All is well.'

'We can be together without a vicar,' he laughs. 'But you will be a real wife with a church paper to say it,' he feels elated and excited as she rests her head on his shoulder.

'My dreams will come true. Every summer we can be together like this in the grass loving and loving,' a small tear drops from her eye as she feels the happiness.

'Four summers and my name will be on the cottage,' he says with satisfaction.

'But we have to wait for Wigmore to return. After lent, May Day he told Martha,' says Livy as she turns and kisses his cheek.

They lie in the grass looking up into bright white clouds that are piled high and move slowly away like stately grandees.

'Wigmore wants us to find a Holy place to wed, a place with no evil only good. I know where it could be,' she says in a soft voice.

But Seth's attention is on the sound of a distant bark.

'Listen!' he says quickly. They listen but the only sound they hear is birdsong and the hum of insects.

'Hollywell is where we can be married.'

'Where Fisher may be,' says Seth.

'I am going to find him. He has been mad I know, but he is my father. Martha knows nothing of him, the Hollywell Fisher people are secret, he may have died and been buried down there. But we are going to see....' Livy stops talking as Seth lifts a finger and they listen again.

Yes, they can hear the dogs barking. Seth lifts his head and peers out from the grassy hollow. The dogs are circling a group of stray ewes; dedication to his animals rules his life.

'I must see to them,' he says hurriedly dressing. 'Hollywell will be the place. If you find Fisher come to tell me, but run if he tries to take you again.'

'Don't leave me like this, Seth.' pleads Livy. 'I'm wanting you.'

'There will be many more times, my love, be patient.'

This night the silent visitor only shows itself as it drifts between broken cloud. It looks down year on year saying nothing but listening to the myths and falsehoods that try to give it meaning and explain away its presence. The damp earthy night mist is back. It drifts about in the orb's grey light. It drifts into the Applegate cottage around the sleeping occupants. But Livy is not asleep; she lies on her bed, her body wants sleep but excitement keeps her eyes open.

'He is willing,' she whispers. 'He will marry me. I will be a wife,' the thought fills her with emotion, her small fingers twisting a curl of her hair. Her bedside companion is silent.

'Martha has said it. One more winter and we can marry. We can marry. I'll be the wife of a shepherd. Never in service. A proper wife,' she whispers quietly.

Beth's eyes flicker open.

'Shush, Martha will hear,' whispers Beth. 'Have you told Seth?'

'Yes, I have told him. A Holy Place said Wigmore. He has been told Vicar Lod doesn't believe Martha's story, it won't be in St. Mary's church, but we know it's true and honest. If the church doesn't want me, I don't want the church,' Livy says as she turns her head to face Beth, their noses almost touching.

'If you are with Seth what will happen to me?' Beth breaths into Livy's face.

'She talks of the thatcher and her lessons a lot. I think she may like him.'

'But she talks about his fallen cottage?'

'I don't think that troubles her. They could get married with me and Seth.'

'Does he love you?' asks Beth.

'I think he has loved me for a long time.'

'But he must tell you to know for certain.'

'I may be with child soon, Beth. We have loved and loved. I am tired and happy.'

'Martha will hear us ....Shush,' Beth whispers as they hear Martha turn in her bed. 'She talked of the thatcher when you were away to Seth. Said she knows him now.'

'Seth knows we will look for Fisher. He may be a corpse. But we must look. Will you be with me when I'm at the Hollywell searching for him?'

'I'll be with you. But Charles. Where is he now?' asks Beth in a distant far away voice. 'He may have died too.' she says suddenly in a fearful voice.

'No. No. He has no reason to die. He is young like us. Don't fret so Beth.'

The girls lie in silence until Livy says with emotion.

'We will find Fisher. It's something I need to do.'

'If he had passed you would have felt it in your dreams.'

'My dreams have told me nothing. The sheep took Seth away when we were to love. He left me quickly. Stroke and comfort me, Beth. Wake my spirit.'

Livy feels a gentle hand on her thigh that explores her body and strokes her.

'Be quiet Livy or she will hear,' whispers Beth, as small sighs come from Livy's lips as her body trembles.

'She has made the noises in the night. She said she was in her dreams,' Beth says in a soft voice.

A night working spider repairs his damaged web across the shutter as the grey nightly visitor moves through the stars.

'Sleep now, Livy.'

The two girls hold each other until their gentle breathing proclaims them both away in their dreams.

Chapter Twenty

Love letters

The reeds of Pemsey marshes are stiff, unbending and strangely quiet. For several days an icy north wind has blown across the marshes bringing snow and turning the still water to thick ice. Amos Reed the hardworking thatcher is preparing his cottage for the winter with fuel, victuals, and a plentiful supply of rush candles. All he can do now is to maintain body and soul and wait. He stands in the parlour of his tumbled cottage looking around trying to decide what else can be done to preserve the warmth of his small fire. He checks the shutters and decides which one will not be opened again before spring. He pulls straw from a bundle under his arm and pushes it forcibly into the crack between the wooden shutter and the wall. He considers the furniture and moves the settle closer to the hearth and looks at the remaining furniture. Two stools, a dark wooden chest, a bench and the table. His eyes rest on the old table. A square heavy oak table that has been in his family for generations with symbols and marks carved into its thick wood. Games of strength have been fought on it, babies have been born on it. He wonders if the letters MARTHA, that he has learnt, will be added to it. He remembers the last tutoring with her, when the table had to be moved back into the cottage when sitting in the open threatened freezing hands and feet and how she anxiously looked around the small room as he lit the fire. He had received much tutoring from her before the winter had set in and the marshes had resounded to many night time songs as he revised in the darkness. His alphabet was known, his numbers were coming, his next challenge, Martha had judged, would be to decipher unknown words.

The Meads hamlet sits silently under falling snow. The nights are long and dark, the days short and cold. Icicles form along the eaves of wet thatch and grow like strange plants. The birds are silent, puffing out their feathers as they wait. The farms and orchards of the hamlet wait. The people of the hamlet wait. The sun sinks lower and lower until the huge astronomical clock chimes its giant bell and the coincidence of planetary orbits and spins begins lifting the sun higher and higher above the horizon. The long dark winter nights grow shorter. The icicles melt, drip and fall. Wildlife wakes, shutters are opened and people joyfully celebrate the coming of spring.

On the marshes, the surface of the water now ripples and the reeds rustle as Amos the thatcher opens a draughty shutter to clear the smoke from his parlour. He looks out to his ditches and his new piece of land. He feels a thrill. He feels proud and elated. Abe's wagon had stopped visiting the marshes when snow was on the ground; there had been no messages from his tutor. He thinks of her, he sees her brown soft happy eyes.

255

He remembers watching her arrive on Furlong for their first lesson, how overbearing she was at first and their last lesson by the fire in his parlour when they laughed. His mind drifts back to reality as he looks at his reedbed for the year and the tethering rope that leads to his willow eel basket.

Martha is watching Abe's wagon. It stops on the track outside her cottage, Abe sees her watching and signals her to come to him.

'What have you got for me, Abe?' she asks.

'First trip to marshes,' he says as his pipe rattles. 'Gave me message for tutoring to start again day after morrow,' he says as he removes his pipe and spits.

'Did he say anything more?' she asks.

'Nope, s'all he said. Water's high but tracks still there.'

Martha was expecting the message and is relieved it has finally arrived. She knows his learning will soon finish and their informal contract will end with Furlong returning to the marshes. A heart-breaking prospect for her girls and a setback for her tutoring which had found more scholars with the help of the steady cob. On the appointed day she is up at sunrise, packs her bag and walks through the bright crisp morning air to collect Furlong who has been stabled at the inn.

'Abe told me you would be away to the marshes again,' she hears as she mounts Furlong and sees Nell at the door of her inn. 'Looking after that thatcher man?'

'He's learning,' replies Martha stopping the cob at the door.

'Innkeepers know all. Constable Cheer has talked to me about pastry maid. Cupids busy amongst the pies so he'll be wanting to stake his claim on the lass. Have you got a Cupid in that bag of yours?' asks Nell looking quizzically at the bag over Martha's shoulder.

'I haven't decided. Sometimes he's in there.'

'Don't let him jump out. Thatcher worked on that,' says Nell pointing to the thatch over her inn, 'New coat, that's what he left for me,' she points to a woven reed fox with a bushy tail that struts across the ridge.

Martha's face slightly frowns but she says, 'I like it. He left us nothing to look at so you are lucky for your fox.'

'Good at his trade. People ask about it.'

'Of course,' Martha says without a frown. 'But my cottage didn't get a fox on the roof.'

'I asked him for a ship but he said he was no sailor. There are some saying clergyman will be back for marryings at Hollywell.'

'They may be right,' are Martha's last words as Furlong trots into The Street.

She relaxes as the cob needs little guidance as it leads her through the cool morning air onto the marshes and negotiates the narrow tracks that lead to Amos' cottage. She pulls Furlong in and stops on a spot where she has a good view of his cottage. Looking at its tumbled roof, its abandoned thatch and general disrepair makes her feel uneasy but she knows that within the small parlour there could be warmth and security but there needs to be room for her growing family. She notices a change and her eyes fix on it. His old thatched hurdle showing his craft is still there with its fox but now there is a second fox following the first.

'He's a clever skilful man,' she whispers to herself.

She ponders the fox and the man. A man who has a passion for his craft may not need a wife, but she won't want a man without one. A fox is clever. A fox is cunning. A fox lives with a mate. These indefinable random thoughts flit through her mind as she approaches the cottage.

'The fox,' she says as she dismounts. 'He's got company.'

'A mark of my craft,' he says looking at it with satisfaction.

The tutoring of Amos continues. He has counted beyond one hundred and is capable of writing words for short sentences. He remembers his first skirmish with the twenty-six and with a justified sense of accomplishment has proposed to Martha that their informal contract is coming to its conclusion and that her next visit will be the last. She knew this open-ended agreement must end but she didn't expect it so soon. She had commented that he still had a lot more to learn but agrees to one more tutoring which will be the last. She had looked at him as he spoke of the last tutoring and thought she saw sadness. She returns to her cottage and disappoints Beth and Livy with the news that Abe will be returning Furlong to the marshes after the next tutoring.

The following nights are long for Martha. She tries to sleep but her mind looks for answers and when they are found they are doubted by her heart and abandoned. He has made obscure allusions to friendship but perhaps nothing else is there for her. At the start of the tutoring, she had felt tense but as time passed, she had become more relaxed in his company, they had talked as close friends. Were his thoughts still with his lost family? As she lies in the darkness of the night a dim light creeps slowly across her body. The strange night visitor is making its appearance. She gazes at the silver orb, she knows it well. She wants to touch it, she wants the large dependable orb to hold her safe. She knows there is nothing to fear, she watches it captivated by its magnificence as it drifts across the heavens. She remembers what Lizzie had said to her on that freezing winter night and makes a decision.

'I'll wear the white cap,' she whispers to herself.

She closes her eyes to sleep but as the silver orb looks at her more thoughts tumble through her mind. He aroused me when I had taken off the black cap, that time in his cottage when we laughed together and he stroked my breasts. Why did I do it, raising my gown for him, we were like man and wife then, but will he need me as a wife or will I be forgotten. What sort of man sins with a widow, a man of no faith, Lizzie says he's an empty man. I don't want to be an empty woman, God save me from emptiness of widowhood, a weak woman. No, I'm not a weak woman, my children are mine but they will be his, they will belong to him. God, he must love them and me, or I will be dead with sadness; sadness, I know a lot about that. My children need a man to care for them.

Her eyes open and she repeats, 'I'll wear the white cap.'

Her eyelids flutter. Her eyelids close and she finally drifts away into dreams.

The orb leaves her and drifts across the blackness of the heavens. A light appears in the east as the sun sweeps the night away with its golden light. Martha prepares herself for the last lesson and makes her way to the inn to mount Furlong.

'Last tutoring now. He doesn't want more so she'll be back on the marshes' Martha shouts to Nell as she strokes the cob. She looks up enviously at the fox high on the thatch of the Ship Inn. 'I may have one on my roof someday.'

'The Hunt will never get it up there,' says Nell with a determined laugh. 'Constable's been drinking here. He's full of

259

the maid's pastry. He says to tell you they want marrying same time as Livy at the Hollywell.'

'Clergyman Wigmore is willing to marry. He'll want something for his purse,' advises Martha leading Furlong to Nell who stands at the doorway of her inn.

'Constable's an easy man now I've found him the maid. She says she wants him so it'll be a good nest,' says the innkeeper.

Martha is pleased for the two in the nest but feels slightly dejected as she once thought the Constable had looked at her.

'Is he still in there?' asks Nell looking at Martha's bag over her shoulder. 'Little Cupid?'

'I don't know but I hope so.'

'That white cap of yours tells me he's still in there,' says Nell. Martha looks past Nell into the parlour where she sees the large figure of Gaunt listening to their talk.

'Got a new man to roll things along?' she says to Nell.

'His dreams are from the green wood if you ask me. He's slept under it too long. Bring the thatcher for some ale.' instructs Nell as Martha turns the cob towards The Street.

The cob follows the familiar path down to the marshes and makes her way between the new ditches. A frown settles on Martha's face as the cob trots past familiar landmarks that mean more to her on this last journey. She used to prepare a new activity for every time they met, but for today little has been planned.

'Not inside this day. The weather is good. The table on the grass,' she says as she dismounts. 'I'll be sad without this girl,' she confesses to the thatcher as she rubs a hand across Furlong's warm back.

'Hitch her to Abe's wagon,' says Amos.

She waits for him to comment on her clean white cap. But it doesn't come.

'I've missed her too. But perhaps you'll meet her again sometime,' he says with a slight smile.

The table is not an easy thing for even a labouring man to move. Each time it has been called for he is involved in an ungainly struggle as its width is only just within his grasp and when he can hold it he can't see where he's going. He distinctly dislikes Martha watching him as he struggles.

'Martha. Come here.' He calls as he stands by the table.

'What do you want?' she asks.

'Come here,' he repeats.

After a short pause she comes into the parlour.

'Why do you call?' she asks.

Amos nods towards the other side of the table.

'Take hold,' he says nodding again.

'You would like some help,' she says as she takes the bag off her shoulder.

'I would always like your help,' he says looking at her.

Martha smiles, lifts her side of the table and thinks of what he has said. To get the table through the door Amos volunteers to walk backwards and as he does so his heel comes in contact with the edge of the door stone. He stumbles backwards but manages to stay upright and keep hold of the table.

'I don't tutor people for carrying tables,' she says with a laugh.

He looks and smiles but he doesn't laugh. The table is placed on the grass in spring sunshine. They hear a shout.

'Mossy!' a voice calls.

'Here.' replies the thatcher.

Two labourers appear with spades and axes. Amos leaves Martha and takes them to where a number of hazel poles lie on the ground. After some pointing and gesticulation, he returns to Martha who is sitting at the table.

'Opening up the ground for some stone,' he says as he joins Martha at the table.

'So I'll have to say goodbye to Furlong,' she feels her reply is not how she feels and adds. 'Unless you need more tutoring.'

'Furlong will be busy here,' he replies. 'She's needed to haul the timbers. Hitch her to Abe's wagon,' he repeats.

Alphabet characters are spread randomly across the table. Amos looks for his favourite letters and spells,

'THATCHER', he smiles at it. Martha changes it and leaves the word,

'FOX', he looks at her puzzled.

He plays with the letters and leaves,

'ROOF',

Martha nods her approval then changes it to,

'ROOF FOX'.

The simple exercise continues till Martha pulls from her bag a scrap of newsprint and lays it on the table.

'From the Lamb Inn where travellers from London leave them,' she says as she smoothes it flat. 'Let me see if my journeys to the marshes have been of some worth. '

He looks at the paper. He looks at Martha. She says nothing but nods towards the piece of paper. He looks at the print, moves a finger slowly along each line and speaks each word.

The London Evening-Cryer
Tuesday, June 17, to Thursday, June 19, 1738

Oxford – The Innkeeper of the Merry Fiddlers watched the coach from London stop in his yard. As passengers carried their luggage across the yard to the inn he saw a leathern purse fall from one of them and lie on the cobbles. One of the innkeeper's maids came into the yard, hid the purse below her apron and returned to the inn. He found the maid and the purse and they looked inside where they found six pebbles. The Innkeeper asked in the parlour and a man said it was his who then asked, 'Where are the six crowns?'

Martha is proud of her work and he is surprised at what he has achieved and smiles at the piece of newsprint. Martha wonders if she could be more than a tutor. They hear the labourers talking and the sound of their spades.

'New stone?' she questions, looking at Amos.

'It's for the new walls. They're digging for the stones of the foundations. Another room with stairs,' he says proudly still looking at the newsprint. 'Fallen wall will be rebuilt.'

There's nothing else I can do flits through his mind. He finally looks at her. She knew he would look. She smiles. The lesson is coming to an end and there is nothing settled. He goes inside the small parlour, cuts bread and cheese, fills two tankards and delivers them to the table. They sit in silence listening to the labourers. He plays with the alphabet characters. He looks at her, selects letters and,

'AMOS', appears.

She decides to write and,

'MARTHA', appears.

he adds to her name and,

'MARTHA REED', appears.

Her face feels hot, he looks at her, they both laugh. She flicks her hand across the table, disturbs the letters and all that's left is,

'ARTHEE',

They both laugh.

They listen to the labourers.

'My girl Livy is to be married Mayday,' she says after a pause. 'Married by Wigmore with some from the village. Constable Cheer to be married.'

'Was at the Ship Inn and heard of such. Innkeeper too. So I've heard,' he says.

There is another period of silence until Amos points away to Furlong and says, 'She's needed to pull the roof timbers from the sawyers in forest by the ridge. Can be finished summer then I'll be thatching it.'

'Abe will return Furlong,' says Martha.

'That he will,' says the thatcher looking concerned. He looks again at the letters, picks up a handful and silently places a few on the table,

'FURLONG', appears.

Martha slides letters into place and,

'I RODE FURLONG', appears.

He modifies the letters and,

'RIDE FURLONG', appears.

She would like to ride the cob and,

'MORE TUTORING', appears.

He looks around at his piece of land with its reedbeds and,

'CUT REED WITH ME', appears.

She writes,

'IS IT THE SEASON'.

He writes,

'WAIT FOR THE SEASON WITH ME'.

She slides the letters and,

'MY FAMILY WAIT FOR ME' appears.

He adds,

'BE MY FAMILY'.

Martha reads the message. She looks at it again and looks at the thatcher. He has moved his long hair to behind his silver hoops, he is smiling his broad smile. She tries to think. She looks at the message again. She knows what he means but asks, looking earnest.

'What do you mean?'

'Cut reed with me in the marshes that you know,' he answers.

'My family is more important to me than reeds for thatching,' she says with a feeling of some regret. They hear the labourers talking as they dig.

'Hear them,' he says. 'They're putting this cottage in order with rooms, roof and my reeds to sleep under.'

'I've been a married woman and would need a man of the church to see to it,' she says feeling some relief from uncertainty. But she was not yet where she wanted to be. 'Wigmore the clergyman, I need to be married and safe. My name on paper,' she feels emotionally exhausted, her eyes are damp, a tear falls. Amos has been a father, husband and solitary male. He knows the moods of life. He puts his arm around her and holds her and remembers the nights singing the alphabet song with the waterfowl.

'The alphabet,' he says as he picks up the letters again and places a message on the table,

'SHALL WE GET CLERGYMAN', appears.

Her tears have dried, a smile appears, she writes hurriedly,

'BEFORE REED CUTTING'.

He adds,

'YES', feels it is the end of a journey and adds,

'MY BEST LESSON'.

Chapter Twenty One

A black hand

A gentle breeze carries the plain sound of the curfew bell to Meads hamlet. It is still rung every night at St Mary's church; a hundred year old tradition to clear the streets of the good and the bad. Its sound is now simply a timing signal for the simple one handed clocks that tick quietly in surrounding cottages. It gives the eighth hour after noon.

'The thatcher keeps her,' says Beth as they hear the bell.

She pokes the fire with a stick exposing glowing embers.

'He might be a slow learner or a clever man that wants a woman,' says Livy as she looks for images in the embers.

They hear Lizzie cough in the kitchen and hear the creak of her chair. When the embers are ashes, the girls carry a rush light up to their bedroom, look in to little Jamie and see him sleeping on the floor next to his clay marbles and chalk pebble. The door quietly closes.

'The little man sleeps like an angel,' murmurs Livy.

They inspect the babies in their straw cots, extinguish the candle and fall onto their bed. They watch the nightly orb slowly drifting across the heavens watching all that is proceeding in its dim light. Its shaft of light filters through the shutter and illuminates the dusty floorboards with scattered dried herbs and insects. A brown biscuit beetle has come up from the kitchen below. A grey cloth moth flutters past and small powder post beetles continue their digestion of the beams overhead. They lie side by side and drift away into sleep. The moon drifts higher, there is the noise of the cottage door creaking. Martha has returned from the thatcher and Livy wakes.

'Are you awake?' she whispers in a hushed voice to her bed companion.

'I can hear you. What's to do? Where's the moon?' asks Beth

'Gone way over. Ma's back.'

'Do you like him?' Beth asks in the darkness.

'She says he's a good sharp man,' whispers Livy.

'Sharp? I don't like sharp. He may be cunning,' says Beth wriggling her body at the same time.

'He has a cottage, a good horse and is busy thatching bringing coins for his purse.'

'You are lucky,' says Beth. 'You will never have to go into service and work for some man or woman who may treat you like a donkey if they wish it. I won't like it and will not be good at my work. I love helping Martha but will not love to work for anyone else.'

'You won't need to be a donkey,' replies Livy sympathetically. 'Seth will come of age, the cottage will be his, you may live with us carding and spinning and doing all the other things you do.'

'You will be in Martha's bed with Seth. Modesty will move me.' says Beth.

'Love making can be noisy.'

'To hear Barnabas and Martha loving when we were together comforting ourselves so near them was painless, but to be here alone will hurt my heart with loneliness. Truly Livy I will be sad if I lay here with you and Seth loving and laughing in the dark.' Beth whispers sadly.

Beth senses the threads of her emotion to Livy stretching, twisting and sinking. Martha's footsteps are heard on the stair. They listen to her quietly move about the room, fall onto her mattress and wait for the regular sound of her sleeping breath. Coughing is heard coming from the cracks between the floor boards. Livy has turned her body and with her face almost touching Beth's nose. She breathes silently.

'Can you hear her?'

'I know. It might be the graveyard cough, she might have the lung. She coughs in the day,' sighs Beth.

'Ma may marry the thatcher and you will go with them and be away on the marshes. I'll miss you,' whispers Livy. 'I want Fisher to know of my wedding. If he knows I will feel married proper. He is a strange man and we injured him bad. If he is alive he will be with the Fisher people below the cliffs at Hollywell. We do not know his name but I want to search for him and see him.'

'We will go together to find him,' says Beth stroking Livy's arm. 'Still my sister, you are my best friend, I was jealous of you. Always presents for you, none for me. Bright ribbons he gave you. But I will search with you for the man.'

'He is my father. We hurt him and he may need help.'

The girls lay on their backs and look up through the darkness and are soon back quietly in their dreams.

The clock ticks, the moon slips away and a faint glow appears in the east as a new day is born. Small puffs of cloud appear, change shape and slowly drift by. The Street is bathed in a bright light on this morning as the maids begin their search for Fisher.

'He is my father,' says Livy again to herself with almost disbelief. Before she left the cottage she had collected bunches of herbs that she now carries in a small straw basket. They reach the staircase and peer down at the scene below with inquisitive eyes searching the small black figures.

'We must descend, they're too small to tell one from another,' says Beth after they have satisfied themselves with the view.

The girls cautiously descend the steps occasionally stopping to look below.

'He must have been hurt bad,' says Livy. 'So bad that he may not be able to work a boat. Pity they wouldn't have him in the workhouse. He must be here or buried away at sea.'

'Did you think he would kill you when he grabbed you?' asks Beth.

'I was so frightened when he waved the knife. I stumbled and fell and then I saw Martha. I was shaking and trembling afterwards.'

They reach the bottom of the stair and step onto the pebbly ground of Fisher village.

'If you've come for water, lobsters or any of our harvest there's a levy,' says the deep rolling voice of the Gateman who has suddenly appeared. As he watches them approach, one eye closes, he screws up his face and gazes at Beth.

'If you're gathering oysters, crabs or the like we have a levy made on our crops just like on the furlongs up top.' he repeats jerking his head up towards the cliff top.

'We are not pilgrims to drink your water,' says Livy, 'We have a bible for our souls.'

'Pilgrims and harvest takers here sometime,' the man says still gazing at Beth as she tries to avoid his gaze. 'I'm Gateman here so what's your need?' he asks.

'We have a message for a man. One who lives here,' says Livy.

'Lots of Fishers down here. What's he known by?'

'We have no name but the message is important and we need to see him. He got a broken shoulder summer last,' replies Livy.

Gateman looks away from Beth's face. His eyes focus on nothing, then return to her face.

'That man, Onearm!' he says loudly. 'He's with us. Some call him Onearm, some call him Tarman. Water's not repaired him. Became a wild man. Was going to madhouse but we have him. Woman's gone. Sits all day looking out to sea. Lost in the deeps he is.'

'He's alive then?' asks Livy.

'Aye. Over that way,' he says as he raises his arm to the west.

'We will take no oysters so sleep well in your bed, Gateman,' shouts Livy as they turn to the west.

'Your brother comes for the oysters. I sees him some.' shouts the man after some deep thought when the girls are some distance away.

'He's thinking of me. My disguise must have fooled him,' says Beth with a laugh.

'Onearm or Tarman,' says Livy quietly to herself.

'We will find him now we have names,' says Beth reassuringly as she takes Livy's hand.

They walk a track that wonders between the fragile driftwood shacks and the massive white face of the giant cliff until they are below Whitebread Hollow. Fishing boats have been pulled from the water and sit like stranded fish amongst nets, spars, sail and lobster pots with the black clad figures hurrying about amongst them. The maids are close to a brick and timber smoke house; silently at work with its smoke curling up from its chimney. Here are more black clad figures but these are the Fisher women with white aprons and white caps busy in their work. They pause their work to watch the two maids as they pass.

'We have knives here without hands.' a woman shouts. 'Are your maid's hands too soft for this work?'

'We are not here to work. Our hands are good for our maids work,' replies Livy. 'Where do we find Onearm, Tarman?' she asks.

'If he had two, he would be twice the trouble. Further on, further on,' a fisherwoman indicates pointing further along the track with the point of her knife.

They walk further and soon get the reply they want.

'Tarman's over there,' shouts a woman pointing to a small shack.

Beth squeezes Livy's hand as they cautiously approach a small doorway that is part open.

'Is there anyone within?' calls Livy. There is no reply. She trembles with the thought of being close to her father and seeing his face.

'Is there anyone within?' she calls again.

Beth has slipped her hand away and has peered round to the back of the shack.

'Here Livy,' she whispers as she looks back at Livy who looks nervous and tearful. She holds her hand out to Livy to steady her. Livy's emotions are struggling. She has father daughter bonds that are strong but she still holds memories of the hay meadow that make her tremble with fear.

They stand silently watching. The man is naked to the waist. He pulls a piece of sail canvas flat on the ground, dips a brush into a hot cauldron and begins to paint the canvas with hot black tar. His back is towards them, they cannot see his face. The man's figure is thin. One arm has withered away and hangs like a dead branch while the other is thick and muscular with a hand blackened by tar. His bare back shows a misshapen shoulder and deep scar. Beth's arm is around Livy. The brush is dry and the man moves. A small sound comes from Livy's lips, the man spins round. Livy looks into her father's face. A heavy fearful sadness hangs over his face. She looks into his eyes. Her heart and mind struggle, it is too much and she faints away. She slips away from Beth as her body goes limp and she lies unconscious on the pebbly ground. She is not a stranger to the wild man. He knows her from his days of watching and longing. He quickly pushes his one arm under her and lifts her limp body. Beth cradles her head and they carry the girl into the hut and lay her on a mattress. The shack is small with pots of tar and barrels of salt stacked around a small living space. Beth feels fright as she is now consciously alone with the man.

They both look at Livy's still face then look warily at each other. They both recall the events in the hay meadow and Beth is fearful and wonders if he has a knife. She looks again at Livy's face and sees she is recovering from her faint. Livy's eyes open and she raises her head.

'What has happened,' she whispers.

'Vapours took you away. You're safe now,' comforts Beth in a quiet voice.

Tarman looks on with his sad face but suddenly turns, goes to the table and brings a small wooden box and kneels with it beside Livy. Beth is fearful. The box slowly opens and there inside is not a knife but shiny red, yellow, and blue ribbons. He takes out a ribbon lifts it up and lets it unwind into a curl. The man looks with concentration into Livy face and when he sees her smile he smiles with her. Beth wonders if this is all the man wanted; to see her smile.

Livy recovers from her fears and begins telling the man everything she can find in her trembling mind. The man cries and searched his memory but he can find little, but what he finds he stutters out. They listen carefully to his voice and gradually piece together his sad story of the small boat that was overturned. How his brothers drowned and he survived and was found clinging to the upturned boat. At the end of his tale he holds up his blackened hand.

'I'm Tar...man now. Cannot...boat,' he says in a jagged voice.

The two girls look at the man that had brought horror into their lives in a quiet hay meadow, someone they never wanted to see again. But many things had been told since then. Livy suddenly remembers the basket is not on her arm.

'My basket! Where is it?' she asks.

The basket is found where she fainted away and the bunches of medicinal herbs are handed to Tarman.

'These may bring comfort,' she says as she remembers the reason for the journey that she had forgotten in the excitement of the meeting,

'I am to be married,' she proclaims proudly.

Tarman looks at her. She looks into his face to find his thoughts. She sees a small movement of his lips and smiles.

'Yes. I'm to be married. Clergyman will be here. Down here at the Hollywell, Mayday it is. I would be happy to see you on the day.'

But Tarman does not reply. He has been looking at the box of ribbons. He picks another red ribbon out of the box, holds it up and lets it unfurl into a curl as he watches Livy's face.

As the maids leave Tarman, a sunset sky is low in the west. A hidden moon has pulled the tide over the beach and the sound of its tumbling waves echo from the white cliff.

'He will come. I am sure,' says Livy, relieved her father no longer feels a stranger.

'Let's go to the well before we climb the stair,' says Livy. 'The well can give us luck.'

'I remember the sound of his cracking shoulder. It sounds in my sleep, but it didn't take his life away. He is a lucky man,' says Livy as they place chalk pebbles around the Hollywell pool then make their way back up the timber stair.

Chapter Twenty Two

Hollywell

On this special night the great orb is magnificent; it is full of light. It silently slips along its orbit surrounded by vast swathes of countless spots of brilliant sparkling light in an endless darkness. For the mortals below it heralds joy, warmth, comfort and the unfolding of nature to give them the promise of a harvest. It is here to signal the eve of Mayday.

On this night the shutters of the Applegate's parlour are shut tight for good reason. After a busy day of preparation, important items have been laid out on the parlour table which might tempt a passing fox. Small mounds of freshly baked buns and meal biscuits. A bucket of butter, a bride pie with hidden willow ring, smoked meats and a selection of fruit tarts. In the centre of these life sustaining delights is Lizzie's recipe. A bowl of cherries, plums, gooseberries and pears preserved in thick set honey.

Beside these edible items are straw baskets that wait for flowers to be picked while morning dew is still on the ground. On the floor is a large barrel, some casks, pitchers and wooden tankards. Martha and Lizzie are sitting in the dim light of the fire in the parlour tending ribs of mutton that are roasting on a spit.

'I've seen nothing of clergyman Wigmore,' Martha says after a silence. 'He's been told that I'll be there to be married. Nell told him, I couldn't. Clergymen are used to pain from their flock. He knows Amos is not a church goer, it'll pain him if he never sees me in the pews again. He'll blame the thatcher, call him the sinner.'

'If he's a good man he'll be about. It'll be pain for him to marry those he fancies for his own,' Lizzie replies as she pours hot fat from a spoon over the ribs. 'A man with no religion is an empty soul, Martha. A man with no religion is not a man to marry,' she instructs Martha while looking at the sizzling meat but remembering his shameless wink at a frail old lady.

'He has his religion. Working the wet reeds of the marshes to thatch and filling his purse is his lord and master. He knows all of his trade and works on the Sabbath, cutting reed and trimming hazel for the spars. He tells me all.'

After Martha has spoken there is silence except for the hissing of burning fat.

'The first boy I met talked a lot,' says Lizzie trying to catch the dripping fat. 'When I was a small carefree creature I was seeding a field for a penny when a boy I knew came across the field. I shouted at him to go away and not tread the open ground but he took no heed. He came up to me and started talking about his work, the navy and the army. He began fondling me, I tried to resist but we rolled about laughing and he came into me and then we lay exhausted. All this time my seed bag had been round my waist spilling the seeds. I finished the field with the few that were left. I told no-one but lay awake fearful of what would happen when the harvest came,' Lizzie pauses her story to recollect further.

'Your first child?' asks Martha.

'Yes, that's how the first came about. But seeding became good work after that.'

The last flame of the fire splutters and dies leaving the parlour in darkness. Martha pushes a dry stick into the embers and sees it burst into flame.

'When the crop came up, there in the middle of the field was a circle of a dense thick mass of wheat. ''What is it?'' asked the farmers and later they asked me to seed their fields for three penny. Ma shouted at father calling him a blasphemous liar when she found out that he had told the farmers that I had seen a holy vision in the field. But some whispered witchcraft and put the fear of God in me. That boy was husband for my first four. Died in a brick kiln. Red rough hands he had,' Lizzie's voice tapers to a whisper as she gazes at the embers and her youth.

The large orb has moved across the sky defining the night. Its grey light falls through a shutter onto the floor beside the maids' bed. It throws a dim light that slowly moves across the floor as the moon drifts through space above them. The maids listen to Martha's footsteps on the stair, hear her fall on her bed and wait again for her sleeping breath.

'She's asleep,' says Beth as she turns to face her nightly companion. She brings her face close to Livy's and caresses her forehead. 'Has he told you he loves you?' she whispers.

'You will marry him when the sun's up. I hope you love him. I have love for my Charles and want him to come back. Does love go on forever?'

'I have never said I love my Seth, but I do. We love each other as all the other marrieds do and we will see our names written out to say so. I don't know about forever.'

'Sometimes I think you don't care,' remarks Beth.

'Your Charles will be back, I am sure,' Livy says slightly anxious at Beth's remark. 'He might come back a rich man and buy you a long gown and satin dresses. All the good things you want. You will be happy again.'

'Your names written down may not give you love. I've heard it means he is your master,' whispers Beth.

'Don't say that! You unkind maid. He will never be. I'll not let him,' says Livy raising her voice.

'Shush. She will wake and listen,' Beth quietly whispers. 'Now give me your hand,' she holds Livy's hand. 'He'll be a good man, don't think anything else.'

The maids lie hand in hand, each trying to gaze into their future.

'You will be in this room with Seth after the wedding and I will be with Martha in thatcher's fallen cottage. What about Onearm? Will you let him live here with you. He is your father?'

'All he knows is tarring for the Fisher people. They provide for him. He will stay on the beach where he belongs,' whispers Livy.

'Do you need comforting?'

'Not tonight, Beth. I need to be ready for Seth.'

'This is our last time together,' whispers Beth.

The two lie together until sleep carries them away.

The magnificent orb fades and vanishes from the night sky as a brightness appears in the east. Abe's new wagon is heard stopping outside the Applegate cottage. It has been fitted with a post at each corner and strung between them a sheet for a roof. Abe's passenger is Amos. Nell does not like to leave her inn but on this important day she has no choice. She has Full with her, she arrives at the cottage door.

'What's to be done, Martha?' she shouts.

'Load all from the parlour,' says Martha. 'You too Amos. Put the table on the wagon and load the barrel, casks and victuals.'

The parlour table is carefully lifted onto the wagon. Stools and a bench follow.

'Beth, go with Livy and fetch Jamie and the babies,' calls Martha. The straw cots are gently laid under the table.

The Applegate maids had risen early, left the cottage and sung quietly to themselves as they rubbed their hands in the morning's dew on the grass and wiped it onto their cheeks and foreheads. They had loaded their baskets with sprays of blossoms and flowers. Clear pink white mayflower hawthorn, blackthorn and old crab apple, pussy willow, and many more. Today there are simple bonnets to decorate and blossoms to be tied to the wagon; its poles, wheels, spokes and any part that could take a knot. Seth Applegate has left his flock and dogs with Ebb and is on the Warren track to his marriage celebrations.

'Put the honey bowl on the table where I can see it,' shouts Lizzie to Beth. 'No-one's to touch it till I say's so. It's my recipe. Then the bowl to be licked good and clean.'

Livy has been looking back up the Warren track for Seth to appear. She sees him making his way down the curving chalk track that descends to the hamlet.

'Seth is coming,' she says as she watches the distant figure. She watches him approach the wedding party carefully flicking out his shepherd's crook in time with his stride. He climbs the spokes of a wheel and sits beside her looking at his bride with her bonnet decorated with flowers and coloured ribbons.

'We were up to get the fresh dew,' she says.

'Fresh dew is right for this day. It will be our day, Livy. We'll all remember this day.'

'Are we ready to be off?' asks Abe looking at Martha from under his straw hat.

Martha studies the busy wagon and sees Halfpenny staring up at her,

'Up Halfpenny,' she shouts. 'Let's away, Abe.'

Abe sits in the middle of the driving seat between Martha and Amos. But Amos has a request.

'Come and sit next to me, Martha. Sit next to me,' he says pushing Abe to the end to make room for her.

'Driver should be middle,' complains Abe.

'You're middle enough Abe, let the woman sit with me.'

'Gaunt to pick up and the Constable,' says Martha.

The loaded wagon creaks, lurches forward, then settles to a slow horse's walk. Livy, Seth, Beth and Jamie sit on the table with dangling legs keeping an eye on the victuals that creep about on the table with the shaking of the wagon. Nell tries to sit on one of the stools but the swaying wagon defeats her and she settles to sit on the floor next to the large body of Full who sits leaning against a table leg.

'Hold that bowl of honey. Don't let it fall or any hands go near it.' Shouts Lizzie as she sits beside Nell.

'I've got it,' says Beth as she balances the heavy bowl in her lap.

'My Gaunt to be at the Ditch, God bless his soul. If he's a good man he'll be there if not I'll get him to the clergyman myself,' she says with conviction.

The wagon makes its way down Prentiss Street and arrives at Kent Sheet where they see the Constable dressed in a long blue coat that extends to just above his knees. Its patches, missing piping and some missing fit suggesting a few previous owners. He has one arm round Daisy's waist; the other holds a thick pastry rabbit pie. As the wagon comes to a halt he passes the pie up to Livy who finds space for it on the crowded table and with hands around his bride's waist, he delicately lifts her onto the wagon. Martha and Nell look on with a feeling of immense accomplishment but Nell wonders if she has lost the valuable contact for her London recipes.

'I hope there's room up there,' sings out the Constable in his deep voice as he climbs the spokes and looks at the busy wagon. 'Full load of merrymaking you've got today, Abe,' he says. 'A busy day for clergyman.'

'No barrel tapping today, Constable. More important things to attend to. Isn't that so, Constable?' suggests Nell.

'Drinking today. Ale is for drinking on this day. No tapping but tasting. Have you got good ale for us, Nell?'

'Moons always right for my ale,' states Nell. 'That I can promise you.'

As the Constable looks for room beside his bride she asks him earnestly,

'The ring, Will. The ring. Have you got it? I want to see it again.'

Before he has sat down he thrusts his hand into a pocket and pulls out the ring. The wagon sways, he feels unsteady, he grabs for the table but misses and collapses on the floor beside Nell. Loud cries come from his travelling companions.

'You've been at some strong ale,' laughs Nell as she helps him stand and find his place beside his bride.

'Oh, Will. Are you hurt?' asks Daisy as she squeezes his arm.

'No my love. I am good as a new day. Fear not for my body or my soul.'

'Let us move on, Abe. All's well,' shouts Martha.

It is not long before Daisy remembers her request to see the ring and the Constable thrusts a hand into his pocket again. But the ring is not there and he begins searching through his remaining pockets.

'It's gone! It's gone!' he shouts earnestly as Daisy looks at him with a worried face. 'It must have fallen. We must search for it. Stop the wagon.' he shouts.

The wagon creaks and stops. All corners, cracks and holes of the wagon feel searching fingers. The table is searched and platters are moved. Every crevice is poked and peered into but the ring is not found and Daisy looks anxious.

'We cannot be married without a ring, Will. What shall we do?'

'We will be married dear, Daisy. We will have something for your finger. I am sure providence will be a friend this day.' he says confidently.

Much discussion ensues from all on the wagon regarding rings, vows, omens and spirits until Livy jumps down and unties a ribbon from the spokes of a wheel. She places it around Daisy's finger for its size then plaits it into a bright coloured ring then presents it to the Constable. He thanks her and the wagon moves off. It creaks past Goodwin's Barn and approaches Thomas' Ditch. Nell stands and anxiously looks about. At her Inn she is in control, a pleasant host, but now she frets.

'Gaunt,' she roars. 'Gaunt.'

She searches the figures working in the furlongs but none has the bulk and height of Gaunt. Nell had her doubts when he had asked for marriage but Gaunt had sworn oaths on the bible that if he was title holder he would never interfere with the running of her inn. She would always be the innkeeper. This had been witnessed by the Constable who was now a good ally of Nell in both his informal and official capacity.

'I thought he wanted a wife,' she mutters to herself, but Martha has heard her comment.

'He wants one Nell or he'll waste away,' Martha assures her.

'Whoa there!' calls Abe. The wagon is still as the passengers look for signs of Gaunt. Nell is silent; she is standing with tightly folded arms staring at his small hovel of a cottage. She sees him appear, she feels relieved, she unfolds her tight arms.

'He's moving. He's off his bed,' she says with satisfaction, as she watches his large figure approach through long grass with his dog Jack following.

'No haste leads to heaven,' he gasps as he arrives at the waiting wagon.

Nell lowers her hand, grabs Gaunt and leaning back with the weight of her body she hauls him onto the wagon that sways from side to side creaking and groaning. He manages to find a space and calls to Jack who leaps up and sit beside him.

'Have any strayed away?' asks Abe.

'None have strayed, Abe. Get this wagon down on the beach. It's thirsty work sitting in this sun. Give it some rein.'

Abe gently flicks the rein and the horse moves off.

'It's Wigmore the clergyman.' shouts Livy who has looked back towards the sound of a trotting horse.

'Good day to you good people. Marriage is a worthy pursuit,' he instructs in pulpit fashion as he checks that the four couples have a place on the wagon. He trots alongside the wagon, his black breeches and stockings are partly concealed beneath a black preaching gown that falls loosely down. He is eager to see Martha again and he looks over to her as she asks.

'Would you like to ride on the wagon, clergyman Wigmore?'

Martha pushes herself against Abe and gets all on the front board to move along until there is a space at the end for the clergyman. 'Now you must join us. Hitch your horse to the back.' she says smiling at him.

He complies with this request, climbs aboard and sits looking ahead. The wagon arrives at the head of the track that leads down to Fisher village. A dangerous track that descends on the edge of the vertical cliff.

'Let's go down the slope, Abe. Nowhere else,' Nell shouts as she looks at the edge of the track.

'Oh lord! Look at that, Will. It makes my legs go soft,' exclaims Daisy as she looks at the cliff edge.

Will smiles, enfolds Daisy in both his arms and happily replies.

'Hold me tight dear Daisy and don't look down. You will be safe as the moon in my arms.'

'Down to the beach coming up.' shouts Abe as his eyes study the track ahead and the wagon reaches the steep incline.

The wagon gathers speed as it moves down the incline, it shakes and sways and the passengers feel nervous. Wigmore remembers his last journey with Martha and suspects she may be a bad omen as a travelling companion.

'Abe! keep this wagon straight and even. My bones don't want to be made into splinters,' Lizzie shouts. Abe looks at the steep incline before him with some unease. The amount of unease can easily be determined by the excessive jiggling of the pipe that sits in his tooth hole.

'The old oxen never let wagon go this fast,' he hurriedly admits.

'The clergyman is with us, Abe. Calm yourself?' advises Martha as she watches the pipe with alarm and curiosity.

'How do you slow her?' enquires Wigmore in a faltering voice.

'Never had to slow her afore. Oxen kept pace,' answers Abe. 'Horse and wagon new to me.'

The wagon gathers speed while Abe looks at the spinning wheel beside him.

'Done this afor,' he says lifting up a boot with a grooved sole that he presses down onto the spinning wheel. 'This'll slow my side.'

There is a scraping sound. The wagon slows but lurches towards the vertical drop to the beach. All on board scream with alarm as the wagon lurches from side to side as Abe's boot comes and goes.

'Do something!' shouts Martha as the travellers rock from side to side.

'Needs a boot both sides to keep middling. On the other wheel,' shouts Abe. 'Put your boot on the wheel your side clergyman to slow her or she'll fall apart with the shaking.'

'Do what he says,' pleads Martha. 'Or there will be no souls to marry.'

The clergyman's boots are his own personal property. The only item given him by the church is the protestant bible that is in its special pocket. Old and cared for over many summers with wax and animal grease his boots are his old friends. They have walked many miles together and today they shine from extra greasing. He looks down sadly at his old friends as he hears Martha shout again.

'Do what he says and quickly or we'll all be thrown out.'

'Hold the honey bowl steady,' shouts Lizzie.

'Please do as he says,' says Daisy as she considers the plight of her pastry.

'I'm a man that saves souls with the word. Boots have no mentioned in the good book. May God keep us middling.' he shouts as his shiny boot moves towards the spinning wheel and he looks serenely up to heaven.

A screaming sound comes from the tortured boot as he looks down from heaven and stares with a sad expression at his boot that is getting hotter and hotter.

'Hold it steady! Steady now,' shouts Abe.

The wagon slows. The dangerous swaying from side to side stops and with skill, perseverance and prayer to every ones relief the wagon rolls onto the level track along the beach on its way to the Hollywell spring.

'Is honey bowl still on this wagon?' shouts Lizzie with some concern. 'My recipe it is.'

'Your secret's safe Lizzie and the bowl too,' replies Beth.

'Grooms, have you all got your rings with you?' asks the clergyman. 'Many a time a ceremony has to wait for a groom to return to his thatch and search amongst his trinkets.'

Amos opens his collar where a ring is seen on a silver chain round his neck.

'Mine is always with me,' he answers.

The Constable holds up the red ribbon ring. The clergyman looks at it and says nothing. He has seen rings made of many things in his time marrying at the Fleet. Seth has felt his ring in a small pocket of his smock and nods vigorously.

'A ring Gaunt. Have you got one?' asks Nell seriously watching her future husbands face.

'Don't vex yourself, all is taken care of. It's been safe with me.'

'But have you got it?'

'Look.' he holds the ring for her and the clergyman to see. Nell's face relaxes with relief.

'Your licences are here with me,' says Wigmore tapping a pocket under his preaching gown.

'You'll be needing a ring yourself one day,' says Martha quietly leaning over to him and touching his arm.

'Perhaps that will be my path Martha. But I'll never....' she does not hear his reply as Abe suddenly calls out.

'Hollywell ahead.'

'I can see the spring and stair,' says Beth shading her eyes from the bright sunlit chalk that rises beside the wagon.

They see the black clad men, stooping around their nets, busy with their ceaseless work.

'Not my place this. Not my manor,' says the Constable. 'Outside the parish. I'll only search with military and Rider down here.'

'Not a churchgoer here,' the clergyman decides after scanning the faces.

'They look after their own,' says Nell. 'Sometimes at the inn they talk of the horrors of the storms when loved ones are lost in the deep.'

'Where is my father?' Livy says to herself.

The wagon is now close to the spring. Its clear sparkling water trickles down over brilliant white chalk with the quiet sound of chattering voices. It collects in a large pool, crystal clear and cool on every day. Set out around the edges are numerous offerings; chalk and flint pebbles smoothed by the action of waves, some with scratched symbols and marks. Pieces of elaborately shaped driftwood and rusted metal relics left by pilgrims. Objects bonded with emotion to unknown visitors. The constantly filling pool overflows into a small channel that travels a few paces then disappears into the beach.

The wagon stops. The dogs leap off and sniff the salty beach. The clergyman has a pensive smile as he walks around the pool studying the collection of objects that have been left by the pilgrims. He is familiar with well dressings throughout the country but has never seen offerings at a spring amongst the pebbles of a beach. He feels slightly heroic but looks sadly at a scuffed and disfigured boot. He remembers the ceremony he is to perform and searches for a piece of level ground, collects a bottle from his bridle bag and sprinkles the ground with blessed water.

'Let's get the victuals off,' calls Martha, as the other passengers jump down to the beach. All passengers are eager to help with the unloading. All the pies, meats, buns, butter, biscuits and fruits are laid carefully on the table. The honey pudding has pride of place in the centre. Chalk rocks are rolled together to form a rest for the barrel.

'Tap the barrel,' calls Nell as she passes the oak tap to Full.

'Are we all ready for the ceremony?' enquires Wigmore loudly in his pulpit voice.

'Not yet,' says Martha as she sees Spendwell on horseback trotting towards the wedding group. She did not expect to see him today.

'Martha Applegate,' he calls from a distance.

'Bailiff Spendwell,' calls Martha in return. 'Out of your manor down here. Plenty of herring for the table and lobster down here. Oysters for your strength?' she suggests.

'It's nothing to do with oysters. For you and your maids, Martha. Mistress sent them. Over there,' he points away to a patch of sand where a group recline beside leather cases of various shapes and sizes with their horses tethered to the rocks.

'Music makers,' says Spendwell, 'and I really don't need any oysters.'

'Oh! The music makers!' squeals Beth in excitement. 'The music makers I heard at the mansion.'

'We've no roast beef or wine on this table but you are welcome,' says Martha after seeing Spendwell eyeing the table loaded with victuals.

'Good ale too.' adds Nell.

'Foxes to hunt, fences to set,' he says to excuse himself. 'More music makers today so you'll have plenty of sounds for your ears. Foreigners they are and spies they may be but Mistress asked them to play for getting Charles and Jollyboy back after their fall. They've been asked to play when the victuals are gone,' he says as he heels his horse and trots away.

Beth watches the musicians as the sound she heard at the mansion drifts back to her.

'Where is Jamie.' asks Martha as she looks around the beach for the small boy.

'He's found an oyster,' says Amos pointing to a distant small crouching figure.

'Go and get him Beth.'

Daisy is looking at her reflection in the water of the pool as she runs a hand through the cool liquid. Abe is next to an open fire where tar is melting. He is busily filling his small pipe with tobacco. He takes a burning stick, carefully holds his beard away and positions the hot glowing end over the bowl of the pipe. He draws the hot smoke into his lungs, gasps, and drops the stick back into the fire. He feels the rush of substances through his veins, his body feels uplifted and thrilled. He is not concerned with the marriage celebration and walks out to where rock pools wait for the incoming tide. He sits on a sun-bleached driftwood log and gazes pensively out across the vastness of the sea. The air is still. The sea is a smooth flat sheet of blueness dotted with small stationary boats whose triangular sails search for wind.

'Abe's found a spot to rest himself,' says Seth looking out to the blue water.

'Cooler out there by the water,' replies the Constable.

'Cooler than in this white heat,' says Seth looking back at the white chalk cliff reflecting the hot sunlight. The two men pick their way between rock pools and sit beside Abe. Gaunt has pinched his eyes and watched them go. He is aware that Nell will soon be calling his name to assist her. He helps whenever he can but today, his wedding day, he feels his body deserves calmness and peace and he directs his slow walk towards the log where he joins the three men.

'Martha, I'm going to see what the grooms have found out there,' calls Amos to his bride as he too has seen the men on the log and soon they are moving themselves along the log to give him room.

They sit still and silent like stone sculptures gazing at the sparkling sea like a jewel before them. High in the blue sky the pale ghost of a day moon sits on the edge of infinite space silently looking down at the meditating mortals who look out with resolute faces into the magical enormity. Abe coughs, his pipe is out.

'We never paid,' he says carefully tapping the end of his delicate clay pipe, 'never paid for wives. Tabitha and me were just together bonded. Paid no man of the cloth for a wife.'

There is silence as the men consider what they have heard. Gaunt pulls his mind back from watching a small crab walk sideways through a salty pool and replies.

'Your time was many summers ago, Abe. We pay to be married in heaven by Wigmore.'

There is only the sound of gently lapping waves until Seth has considered a marriage in heaven.

'Heaven,' he murmurs to focus his mind. 'The place for good souls,' he says looking up. 'Good souls. That's not me.

But I'll pay clergy to get mine in heaven. She wants her name on paper.'

'Don't know about a marriage in heaven.' says Abe looking at Gaunt then the bowl of his pipe.

Will Cheer the Constable has looked at the moon, sky and water but always before him is a faint image of Daisy's face. He decides to confess.

'I'm a guilty sinner. Never go to the old stone building. I'm for the vicar and heaven. My Daisy is a fresh shiny rosy ripe apple, she is.'

'Apple guilt fills the clergyman's purse,' declares Abe in a knowledgeable manner.

'I'm not paying a penny to the clergyman. My Nell says the inn will be charitable and pay for licence.'

'Aye. She's bought you. Tabitha and me needed no licence and no clergy. More babes if you have no licence. Licence halts love at the gate. Just a piece of paper,' Abe adds as he turns round and sees Full has also come out to the log. 'One more,' he shouts. 'Come in here, lad,' he signals to Full and pushes Seth and the constable to make space beside him on the log. They are already shoulder to shoulder and he is a wide man. There is a yell from Gaunt who is close to the end of the log.

'Wind's dead, no fish in the nets,' murmurs Seth as he looks out at the motionless small brown fishing sails.

All the men follow Seth's gaze out to the small fishing boats.

'Not a good omen for a wedding,' says the Constable.

'Moon's waxing, good omen,' says Amos.

'When I married my bride we were full ripe,' says Abe. 'Full ripe like a pair of soft plums,' he says gazing out to the fishing boats.

'Best way to be,' agrees Seth.

'Both ripe as ripe. Ready to fall off the tree. A good time it was,' continues Abe.

'I'm Nell's second man. She's my first woman. Not such a young girl now but I'll harvest some of the purse,' declares Gaunt with some sadness in his voice. 'I'll be her soft ripe plum. I've oathed that she will always be innkeeper.'

The hard-working, coin conscious thatcher feels he can give advice to the younger man.

'She must know you as an honest man and trust you if she's to share her purse. That's where your coin will be. Loving is loving, a different business. You may be a soft plum to her but she'll treat you well as she has trust in you.'

'Don't let her work you hard,' adds the shepherd. 'Love needs equal terms.'

'Equal terms it should be. But she's a strong arm. She's no soft plum now,' replies Gaunt.

'My Daisy is my love,' muses the Constable dreamily and quietly to the space in front of him. 'She cooks for me and my boy. She cooks at the hearth with eyes as bright as the morning.'

'My Martha's no soft plum. She's a marsh girl through to the bone, can harvest reed like any on the levels. Knew her then when a small slip of a reed cutter. Now she's more.'

Amos' description of Martha is cut short.

'Hell and flames!' shouts Gaunt as he slips off the end of the log and ends sitting in a salty pool.

Seth stands up.

'Go in there,' he directs Gaunt pointing to his vacant space.

'That I will,' replies Gaunt as his face cringes with discomfort as he sits on his wet breeches.

'How much is vicar charging for a wife?' continues Abe.

'One crown a wife,' answers Amos.

'That'll give clergyman a good night's sleep. Can live without payment.' instructs Abe.

'That was in your day?' repeats Gaunt.

'They've caught you like catching fish out there,' says Abe pointing out to the fishing boats. 'Clergy man's caught you in his net.'

There is another silence as the men consider their future lives, the softness of plums and who's paid for what.

Beth has come out to the men and stands behind them.

'Wigmore has his book and waits for you,' she says in a loud voice. 'And the brides are waiting for their rings.'

'Fish are out there. Need good nets,' murmers Seth.

'We're all fishing. Wives are fishing, husbands are fishing, men of the cloth are fishing. It's time to go,' says the Constable ending their simple journey into philosophy.

The clergyman watches the men amble towards him between the salty pools where small fish dodge their shadows. He feels the solidity and safety of a thick book in his hand as he waits and prays on his holy piece of ground.

'Without wives they're like lost bulls,' declares Nell as she cups her hands to her lips.

'Clergyman's ready. Clergyman waits. Wives wait!' comes from her strong lungs.

The grooms shuffle slightly quicker onto the holy piece of ground and form a rough line in front of the clergyman.

'Have you still got your rings?' he asks again.

The men search pockets, necklaces and nod their heads.

'Can the brides come and stand with their men,' he calls, 'and the service will commence.'

Beth holds Jamie's hand, her other hand is in her apron pocket fondling a small snuff box, at her feet is Halfpenny. She stands beside Martha and Amos.

'Martha Applegate, Amos Reed,' Wigmore looks between them and thinks of Martha dressed in colourful tailored clothes on Ludgate Hill. 'May God's blessing be with you,' he says. Martha nods towards Beth and Jamie, 'and your offspring,' he continues. 'Do you Amos Reed take Martha Applegate to be wife, for all things that God shall provide from providence, in sickness and health, till death shall part you. In the presence of God, you make this vow.'

'That I do,' vows Amos.

'Do you Martha Applegate take this man to be husband, for all things that God shall provide from providence, in sickness and health, till death shall part you. In the presence of God, you make this vow.'

'I do,' vows Martha as Wigmore frowns.

'Place the ring,' says the clergyman.

'I bless you now,' he says as he takes the cork out of a small clay bottle and sprinkles the holy contents over the participants.

Only Wigmore knew that more drops fell on Martha than on Amos. She feels the simple gold band slip onto her finger as the prospect of her new life settles comfortably within her. She had felt abandoned in her widowhood and knew her life with

Amos would be secure for her and her children. She had worked with Amos when they were both children, she knew the reed beds and the people of the marshes and they remembered her. The band had once been on Amos' first wife's finger and they had talked long into the night on the reuse of the ring. Was it right or was it wrong? The decision pleased Amos who felt he had a new family with some thought for his previous one. Seth and Livy are the last to stand on the holy ground. Livy holds the shepherd's crook as he holds her hand and slips the ring over the waiting finger. They exchange vows, hug each other and laugh. The service ends, the clergyman stands apart and watches.

Gaunt fetches refreshment for Nell. Amos is whispering in Martha's ear, she laughs and looks at the distant waves. Daisy loads portions of her pie onto wooden platters. Full sits silently with biscuit and ale stroking Halfpenny who lies on the ground beside him. Amos goes to the wagon, selects a bun, slices it in half with his knife then covers each half in thick set honey. He returns to Martha and passes her half the bun.

'Ha! Ha! Ha!' she shouts and laughs out. 'Heavens it's here! Look what's in the honey.'

Hidden below the honey she can just see the shine of the lost ring.

'Daisy!' she shouts. 'The ring. Your ring went in the honey!'

Daisy and Will hurry over to see the ring shining in the honey. Laughing and chattering they take bites from the bun until they reach the ring.

'You have the ring bite, Daisy,' says Will as he stops his biting.'

She puts the remaining small piece of bun in her mouth and carefully chews. All excitedly watch her cheeks move as the honey is licked off the ring. Her cheeks stop moving and there is a moment of silence. Suddenly her mouth opens and out pops Daisy's small pink tongue and there is the lost ring, bright and shining around the end of her curling tongue. The Constable looks at the tongue with passionate delight. A great cheer goes up and he carefully takes the ring from her tongue and adds it to the ribbon ring on her finger.

'Many have come to see,' Martha says to Nell as they look around at many Fisher people and people they know from the hamlet.

'Even the Gendles and old Moe,' replies Nell.

Also in the throng are Hindle, Reuben, Butcher and Acorn who have descended the staircase leaving Blossom and Barley to manage the inn. Nell stands and with open arms beckons the people to come and join in the celebration.

'There he is. He's come to see me,' says Livy to Seth, as they raise their hands to Fisher and see him raise his tar covered hand.

'Nell!' shouts Beth suddenly. 'The sounds,' she says pointing to the music makers who wait nearby. 'Get them to the wagon.'

'Come over! Come over!' Nell calls loudly waving to the musicians to join the gathering.

All eyes look towards the music makers as they bring their strangely shaped leather cases and stand by the pool of spring water. After their eating and drinking the music makers begin to open their cases and the instruments are carefully taken out. Beth watches as six lute players bring their instruments into the sunlight. Ribs of maple and yew have been steamed, shaped and assembled into pear shaped bodies: some bright with silver. Some have white wood surfaces decorated with fretted sound holes while others are older and darker having been stored in the treasure chests of returning crusaders. The sections of three flared conical flutes are pressed together; the generators of the mellow low octaves. Strange tuneless sounds drift along the beach as strings are tightened and loosened and the flautists exercise their fingers controlling tubes of vibrating air. Eventually the tuning sounds stop. The musicians settle themselves in an arc facing the gathering; some sit on white rocks some stand. There is a patient silence as the players look at the gathering and the gathering looks at the players. One of the players steps forward.

'Music of Netherlands,' he says with a sweep of his arm towards the players.

He turns, picks up a lute and at a signal the musicians create their sounds. The silver wound strings of lutes vibrate in harmony with soaring voices. The flutes add their mellow sound and the air trembles with a pure sound complete and wonderful. The music reverberate along the chalk cliff creating a sound that is too magnificent for hurried frantic dancing: it is music for the ears to enjoy as it mingles with the sounds of nature. Wives and husbands hold each other as they listen and small children stop their play. The beautiful sound drifts amongst the spellbound people as the music makers sing and play. After much enjoyment the players reach the end of their repertoire and their instruments are silent. The gathering is in a hushed bewildered silence. It is a sound that has never been heard before in this isolated rural hamlet.

But then there is another heavenly sound. A sound they know.

'Up there!' someone shouts pointing up the white cliff to the blue sky.

Higher and higher they look.

'Up there higher, higher.'

And there a skylark sings its song.

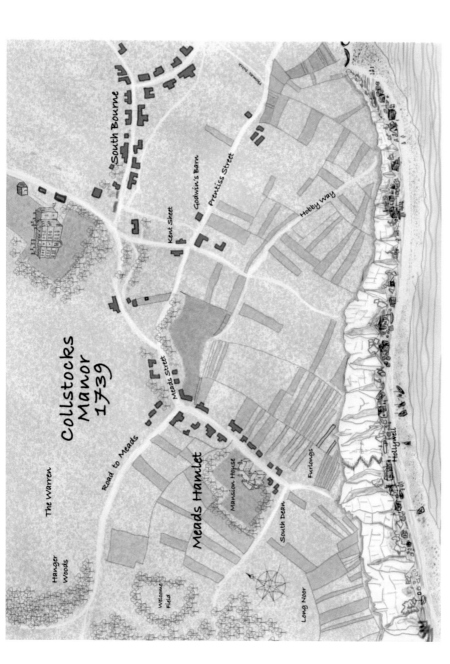

Collstocks Manor
1739

The Warren

Hanger Woods

Welcome Field

Road to Meads

Meads Street

Meads Hamlet

South Dean

Mansion House

Long Noor

Furlongs

Kent Sheet

Godwin's Barn

Prentiss Street

"South Bourne

Hobby Way

Hollywell

Sketch of the 'Old Cottages' at the bottom of Beachy Head Road Eastbourne after Mary Thomas' Diary 1835 – 37. Showing the 'Road to Meads' rising up the South Downs.

Holywell spring

Stair to Holywell

Location of the old
Ship Inn
Meads Street

The Ship Inn Meads Street

Author's Note

The time spent putting these words on paper has been a long journey. A long but fantastic enjoyable journey. It has been a time journey to another world. The lockdowns came and went and all the time my thoughts were with these rural characters living their lives deep in the natural world. Their quiet natural world could be a slaughtering monster or a benevolent companion but their lives were rich in contentment, meaning and purpose. Their close world was a bountiful provider, a world that is unfortunately no more and will never return. However, the downland they worked with plough and oxen and grew their turnips is still with us in our world; it may be under your house or under a black tarmac road; two worlds many years apart.

Would you wish to have lived in their world?

What would they say if they were shown our world?

Life is in retreat from the consequences of global warming as the planet is continually stripped, mined, burnt and warmed. This Georgian Meads novel is fortunately in the time before the industrial revolution; before the smoke and the soot had darkened the skies. It is hoped therefore that this novel will bring some solace to the discordant world of today where there are many challenges to be faced for existence.

This book was prompted by the discovery of two items in the National Archive. When the year 1739 dawned the residents of the rural hamlet of Meads were not capable of writing a record of their daily lives. They had grown to adulthood without any opportunity to sit behind a desk in an educational establishment. Fortunately in the bustling streets of London where daily labouring was not a necessity there was knowledge to be had in the nascent institutions and coffee houses. Many had begun to use their knowledge and one of these was the surveyor who came to the hamlet and spent time busy with his measuring chain to prepare the financial map of Collstocks Manor which this story is based upon. It's thanks to this unknown surveyor that this story can now be told. Thanks also go to Mary Thomas of Ratton, a Victorian diarist and artist who helpfully left an expressive sketch of the old cottages in Beachy Head Road, Meads in her diary of 1835 - 37. The 'New Cottages' appear in a map dated 1876. The historical records these people have left us are part of the National Archive and are available to view at The Keep, Brighton. Due to copyright and licensing restrictions both items have been redrawn for inclusion in this book. The manorial map names Holywell as Hollywell. The map in these pages is an extract from the original. All artwork is by the author.

Map of Collstocks Manor ESRO reference: R/L 40/3/2RR/2
Sketch Book of Mary Thomas of Ratton ESRO reference: AMS 6185/273

I would like to clarify a situation which no doubt relates to many first time writers who are absorbed in their characters and story line. An excess of enthusiasm has resulted in previous copies of this book going to the printer before any significant proof reading had been carried out. This omission has now hopefully been corrected with print run (c) which now follows a more established sense of spelling and grammar.

No artificial intelligence has been used for any part of this book.

C W